The
Stolen Queen

Lisa Hilton is the author of four historical biographies and two historical novels, *The House with Blue Shutters*, which was shortlisted for the Commonwealth Fiction Prize and *Wolves in Winter*. She has made several historical programmes for television and is a regular art and book reviewer. She lives in London.

Also by Lisa Hilton:

The House with Blue Shutters

Wolves in Winter

The
Stolen
Queen

Lisa Hilton

CORVUS

Published in trade paperback in Great Britain in 2015 by Corvus, an imprint of Atlantic Books Ltd.

Copyright © Lisa Hilton, 2015

10 9 8 7 6 5 4 3 2 1

A CIP catalogue record for this book is available from the British Library.

Trade paperback ISBN: 978 1 84887 469 5
E-book ISBN: 978 1 78239 407 5

Printed and bound by CPI Group (UK) Ltd, Croydon, CR0 4YY

Corvus
An imprint of Atlantic Books Ltd
Ormond House
26–27 Boswell Street
London
WC1N 3JZ

www.corvus-books.co.uk

To Kate Williams.

PART ONE

INTRODUCTION

IN THE TIME WHEN I WAS STILL A CHILD, IT SEEMED to me that my father's city of Angouleme was an island, a floating city gathered in the folded waves of the Charente Plain. From harvest until Easter, the fields that stretched below the ramparts were bleak, wind-scoured, pitted here and there with lonely clumps of juniper that I would make-believe were rocks where mermaids might sing, wriggling up from the froth of chalky soil which tipped the winter rains into a silvery net of tiny streams. I had not seen the sea, then, but on bright days when my nurse Agnes would take me to walk in the garden I would scramble up on the wall and claim I could spy it, a tinsel ribbon at the edge of the horizon, and I would make poor stout Agnes puff along after me as I played at being a pirate princess, defending my kingdom against dragons or the wicked hordes of heathen soldiers, pulling up the beach in their black-sailed ships, vicious scimitars glinting deep in their beards, clutched in gold-tipped pointed teeth. Agnes grumbled that it was no game for a young lady, and why couldn't I sit nicely under a rosebush and attend to my needlework like a Christian child, but I argued rudely that I was I not a Courtenay and a great lady besides, and that serpents and infidels were very much my business. Agnes had nothing to say to that.

My mother's people were a crusading family, royalty from Outremer, the kingdom across the sea where the bravest knights of Europe fought in the bloodstained desert to preserve Christendom from the wicked wiles of Saladin. When I was big I was going to take ship at Italy and cross those deserts myself and live in a pink marble palace with a hundred courtyards full of fountains and a troop of monkeys with gold collars to bring me pomegranates and sherbets made with jasmine syrup and mountain ice. Agnes said monkeys were nasty beasts, she was sure, full of fleas and worse, and that she had no intention of getting on a ship and then where would I be in my pink marble palace with no one to mind me? So then I would sit quietly, to please her, and pretend to study my missal, but in a while my eyes would wander up through the wide sky above my father's house to the façade of the cathedral, alive with its tumble of stone flowers and beasts, and my sensible wool cloak would turn to mail across my back so that I could feel its dusty weight, and the sharp wind that whipped up from the river below the city would be full of the scents of saffron and incense and the cupolas at the corners of my grandfather's church would shimmer in a mirage, becoming the towers of the Holy City itself … until the bells rang for the tenth hour and I had to snatch up my book and run to wash my hands as Agnes called me to dinner.

I was playing there, up on the walls, the day the silk merchant came. April, and the waters of that fancied ocean beneath me were turning from grey to the palest golden green.

'Look, Agnes, he's here, he's here!'

Childhood has a different calendar, I think, not marked by the feasts of the Church or the regular shift of the seasons but by the smaller, more personal rhythms of a world of which we are still the centre. For me, the new year began when the new sunlight softened merciless Poitou wind and I began to watch for the silk merchant on the road from the south. He was Venetian, from that city that really did float on water, where all the wealth of the East was gathered to be floated along canals the colour of the silk man's strange aqua eyes. I loved to hear my mother tell me of Venice, the Crusader's gateway, from where the men of her own family, the Courtenays, had set out to fight the heathen, where mysterious ladies waited in gold-panelled rooms, combing out their hair in pearl looking glasses, with the silk sleeves of their gowns trailing all the way to the ground. My mother had a looking glass, and if I was very careful she might sometimes allow me to peep at myself in it. She said that in Venice the light was conjured into so much glass that the whole city shimmered like a vast mirror, a vision of Heaven at the edge of the world.

Even Agnes was excited to see him, looking carefully round to see that none of my father's grooms were nearby before hoisting her skirts, showing a glimpse of blue cloth stocking, to climb up beside me. She put her arm around me as we watched, and I remember her smell, the lavender in her linen under the darker odour of her winter gown, mixed with the olive oil of the Castile soap she used to scrub us with in the bathhouse.

I pointed along the road to where the silk man's mule laboured like a fat bluebottle through the swampy hollows left by the winter floods. 'Look, there he is!'

'I see him, Isabelle, yes. I see him, little one.'

If I had listened, perhaps I would have caught something different in her tone, but I was too excited to care.

'But there's someone else, Agnes, look!'

I felt her stiffen beside me, a sudden tension in her gentle arm, and she looked round wildly for a moment until her eyes dropped back to the road, and seeing that the second rider was alone, she let out her breath and hugged me closer.

'What's the matter, Agnes?'

'Nothing, my treasure. I wonder who that is?'

The Poitou roads are almost impassable in the wintertime. Our supplies and messages came up the river on barges. It was not until the world dried out that the time came for the men to move out for the campaigning season. It was too early for there to be anything to fear from the road, even I knew that. Agnes was always worrying. I peered as far as I dared over the worn stone, my feet dangling in the air behind me. The horseman was gaining on the mule, I could see the red and gold of his surcoat through the splattering of road mud. He was riding crazily, paying no mind to the treacherous ground, his body hunched high over the straining shoulders of his mount so that I could imagine the poor beast's sides slick with sweat and blood from the cruel spurs. He came up behind the silk man and the mule skittered clumsily from his path, I heard a shout of protest as the packs were pelted with dirt. I wanted to giggle, but Agnes would not have liked me to laugh at another's misfortune, so I made my face solemn and said that I hoped the poor silk man's wares were not spoiled.

'Still, he must be important. He will be coming for my father.' I felt proud as I said that, knowing that my father was the most important man in his county of Angouleme and La Marche. Aymer Taillefer, Count of Angouleme, as the heralds called when he entered the cathedral for Mass, one of the greatest vassals of Philip, king of France. My father's people had held our lands since the time of our ancestor, the Emperor Charlemagne. They had fought the Norsemen when they ventured into this part of France, and the meadows beneath their city were full of iron, my father said, from their swords and from their blood. Our name meant 'iron cutter,' after the Count of Angouleme who had sliced a Norse chieftain in half to his waist, cleaving his helmet and breastplate with a single great blow of his sword. The Taillefers belonged to Angouleme, and Angouleme to us, and one day this high city would be mine, for I was my father's heiress.

'Come away now, Isabelle.'

'No! I want to see.'

'The silk man will be here soon,' she coaxed. 'We can go to the kitchens and see about some food for him. And then you can choose your gown.'

I struggled out from under her arm. 'No, I want to stay here. Look, they're opening the gates!'

7

'You'll fall, you foolish child! Come back, now.'

Reluctantly, I let her lead me down to the kitchen buildings but not before I had jumped three times from the wall into her waiting arms. And then we were in the kitchens, where I was rarely allowed to go, and all the cooks and scullions bowed through the smoke and steam and said 'my lady', which I liked very much, and we picked out a cold duck and some soft manchet bread for the silk man, and I grandly ordered some spiced wine for my visitor and was given a piece of pink marchpane to suck, so that altogether I forgot about the messenger so eager was I to see the silk that Agnes would sew into my birthday gown.

*

I waited and waited in my mother's room, where we would always look at the fabrics together, but even after the silk man had unloaded his wares and washed and eaten and prayed, my mother did not come. I fidgeted with the hangings on her big carved bed and poked in the rushes with my toes and made a nuisance of myself until Agnes snapped at me and told me to sit quiet.

'But *Maman* said she would come! She always comes. Why is she late?'

'I don't know.'

'Well, send to find out then,' I said imperiously, so Agnes spoke to one of my mother's maids, who had gaggled in the doorway, as eager as I to see the cloths and slippers and ribbons. In a while she slipped back and whispered in Agnes's ear.

'Maman says you can start without her, Isabelle. She's very

8

busy, and you're a big girl now. Old enough to choose your own gown.'

I thought about crying. It wasn't fair. My mother always looked at the silks with me and told me stories about where they came from and it wouldn't be the same without her. Still, the maids were watching, and Agnes's face was tight with something I didn't recognize, and I knew that she minded for me and that I should behave graciously.

'Very well.' I took a deep breath and motioned my hand to the silk man as I had seen my mother do. 'You may show us what you have brought. We will see if it pleases us.'

I caught a giggle from one of the maids and glared at her. She bobbed a curtsey and said, 'Excuse me, my lady.' I felt better. I clapped my hands, trying to feel as happy as I had last year, and the year before.

'Come along then!'

For a moment the girls hung back, but then they fell upon the opened packs like a flock of pigeons, pecking and exclaiming, running rainbows through their fingers and holding up the jewel-coloured cloths to their faces. I pointed to a heavy red as it slithered to the floor. 'Where does this come from?'

The silk man's skin was dark like old leather, but I thought I could see that city of sparkling water and glass in his curious eyes. I liked the long lilt in his voice when he spoke, the slim suppleness of his vowels, poking through our language like the slender prow of a boat. 'From Venice, my lady. My city.'

All the same, the red was too weighty and sombre, like something a priest would wear.

'Show me another.'

He pulled out a length of golden orange, holding it up to the light so that the colours danced, then spread it across my knees so that I could make out the delicate blue embroidery, a shadow pattern of foliage.

'This is from the meadows of Anatolia, my lady. The women there labour for years on a single piece of cloth. It will be as though your skirts are a field of flowers.'

Agnes looked disapproving. 'You may set that aside for my mistress. It is too fine for a child.'

I didn't mind. It was beautiful but it was not my birthday gown. The maids had gathered beneath the casement exclaiming over a piece they held between them but when I looked again I was puzzled, for it seemed there was nothing in their hands.

'That one,' I demanded.

Agnes often reprimanded me for my eagerness, for poking and snatching, breaking things or making them grubby, but when I saw the silk the maids were carrying I held myself back, afraid to touch it. I had never seen anything so beautiful. The tissue was so fine it might have been a lady's skin; the veins on the girls' hands were visible beneath it. It was not quite white and not quite silver, densely woven like damask, but it seemed as light as a cloud. It was definitely something that a mermaid would wear.

'Please, where does this come from?'

'Oh this, my lady? This is not for sale.'

I thought I knew all his merchant's tricks, like when Agnes took me to the fair on Lady Day and the stallholders pretended

10

they had nothing to spare because they knew we were rich. I thought I would pretend to be patient. 'But please, tell me where it is from.'

'This silk is from Persia, my lady. There is nothing like it for sale from Naples to Paris. And it is a gift, a gift for the queen of France herself.'

'Really? For the queen?'

'For Queen Agnes, yes. She was a princess of Dalmatia, you know, which is a Venetian territory. Her Majesty will value this greatly, so you see I cannot sell it, even to such a pretty little lady as you.'

'Is that so?' It was my mother's voice. The silk man folded himself into a bow so tight I thought he would spring back like a spinning top, and the maids' gowns rustled as they bent deep curtseys, but I rushed into her arms.

'Maman, Maman, here you are! I knew you'd come! Look at this, Maman, he says it's for the queen!'

My mother squeezed me so tightly that I was lifted off the floor and she buried her lips in my neck, kissing me until it tickled while I rubbed my nose into her shoulder.

'How much?' she asked.

'But Maman, it really is for the queen, we can't buy it!' I explained.

'Do you like it, little one? Shall you have it for your birthday gift from me?'

I hesitated. I wanted it, of course I wanted it, but there was something about it that made me afraid. It was a costume for a pink marble palace, like something from a story that I didn't quite want to come true. When I looked at it, it made me feel lonely.

'Won't the queen be angry, Maman?' I hesitated.

My mother smiled. 'I daresay the queen has plenty of silks to choose from. And this is white, the colour the queens of Eastern France wear for mourning, you know. Perhaps she will not like it, just now.'

As my mother spoke I saw Agnes's eyes seek her face. She raised her eyebrows, questioning; my mother replied with a barely perceptible nod.

'So you would have it, then, my darling?'

'Of course, thank you Maman, oh, thank you!' I tried to hop with happiness, to show my mother I was delighted but there was a strange cold feeling inside me, and as the silk man moved to lay the cloth on my mother's bed I hated how its lightness stirred in the breeze from the casement, like a living thing. A shroud, I thought, a creeping shroud that would swallow me up and suffocate me. I wanted him gone, I wanted to choose another gown, anything, yellow or blush or green, I didn't care, but I smiled and held my mother's arm as the silk man bowed his way out to the strong room where my father's clerk would mark the silk on the tally sticks. The maids fluttered out, exclaiming over their ribbons and kerchiefs.

And then, when we were alone, my mother told me slowly and sadly that King Richard of England was dead, and that I was to be married. I was nine years old.

CHAPTER ONE

My mother had told me the tale of Melusina many times. 'There was a king,' she would always begin, 'who loved his wife very much. When she died, he raved in his grief, and his only consolation was found in the forest, where he hunted for hours every day, exhausting his horses as he tried to ride away his tears. One day, the sorrowful king had outrode his groom and squire and found himself alone in a strange part of the forest. He heard trickling water, which reminded him that he was very thirsty, so he stopped at the spring to refresh himself. As he stooped over the clear water, he heard a woman's voice, singing.'

My mother would change to the langue d'oc here, the language of the musicians, to sing the words the king heard. Sometimes she sang from one of my favourite songs, 'He alouete, Joliete, petit t'est de mes maus,' putting the words in the mouth of the beautiful fairy, Pressine, who waited by the well for the king.

'And then, as he saw her, the king's aching heart was healed. In time, Pressine became his wife. When it was time for her to give birth, Pressine told the king that he must not come near her, and she was delivered of three baby girls, Melusina, Meliore and Palatine.'

'Did she love them, Maman?'

My mother would kiss me on the nose. 'Very much but not as much as your maman loves you, little one.'

Then the story told of how the king, hearing of the births, rushed to congratulate his wife, breaking the rule she had given him, and **Pressine** said sadly that he had not kept his promise to her, and that she must leave his castle at once. And then a great storm blew, with clouds like ink and rain so thick the sun disappeared, and when the storm had gone, so had the queen and her daughters.'

'Where did they go?'

'To the Lost Island, where no one but the fairies has ever been. But each day, the queen carried her daughters to the peak of a mountain, where they could look down upon their father's lands, and she would tell them that they might have lived there, and been happy, except that he had broken his word.'

'Was she sad?'

'Very sad, my darling. But she had to keep to the fairy law,' Mother would explain.

Melusina was the most beautiful of the three fairy princesses, and the most curious ('who was she like, little one, I wonder?'). When she was grown up, she asked Pressine what it was that her father had done. When she heard of how he had spied on her mother and defied her, Melusina decided to punish the king. She stole away from the Lost Island into his lands, and there

14

she used a spell – remember, she had fairy blood – that imprisoned the king and all his barons inside a stony mountain cave. When Pressine discovered this, she was angry, in turn, for she loved her husband still, and longed for him, despite his error, and punished her daughter with another spell – a curse. Every Saturday, Melusina would turn into a serpent, and this would continue until she found a man to marry her who would agree never to see her on that day.

'But Maman, why did Pressine put such a wicked charm on her daughter, if she loved her so?'

'Because sometimes mothers have to do very difficult things if they believe they are right. Melusina was different from other girls: she was a fairy. So her mother knew that only by obeying fairy laws could she keep her daughter safe. Shall we see what happened?'

'Oh yes!'

'Well then, Melusina set off alone, and she travelled through many forests and many mountains until she came here, to Poitou. The fairies were very happy. They had been expecting her and wanted to make her their queen. They came to dance with her in the woods at Colombiers,' she would continue.

Now she was arriving at the part that I liked best. 'Tell me about the changeling, Maman. And the murders!'

'Are you telling this story, or I? Now, in the forest that very day was Raymond, the lord of Lusignan. Raymond was unhappy, because he had accidentally committed a crime. He had been hunting with his uncle, and as they bearded the boar, it had turned aside on Lord Raymond's spear and plunged its deadly tusk into his uncle's flesh and killed him stone dead. As Raymond wandered sadly through the forest, he saw Melusina, who was so beautiful that he fell in love with her at once. Only by marrying him, he swore, could Melusina be so kind as to assuage the wound in his heart, which was likely to be as fatal as the boar's tusk. Melusina said that she would surely marry him, upon the condition that he never looked upon her on a Saturday. Raymond agreed, and so they were married.

'Then Melusina had the fairies build a great castle near to the spring where they had met, but she warned Raymond that if he broke his promise she would leave him and they would both be very unhappy. Raymond was so ensorcelled by Melusina's loveliness that he did not even care when their first-born son, Geoffrey Spike-Tooth, was born with a boar's tusk protruding from his upper lip. But Geoffrey was as ugly inside as he was on the outside. He was cruel to everyone in the castle, but most of all he hated his younger brother who was very holy and pious and had gone to live with the monks in the abbey at Malliers. Geoffrey Spike-Tooth was also jealous of his parents' happiness, and he plotted against Melusina. He decided to spy upon her in her privacy on a Saturday.

'On that day, Melusina would shut herself up in her rooms, taking no food or drink, allowing no one to attend on her from dawn until sunset. She had a great bath in her chamber, and filling it was the last task her maids were permitted before their mistress retired. So Geoffrey Spike-Tooth disguised his ugly features in a plain gown and a hood, and carried a jug into Melusina's rooms as the maids brought the water, then he hid himself under the bathtub and waited, spying out under the bath cloth.

'When Melusina got up from her bed and lowered herself into the bath at dawn and the first ray of the sun crept through the window, her legs were transformed into a serpent's tail, all blue and silver scales. All day the wicked son lay under the bath while the fairy splashed in the waters and, at nightfall, when Melusina walked back to her bed and called for her maids, he escaped and rushed straight to Count Raymond. When the count learned the truth, he did not rage and turn his wife away, as Geoffrey Spike-Tooth expected, but grieved, because now that he knew the truth he risked losing his beloved wife forever.

'Enraged at the failure of his plan, Geoffrey Spike-Tooth travelled to the abbey at Malliers and set it on fire. The good monks and his own holy brother were burned. Melusina heard this dreadful news and rushed to her husband's chamber to comfort him. But now, the story says, my little one, that the poor afflicted father was convinced that the fairy's curse was on his family, and he accused poor Melusina before all the courtiers.'

My mother would draw herself up tall and make her voice very deep and stern.

'Out of my sight, thou pernicious snake and odious serpent! Thou contaminator of my race!'

'Oh Maman!' I would burst. 'And then?'

'Then, Melusina was so shocked that she fell down in a faint but when she awakened, she solemnly told her husband that she must leave him, just as her own mother Pressine had left her father the king for the breaking of his word. Her fate was to wander about the world forever, invisible as a spirit. Only when one of her own fairy kind died at Lusignan would she become visible again.'

'And now the curse!' I would shriek, delighted at the deliciously terrifying climax of the story.

'And now I must depart from you, faithless husband, that thou, and those who succeed thee for more than a hundred years shall know that whenever I am seen, hovering over the castle of Lusignan, then it will be certain that in that very year the castle shall have a new lord. And though people may not perceive me in the air, they will see me by the fountain, especially on the Friday before the lord of the castle shall die ...'

*

And so, like every child in Poitou, I knew the story of the Lusignan ancestress, the serpent-woman Melusina. She haunted this same castle, flapping round the battlements on stormy nights, protecting her descendants with her demonish powers. But if ever she was seen, it meant death to the Lusignan lord.

They are black, the Lusignan men. Their hair is the colour of the river in winter, sucking the light around them, their tip-tilted almond eyes like nuggets of charcoal in sallow, horn-tinted skin. And they are tall. So tall that when Lord Hugh stepped down from the dais in his hall to greet us after our journey my father's head only reached his shoulder. My father had put off his hauberk as he dismounted, to show that he came in peace to his old enemy, and Lord Hugh, also, wore no armour. But where my father's mantle was travel-stained wool, bunching over his round belly and gathering under his red beard, which fell to his chest, Lord Hugh wore white silk, spotless as an altar cloth, and a short green cloak clasped at one shoulder with a huge gold brooch shaped like a serpent, and his shaven face was all clean, hard planes. A little behind him stood his son, Hal, nearly as tall but narrow and gangling, a sapling next to his father's massive oak, with the same pitchy hair falling fashionably long, the tips curling to touch his soft, sulky mouth.

The Lusignans and the Taillefers had always been enemies, for my father was King Richard's man, defending his lands against the rebellious lords who sought to chip away at the empire of the English king while he was in the Holy Land. But now, my mother had explained as we bumped along in the litter, the leathery smell of the curtains wafting over us, the Lusignans were our allies, ever since King Richard had made Lusignan knights kings in Cyprus for their service on Crusade, and a marriage, my marriage, between our houses, would seal our loyalties and protect our lands together under the leopard flag of the Angevin kings. It had been King Richard's wish that a match be made, before he was struck down by a crossbow wound in his shoulder and died without children, leaving his crown and his dukedoms of Normandy and Aquitaine to his brother John. At least, that was what she told me then.

It seemed unreal to me, all this squabbling about lands, and yet at the same time it had always been as much a part of my life as hearing Mass or doing my lessons. Fighting was what men did – they rode out as soon as the roads were clear in the spring and returned with the fogs of autumn, and I would hear my parents talking as I dozed in the solar after supper that such a county had changed its fealty again, or that the French armies had taken a castle from the English, or they from the French. It was a game, I supposed, that great people used to pass the time, as shifting and impermanent as the quarrels and alliances of a childhood afternoon in the garden. Men fought and women married, that was what my mother said, and with our marriages we would weave peace between the counties of France. It was men who made war, Maman explained, but it was women's holy duty to make peace, for that was what God commanded.

'See how handsome he is, Isabelle,' whispered Agnes. 'Don't be afraid.'

I did not think him handsome. I thought he looked stupid. I wanted to rush and hide in my mother's skirts and beg her to take me home to Angouleme, but she was moving forward, inclining her head graciously to Lord Hugh, though not too low, as she was a granddaughter of the king of France. I gave Agnes's hand a tight squeeze before I stepped into my own curtsey, as my mother had taught me, only wobbling a little when my knees touched the rosemary-scented rushes. When I looked up, he was standing over me, impossibly high, smothering my hand in his great hard palm and leading me forward to present me to Hal.

'The Lady Isabelle.'

I curtsied again, with no shaking this time. I bit my lip and thought of the Courtenays, princes of the desert, and of my father's people, the Taillefers, the iron cutters, who gained their name from the slashed chain coat of a long-ago Norman sea king. I would not let this boy see how scared I was. I could feel my mother watching me approvingly as the servants brought wine in silver cups and we moved to take our seats.

'To King Richard, may God save his soul,' offered my father as he took a deep drink.

'And to our new King John, may God preserve him,' replied Lord Hugh. Then they both laughed and sat back as though they had said something secret and clever.

'Have you no words of welcome for your bride, Hal?' smiled Lord Hugh. His lips were curled upwards but it was a snake's smile, I thought, with no kindness in it.

Hal muttered something through his fringe about my being very welcome to Lusignan.

'Perhaps you would like to take Lady Isabelle to the garden, Hal? To become better acquainted,' suggested Lord Hugh.

The men rose as I stood and let Hal hand me down, Agnes bustling behind. We were not half the length of the hall when I could hear the adults' voices begin, urgent and close. Hal led the way carelessly between two men-at-arms in green surcoats, not giving a glance to the horrible blades of their axes, then down a narrow passage to a small door which gave onto a walled garden. The air was warm between espaliered peach trees and a soft lawn that looked as inviting as a velvet carpet. It was such a relief to be in the air after the smoke and scents of the dark hall that I began to feel a little better. Perhaps Lusignan was not such a bad place after all, even though it was full of Lusignans. Agnes gave me a warning nod, which I knew meant I was to behave, and seated herself on a sunny bench, her eyes falling closed straightaway with exhaustion from the journey.

'What shall we play?' I asked Hal.

'Play?'

'Yes. You could be Saladin, if you like, and I will be Peter de Courtenay and attack you in the tree. Or do you prefer hunting? I can be a bear. Or we could have a sword fight, if we can find some good sticks ...'

'Why would I want to play with a stupid little girl? I don't play, anyway.'

He wasn't that much older than me. 'Well, we could dance then. I can do *les grâces*, can you?'

'Dancing?' he sneered. 'How about this for dancing?' He kicked me hard on the shin so I fell over and I could feel the scrape of his boot even through my gown. I rolled on the lawn, which was not so velvety as it looked, and I thought that Agnes would scold me for spoiling my clothes, and then I felt a great wave of tears build up inside me and I was so angry that he might see me cry that I jumped up and threw myself at his nasty sneering face, and when he toppled over next to me I grabbed his arm and sank my teeth into his wrist as hard as I could so that he screamed.

'Who's the stupid girl now then?' I jeered. 'Ow!' He had a handful of my hair, wrenching it so hard I thought my scalp would peel off. I rolled over on top of him and banged my knee into his stomach to wind him. 'Let go! Let go! Or I'll bite you again.'

'My lady! Stop this at once!' called Agnes, but I was weeping furiously now, I could feel my face all hot and smeary, and I didn't care about that, or the state of my skirts, I was going to fight him like a Taillefer and make him surrender. But he was much bigger than me and he tipped me over easily, sending me sprawling. He was walking away, shaking his arm.

'Angouleme bitch.'

'How dare you?' I howled, scrabbling myself upright. I ran at him, grabbing at his cloak before Agnes could reach me and jabbing the point of my elbow at the soft place between his legs. He screeched and dropped to his knees, clutching himself, so I kicked at him and shouted, 'Infidel dog! Submit!' When I looked up I could see the axe men laughing and my parents' horrified faces peering through the garden door. My mother flew towards me and grabbed me like a kitten by the scruff of my neck.

'Agnes! How could you let this happen? And you, Isabelle, for shame! You shall be whipped!'

I had never seen her look so furious. It made me cry harder.

'But he kicked me, Maman! I only wanted to play.'

'Lord Hugh, I must apologize. She has her father's temper. She is willful but she is a good child.'

I was being picked up, swung through the air until my dirty face encountered Lord Hugh's white-silk shoulder. 'Your coat, sir,' I mumbled, finally remembering my manners, but he held me tight against him, so tenderly that I could not stop the tears, and I felt that huge hand awkwardly petting my head.

'Madame, it is my son who should be ashamed, to treat a lady so,' apologized Lord Hugh. 'Hal! Apologize to Lady Isabelle immediately!'

I could feel the rumble of his voice deep in his chest, against my body. I peered through my dishevelled hair down at Hal, who made a deep bow and said, 'I beg your forgiveness, Lady Isabelle.'

His father's hand shot out and cuffed him round the ear. 'None of your cheek, boy. Say it like you mean it. And shame on you for losing a fight with a little maid.'

I tried to catch Hal's eye as he repeated his bow, to show I was sorry that we were both in trouble, but he was not enough of a child to remember that we should be allies. All I saw in those deep slate-black pools was hate.

Lord Hugh set me gently to the ground. 'There, Isabelle. You are very welcome to the family. Now run along with your nurse, you must rest. Do you like marmalade?'

I nodded.

'Then you shall have some. Go along now.'

Still panting and snorting with tears like an exhausted pony, I took Agnes's hand and let her lead me away, grim faced. As soon as we were indoors she looked at me and sighed.

'Oh Isabelle. How could you? Hal is your betrothed, and he will be your master. How could you be so wicked, little one?'

I didn't care about Hal and I would never let him be my master. As I trailed along after Agnes I thought on Lord Hugh. He was not a kind man, I could see that, but he had been kind to me for all that he looked so grand and stern. Perhaps because Lord Hugh's family were Crusader kings like mine, he saw that my blood was brave and fearless, that I was a Courtenay as well as a Taillefer.

I wished I had remembered to tell Hal that I knew all about Melusina and that I knew he was the grand-something of a snail like the one on his father's brooch; that he should beware, in case she came flapping her wings after him. Although the Lusignan castle seemed huge after the broad, light-filled rooms of my father's house, I was not a bit afraid of some old serpent, at least not now, in the daytime, with the sun glowing through the horn panels of the casements and the scent of apple blossom from the orchard. I did not much like the thought of being married, but Lusignan was not so very far from Angouleme. I should have to stay here until the ceremony was conducted when I was twelve, which seemed an impossibly long time, but Agnes would be with me, and as soon as I had been educated as a wife I thought I could go straight home for good because I would be a grown lady and no one should be able to stop me. And perhaps King John would take the cross like his brother, and stupid Hal would sail to the Holy Land and be killed by an infidel, which was also a satisfactory thought. Perhaps I would go, too, and rescue him from a dank and horrible dungeon and then he would have to be grateful to me, like a true knight, because I would save him for honour's sake even though he had kicked me, and then we would see who was the stupid girl.

So I lay on the little white bed which had been prepared for me while Agnes clucked and ordered alum to rub down my grass-stained skirts, and dreamed of myself and Lord Hugh at the head of a conquering army, storming a citadel, scrabbling up broken walls with our swords on our backs while Greek fire boiled down over us and the besieged crawled out to beg us for mercy. My mother would be there in a flowing gown in a courtyard full of fountains, and King John would grant

25

me the castle all of my own, forever. And then the marmalade came, raspberry, in a silver dish with an ivory spoon, and I lost myself in a sunny doze of sugar, trapped as sure as a nectar-sozzled fly who notices only too late that her wings are sodden with sweetness.

The betrothal ceremony was held the next day, before my father and Lord Hugh rode for Normandy to greet the new king on the borders of his dominions to swear their allegiance. Agnes had washed my hair with ashes and lemon juice and combed it out so that it hung below my waist. I had white silk slippers chased with silver and my new white gown. I shuddered a little as its cool weightlessness enfolded me, but Maman told me I looked beautiful so I tried to look happy.

Sulky Hal scowled through the words the priest repeated to us, the *verba de praesenti* that meant we were bound by God to be married, but I did my best to speak up clearly and smile graciously when he slipped a tiny gold ring onto my finger, and all the Lusignan court bent in a windblown cornfield of bows to acknowledge me as their new lady, which I liked very much indeed. Then there was music, and tumbling jongleurs, and a castle made of coloured wafers, almond paste and candied oranges. My mother handed me small purses of coins to hand to the poor people who shuffled into the courtyard to receive the scraps from the betrothal feast. The Lusignan knights paraded in their green surcoats, with their horses hung in the same, and I had to admit that Hal looked very well mounted up high with his chased leather buckler. He was to ride with his father that night. Then the men clattered down to the gatehouse where the baggage wagons waited and dismounted for the priest to bless them, and my father caught me in his arms so my face was squashed in his familiar stinky beard and told me to be a good girl and mind my mother. Lord Hugh reached down from his saddle to take my hand. 'I will see you very soon, Lady Isabelle. I hope you will be content here at Lusignan.'

'I'm sure I shall, sir.'

He leaned forward conspiratorially so that I startled at the flash of the gold serpent at his throat. 'And mind you are not too obedient. I have great plans for us, Isabelle, great plans.'

I looked modestly at the toes of my slippers as he kicked his horse into a trot, and leaned my head against my mother's side while we watched the men wind away down the road as we had done so many times before. The spring sky was still light and although the day had been so eventful I had that feeling of flat-ness that comes when others set off on a journey and one is left behind. My mother pulled me to her and hugged me fiercely, so tight that I could feel our heartbeats meld for a moment in her embrace.

'Don't be sad, Maman,' I said stoutly, 'Papa will come back, he always does.'

'I'm not sad, little one,' she murmured, her lips in my hair. As though she was speaking to herself, I heard her whisper, 'We still have a little time.' She released me and looked the way they had gone.

'Will they be away long, Maman?'

'Normandy is very far, little one, and there will be a great deal of business to be done. Things will change, now that King John holds his brother's lands … if he can hold them.'

'What do you mean?'

My mother looked weary and distracted but she answered my question patiently, as she always did. 'King John of England and our cousin King Philip of France are enemies. They have always disputed the rights of the English kings to their holdings here but King Richard lived here most of his life when he was not on Crusade. He was known, understood. This John is English, he speaks English and he conspired with English lords to overthrow his brother. And there is another heir to the crown, Duke Arthur.'

'The son of Duchess Constance of Brittany?'

My mother smiled. 'What big ears you have, my treasure! Well remembered. Yes, Duke Arthur claims the crown because he is the son of King John's elder brother. If he declares for King Philip it will go badly for the English.' She sighed, her eyes were far away on the road with my father, I thought. 'But this is not your affair. You are betrothed now. We will do what women do – we will wait.'

I was pleased that I should not be seeing Hal for a good long time, at least. 'And you shall stay here until May Day, Agnes says?'

'Yes, little one, until the May is brought in.'

I couldn't understand why she looked so thoughtful. My father was often absent, and this time he hadn't even gone off to fight. 'Anyway, I'm here. And we can play every day,' I announced firmly.

'Of course we can, little love, of course we can.'

My mother's women were waiting to attend her to supper, she kissed me and promised to come to tuck me into bed, but as she walked slowly back to that huge castle, so vast compared to our home in Angouleme, I could see that the straight reed of her spine was held with effort and her head leaned wearily to one side. Perhaps she wasn't worried about Papa, perhaps she was sorry that I should stay at Lusignan when she had to leave. But though I loved my maman better than anyone, I was accustomed to spending long periods without her, and the thought of her sorrow slipped from me as I too walked up to the castle, imagin–ing what a great lady I should be, and how I should make stupid Hal sorry and respect me when he came back home.

CHAPTER TWO

For a long while afterwards, I thought that what I saw at Lusignan on May Eve was a dream. And longer still, after I stopped believing it, I told myself that I still did.

Agnes had put me to bed early. I was excited at the thought of waking at dawn to watch the village girls dancing in their spring ribbons with sweet-scented boughs in their arms. I chattered and wriggled until Agnes sent down to the kitchens for a posset, and when I had licked the last of its milky, honeyed sweetness from the bowl, it seemed that I slept, but I could not have been sleeping because here was Agnes drawing back the bed curtains and lifting me up in only my smock. I lolled drowsily in the cushions while she untied my plaited hair so that it hung around my face, pale as new corn in the light of her candle. In my dream, Agnes was in her smock, too, and her hair was unbound, with thick grey streaks running through its nut-brown polish. I ran my fingers through them as I rested against her shoulder, squirming as we came out into the cool night air. It seemed very dark and I thought, later, that I must have been asleep since I did not think to ask why she had woken me, or where we were going. Then I was swung through the air and I could smell horses and a man's sweat, clean and sharpened by the night, but though we were moving I heard no hoof beats, so I thought placidly that we must be flying, and closed my eyes to the soothing rhythm.

So we rode, or flew, and when I opened my eyes again, or dreamed I opened them, we were in a clearing by a river, moon-light scudding over the ripples like the grain in black silk, on a little pebbled beach overhung with trees. The stones crunched below us as someone came to tie the horse and I sensed other horses, waiting in the darkness. As I was carried down, I could see that their legs were bunched in pale rags. I tried to twist up my head to see the man who carried me, but the hood of his cloak was thrown over his face, and though I told myself in my lulled state that I ought to be afraid, my body was soft and loose and I left my head nestled comfortably against his shoulder, hard beneath the thick wool. I sensed other people moving around us. We were making for the glow of a huge bonfire further down the shore, crackling and throwing up billows of smoke and the scent of wood ash. And still, I was not afraid, even when I saw what waited there.

Next to the fire was a great boulder and on it stood a horned man. A stag's antlers were fixed to his head, which was covered in a kind of leather mask, and long dull robes enveloped him to his feet. Around him in a circle huddled more cloaked shapes and beyond them, in a clutch of faces illuminated in the dancing firelight, I recognized Agnes. Several of my mother's maids seemed to be there also, and other faces, too newly familiar from the castle and the village, though they were working people to whom I had never spoken. They moved aside to make way for us as I was carried to the boulder, where the horned man towered above me. Whoever was carrying me set me gently down, my bare feet flinching against the rough stones, as the first circle of shapes rose up and gathered around me. I staggered a little, dizzied by the light, turning my head slowly.

'Who brings this child?' the horned man was speaking. Though his voice was muffled by the mask it seemed familiar to me.

'I do.' In my dream, I knew my mother's voice and thought, as is the way of dreams, that I was safe, because she was there. Her hood had fallen back a little as she moved to take my arm and I saw that her hair too was loose, its heavy waves dark gold.

'Do you come of your own free will?' He was speaking to me. I nodded dumbly.

'You must answer,' my mother's voice floated towards me from far away, as though it twisted among the logs at the heart of the fire.

'Yes,' I responded.

'Do what I desire,' the horned man said.

Mother's hands were on my shoulders, pressing me to my knees. I was so cold now that I could not mind the sharp stones through the fine lawn of my smock. Her voice wound into my ear, 'Thou art my god.'

'Thou art my god,' I mumbled.

The horned man held out his hand, and as my mother reached up to receive what was in it I felt other hands untying the laces at my back until the shift fell from my shoulders and I felt half my back scorch suddenly in the fire heat. My mother held my left shoulder and turned her face away, the hood falling forward, covering her, as I sensed a sudden, sharp pain above my shoulder blade, a pain that swam from me even as it cut me, as though I were dreaming the hurt of another's body. My mother gripped me tightly, so tightly her arm shook, and her fingers digging into my skin hurt more than the strange new pain that rippled across my back. The horned man reached down once more and I saw that he held a long, thick awl, its sharp point disappearing into the darkness as he brought it to the mouth of the mask. Arms pulled me to standing, though I could barely straighten my stiffened legs. The horned man then knelt, leaning down from the boulder so that the smell of his robes was over my face and I knew they were not cloth but animal skin, stiffened and reeking. He placed his palm over my face, its heel against my mouth, and as I gasped for breath I drew in a thin, irony liquid. He turned his hand and extended the fingers, like a bishop, I felt my mother's hand inclining my head to kiss it. I wanted to spit and smear the juice from my face, but as I tried to clean it on my smock the group behind us began to clap and cheer, so I turned my head to the firelight and tried to smile into my mother's eyes.

And then, the dream broke into fevered fragments, so that one moment I was sitting on Agnes's lap, with a cloth before us, with food and jugs spread out, and she was feeding me a piece of chicken with raisins; then I was lying in front of the fire, my eyes spinning, as a strange music woven of flutes and harps and clapping hands drew each one of the muffled figures up into a dance that coupled them back to back and whirled them around the fire against the path of the sun; then my mother climbed on the rock, her streaming hair mingling with the fire as she threw away her cloak, tall and slender, her thigh bound with a red cord, and the other women likewise, so that they were naked in the orange flames, their bodies smoothed and silvered, cast in their hair, with deep hollows between their legs. The horned man moved among them, a lantern burning between his antlers, turning them two at a time in the dance, spinning like the stars in the invisible heavens, and they were laughing, beating time with their feet and singing in a language I had never heard. Then I must have slept truly, for when I woke the figures around me were sleeping in the first pearl glow of dawn, their bodies covered once more with dew-dampened cloaks, and the horned man was gone. In his place was Lord Hugh, curled on the boulder with the gold serpent wound at his throat.

For a while I watched him sleeping. My mind was spinning, my body tight and chilled, though someone had thrown a cloth over me as I slept. As I sat up, Lord Hugh opened his eyes and stared back at me, those dark eyes swallowing the first rays of the sun as he blinked slowly. As I made to sit he bounded down in one movement and lifted me to my feet, calling 'Isabelle! Good morning!' and as I creaked into my curtsey the shapes around me stirred and sprang up as though the stones were suddenly alive, so that when I raised my face to his it seemed that he had summoned the morning, and all around us the women began chattering, splashing their faces in the river water, braiding up their hair, producing baskets of bread and cooking pots as though we were on a picnic.

'Where is my mother?'

'At the castle, of course,' replied Agnes, looking her usual, neat, daytime self.

'But she was here … we were all here, in the night.'

'Silly. I brought you down for the maying and you fell asleep. The others were resting – they'd been out gathering the boughs. Don't you remember?'

I looked about and saw that there were piles of plane twigs lying about, their leaves uncurling in the early warmth to release their fresh, sticky scent. Some of the village girls were seated, twining apple mint, mayweed and bryony into garlands for their hair.

'Yes. Perhaps. Agnes, I had such a funny dream!'

'Come and have some food. There's milk and fresh honey-comb.'

'But Lord Hugh … is my papa here with him?'

'Not yet, little one. Come and eat.'

It was not until later on May Day, after we had breakfasted and walked to the village to make the churchyard gay with May blossoms, skipping to the wooden whistles that Agnes said were the custom at Lusignan, until after my mother and her maids had watched the dancing, her face now as bright and clear as the morning, that I felt it. Agnes had sent me to make myself neat for dinner, as Lord Hugh was in the castle, and as I reached up to comb my hair, I felt that sharp pain in my shoulder.

'Owwww! Agnes, it hurts. Are there fleas in my bed?'

'I should think not!'

'But it hurts.'

'Let me see.' She unlaced my fresh smock and peered at my skin. 'A spider bite, maybe. From when you were resting on the ground this morning. I have some mallow balm, that will soothe it.'

I didn't believe her. When the adults had gone to their sleep after dinner I went to my mother's room. I wanted her looking glass. The maids must have been in the dormitory as my mother's chamber was empty, smelling of beeswax from the scrubbed boards covering the floor. The cushions were plump and neat, my mother's wooden chair, her chest and travelling boxes neatly arranged. I hunted among the combs and pins laid out on her box, but the looking glass wasn't there. Perhaps she had combed her hair before lying down and had it in her closet. I pushed open the door, quietly so as not to wake her, but as I stole inside I tripped over her slippers which had been discarded at the foot of her big, curtained bed.

'Isabelle!' My mother was seated in the window, her hair uncovered and her feet bare. Lord Hugh was hunched in close to her, they sprang apart as though I had caught them whispering secrets. 'Isabelle! What are you doing creeping about like this?'

'I'm sorry, Maman, I just wanted—'

'Can't you see that I'm speaking with Lord Hugh? Where is Agnes? Why are you wandering about by yourself?'

I did not understand why she should be so cross. At home I

was always running in and out of her chamber. Perhaps it was because I was betrothed, now. 'I came to look at your glass, Maman. A spider bit me, Agnes says. I'm sorry.'

'Run along now,' she said more gently. 'We can have the apothecary take a look if it troubles you, later. Off you go.'

I shuffled disconsolately down to the garden, my shoulder still stinging. I felt like crying, but I didn't really know why. Yet that was how it was for the time until my mother departed and left me alone at Lusignan. We went to Mass together each day, she heard my letters with a set of polished ivory blocks Lord Hugh had given me, I walked with her on the ramparts and she came to kiss me before drawing my bed curtains at night, but my maman seemed to be somewhere else. Before, she had loved telling me stories but now when I snuggled into the pillows and begged her to tell me of the great battles of the Crusades once more, she would sigh and smile, and blow out the lamp. 'Maybe tomorrow, little one.' And though she was as beautiful as ever, the most beautiful lady in Poitou, the maids said, her face looked drawn and her eyes were never still, dashing like butterflies under her dark lashes, as though she was watching for something that wasn't there. I wanted my mother. I wanted more than anything to curl up against her side, smelling the rosewater in her linen, and fall asleep with her lips warm on my brow, but I was strangely afraid to go to her chamber, and when once I tried, there were two maids outside the door who told me that the countess was not to be disturbed.

*

My bridal chests were arranged in the closet off my own chamber. They contained the linens which had been spun for me since I was born until the day that I married, pressed and packed with sweet smelling herbs, the betrothal gifts my mother had accepted from the Poitou lords who had sent plates and carpets to mark the union of Lusignan and Taillefer, and the jewels that my father had presented to me for my wedding. I had never taken much interest in their contents but now I waited until Agnes was resting and filched the bunch of keys that she wore on her girdle and unlocked them, rooting carelessly through their contents until I found what I needed. Two pewter dishes, traced with rievaulx at their edges, a gift from one of my father's stewards. Not the finest things I owned, to be sure, but I propped one on the chest top against the wall and sat with my back to it, my gown unlaced, holding the other in front of my chest, tipping it against the light until I caught a wavering glimpse of my pale skin in its dull sheen.

The dish was heavy, and the reflection poor, not nearly so good as my mother's glass, but with patience, allowing my eyes to travel over and over the line of my shoulder, I thought I could make it out, the little wound I had explored so many times with my fingers under the bedclothes at night. It no longer pained me but the smooth plane of my flesh was scarred up beneath my hand, and in the silver glow of the dish I could see the form of it, a thin wavering line that looked to me, as I twisted and strained, like a serpent's tail. Quietly, I replaced the dishes, stuffing them into a wad of woollen blankets, then fumbled my way through the keys until I found the one which opened the armoire.

This was the finest chest, worked in walnut intarsia the colour of gold and cinnamon, lined with cedar inside. My marvellous white betrothal gown lay on top, carefully rolled away by Agnes. Spitefully, I took my knife and made a little cut in the hem.

And each day after that, I sliced away at it a little more, until it became a habit that I craved, the whisper of the fabric as it slipped compliantly apart. I would never wear it again. When Agnes took it out to be cleaned it would collapse like a handful of snowflakes and I would say that the mice must have eaten it, for somehow I blamed that shimmering tissue for taking my mother from me. Its curling white edges haunted me like the moonlight of my strange May Eve dream.

So with each cut, I hardened my heart a little against my mother, though I did not know it then. I did not mention the strange wound, either. I told myself that I must have been scratched on a May bush, and that it would heal. But in the last days before my mother's going, I could not sleep. When I closed my eyes I would see the horned man reaching down towards me in the vagrant light of the flames, and I woke sweated and twined in the bedclothes, calling for Agnes. But when she came, it was as I had seen her on May night, naked, with her hair tumbled about her face, and I came truly awake and screamed so loud that the guards rushed in, all the way from Lord Hugh's chamber with their axes raised. My mother appeared, dreamy in her nightshift with a cloak thrown over, but when she knew that I was safe she scolded me.

'It was only a bad dream, Maman. Did you think a Saracen assassin had climbed into the castle?' I was trying to please her,

39

to make her smile with the memory of our stories, but the look my gentle mother gave me was sharper than any pagan's dagger and she berated me for shrieking like a silly child.

'You are betrothed now. Learn how to conduct yourself, Isabelle. You will stay in your room tomorrow. I shall send my confessor to pray with you.'

I would not weep in front of her, I bit my lip proudly and held the tears in, but when she left I hurled myself back on the bed and cried silently until the whole room seemed to shake with my misery. What had happened? Where had my mother gone?

When it came time for her to travel to Angouleme I took leave of her formally, thinking of nothing but holding my spine as erect as a poplar as I curtseyed to the ground and wished her a safe journey. I kept my eyes there while she was helped into the litter, but when she called my name I lifted my head as eagerly as a puppy, and from where I stood below the leather curtains I glimpsed the pale flesh of her leg where her light summer gown had become trapped in one of the litter's poles. As a maid moved to free it, I saw a red garter tied beneath her knee, but my mother wore no stockings that day.

'Isabelle?'

'Yes, Lady Mother?' She settled into the litter, pulling her skirts tight about her and reached down to stroke my cheek. 'Maman.'

'This is very hard, little one. Remember the story of Melusina, and her mother Pressine? Sometimes … sometimes mothers have to do difficult things. Things that their children might not understand, things that seem … unkind. But I love you, Isabelle. Remember that I love you. Remember that.'

I was not to see my mother again until the day I married. I wanted to climb into her arms and beg her to take me with her, but I stood there sullenly, as stupid as a toad, and in a moment she sighed and turned her face away and signed for the litter to move off. I watched her until she was out of sight, winding down the steep slope beyond the curtain wall, but I did not wave or call my love after her. When the sounds of the horses died away the maids turned and curtseyed deeply to me, for with my mother gone I was the first lady of Lusignan. I acknowledged them coldly, for was that not what it meant to be a lady? I should be as aloof as the queen of France, my cousin, so that no one should guess how the pain of my mother's departure twisted inside me a coil of pain that burned in my flesh as sure as the serpent engraved there.

CHAPTER THREE

THAT WAS THE DAY WHEN I BEGAN TO GROW UP. IT was not until both my parents had left me that I truly understood that I should not be going back to Angouleme for a long, long time. I tried to make a painting in my mind, like the coloured stories on church walls, to fix my city there forever. Before I slept in my new room at Lusignan, after I had said my prayers, I would screw my eyes up tight and figure it behind them, the sounds of the men heaving loads from the barges at the river port, the bells of the abbey and the convent, which never chimed the canonical hours at quite the same time, the ancient carving in one of the towers where a man's leg stuck out strangely as though there was a figure imprisoned in the stone. I knew that the leg had belonged to Clovis, the first king of all France, who had been wounded in one of the many battles my city had withstood. In memory, I listened for the waterwheels of the mills and the strange singing that came on Fridays from the little building where the Jewish merchants, with their odd tall hats, had made their church. I painted our river, the Charente, in all its seasons, from the low, heavy floods of winter to the *onde allegre* of the springtime rapids. It felt very grand to me that I could bring peace through my betrothal, even if it meant marrying the dreadful Hal, but if I was to be a Lusignan lady I would keep Angouleme inside me, guarding it like a dragon's hoard.

From the moment my mother left Lusignan, I became as docile a bride-in-waiting as Agnes could wish. I no longer scampered about the gardens, muddying my slippers and tearing my gowns. Agnes was no longer obliged to struggle after me as I played at crusading, or tend my scratches when I fell out of an apple tree. I asked her to twist up my fair braids into two prim knots behind my ears and, though I was not yet married, I instructed the maids to sew me short linen coifs to cover my hair. After hearing Mass each morning with the household we would take a quiet walk along the castle's perimeter then sit quietly over our sewing in the boudoir that had been my mother's while Lord Hugh's chaplain read aloud to us. I saw the maids nodding but sometimes the plain shirts we stitched for the poor had little flowers of blood on them where they pricked their fingers to keep awake. I remained alert and upright, only raising my eyes now and then to the clerk when I thought his droning might be something particularly holy. In fact, I could barely make out a word of the Latin and sewing bored me so much I should happily have given all my own fine clothes to the poor if it spared me having to make for them but I could see how pleased Agnes was with the good example I was setting, and I dearly wanted to please her, for she was all I had left of Angouleme.

At least, I dearly wanted to please her during those hours. I sensed rather than knew it, but it seemed to me that men could divide themselves as neatly as a cook quartering an apple. Lusignan swarmed with secrets, with whispered conversations between Lord Hugh's squires, messengers arriving late in the night, a parchment concealed in the chaplain's sleeve, a keening bare-chested man, his back ragged with lashes, whom I saw through my window being dragged through the inner courtyard between two guards as Lord Hugh walked grim faced before him. A little later, as I watched, he returned, rinsing his hands in a ewer and stripping off his bloodied shirt so that the sun gleamed on the pelt of dark hair that covered his back.

In my new, quiet, modest role as Lusignan bride, I learned that a sober countenance and a quiet step were excellent disguises for gleaning knowledge and, I learned, by watching and listening and minding my needle, that the Angevin lands were gravely contested, that the English counties of Anjou and Maine had been declared for the French king and that Arthur of Brittany was planning to claim his uncle's throne. I learned that Lord Hugh was feared, and that he was considered ruthless and greedy for power but, subtle as the serpent he wore at his throat, neither John nor Philip knew which way he would turn his fealty. Yet to me, Lord Hugh remained as cool and courteous as the day I had drawn blood from his son's hand. When we dined or listened to the musicians in the solar he seemed always entirely self-possessed, as though the creeping armies of the two kings, whose men seeped towards one another over

44

the lands of France like rivulets of flood water, were of as little concern to him as the gossiping of the castle washerwomen. So if men could be one thing, and seem another, then why could not I?

Lord Hugh was fond of me, I knew it. He liked what he called my 'pretty ways': how I would rub my cheek against his sleeve and curl up like a kitten in his lap. He admired the grace of my posture and the elegance of my gowns and told me that his son would be a lucky man to have such a beautiful girl as a wife. When he was occupied I was invisible, but in the rare hours he spent at Lusignan he liked me beside him and I studied to please him, learning the Occitan songs he liked from his lutenist or asking him grave questions about the history of his lands, listening to the answers with my head cocked to one side, bright-eyed as a fledgeling. One hot evening in July, I told his steward that I thought Lord Hugh should like to dine outdoors and had trestles brought into the walled garden so that we could eat chilled almond soup and sweet orange-fleshed melons in the shade. I forced the maids to brave the mosquitoes in the river meadows to pick trefoil and bryony – they grumbled about the mosquitoes that bit – and scatter the yellow and purple blossoms over the white tablecloth. I mixed Lord Hugh's wine myself and attended him as dutifully as I should have my own father.

'Very charming, Isabelle. We might be fairies at a hunting party, eh?'

'I should like to go hunting, Lord Hugh. I should learn to ride, should I not?'

'Quite right, I'll enquire. We'll find you a nice quiet palfrey, we don't want to scare Agnes.'

I wriggled into his lap and twined my fingers around the serpent brooch. 'I don't want a nice quiet palfrey, Lord Hugh, I want a real horse.'

He drew back his head and looked at me, blinking as though he suddenly saw me for the first time. 'Yes,' he answered slowly. 'I expect that you do.'

'So may I?'

'What about your chaperone?' he whispered in my ear so that I felt his lips warm and dry against my skin. 'I can't see fat old Agnes heaving herself onto my destrier!'

'She doesn't have to come,' I teased back. 'And if you wish it, my lord, what can she object to?'

'Then you shall have a real horse, Lady Isabelle. And you shall learn to ride.'

He fluttered his fingers in an elaborate courtesy and I giggled, prettily, because that was what he expected. And in a few days he gave me Othon.

Often, in the evenings after supper, Lord Hugh's Aquitaine musician would recite romances for the company; plaintive stories of sighing knights who pined for beautiful ladies. I had never paid them much mind, preferring those tales of magic and adventure that my papa had sometimes told me. When I first saw Othon, he seemed to come from one of those stories. He was a bay gelding much too big for me with huge black eyes, Lusignan eyes, and the prettiest white blaze on his nose. From the way he lowered his head as I stepped up to the mounting

46

block and the delicacy with which he snuffled a palmful of hay from my hand I could see that he was a very intelligent horse but from the flare of his nostrils and the strength of his hindquarters I saw, too, that he was wild when he chose it. 'I shall call him Othon,' I declared.

'What kind of a name is that?' asked Agnes. She had consented to my learning to ride but she was not pleased.

'A very good old name, Agnes,' I said haughtily. I didn't say that it was a pagan name, or that I remembered it from my papa's stories of the Norsemen who sailed down from their icy kingdoms to conquer France hundreds of years ago. The Taillefers, my family, had defeated the Norsemen. The stories of the Norsemen spoke of a magical horse, the best among gods and men. A steed that ran between the earth and the sky with mysterious signs carved into his bridle.

'Is he a suitable horse for a lady?' Agnes asked the groom who held Othon's bit. I caught his eye.

'Very suitable, madame,' he replied courteously, his face grave.

'And your name?'

'Tomas, madame.'

'Very well, Tomas. You may begin Lady Isabelle's lesson.'

From the moment Tomas handed me into the saddle, I knew that I didn't need to learn. I had pretended to have a horse of my own for years, riding broomsticks and branches, to Agnes's despair, for was I not a Courtenay and a Taillefer? It was in my bones. I knew it as soon as I squeezed my knees against Othon's flank and felt him settle beneath my weight.

I knew how to hold the rein just so as not to hurt his delicate mouth. I knew how to listen through my sinews to the rhythm of his blood. I leaned forward to whisper in his ear, 'Just a little time. We must be quiet, Othon. And then we shall fly, you wait and see.'

So for several afternoons, Tomas walked us around the yard under Agnes's measuring eye, calling out instructions and pretending to correct my posture and my handling of the bit. I could see how impressed he was with the way I rode, and that made me want to be even better. As we dutifully turned circles and figures of eight, I let my mind loose as I had not done since my mother left, dreaming of tournaments where I would disguise myself as a knight and charge down the list, unseating the famous champions of France, and then, tearing off my helmet, I would reveal that I was Isabelle, the finest horseman in France. King Philip would be astonished, the musicians would make poems about us, and I would wear the queen's favour in my braids. I would lead our men in battle and bring peace to our lands, and Hal Lusignan would beg for the favour of being my squire.

My splendid dreams ended with a bump. Othon had thrown me, and I lay in the schooling ring, with sawdust all over my face. I jumped up before I had my wind back, desperate to show Agnes that I wasn't hurt, but she was already bustling towards me.

'Isabelle! Oh Isabelle! You are too bold!' She petted me while she scolded, and though my eyes burned with tears, they were of rage, not pain nor fear. How dare Othon behave so rudely? I rubbed my face and saw old Tomas laughing at me, which made me angrier than ever.

'They can feel it, my lady, if you are too proud. He was just showing you who's master.'

'He is my horse!'

'Indeed. But if you take your whip to him he won't respect you. Old creatures, horses. Look at him now.'

I stepped up to Othon and rubbed his soft nose. He was pulling naughtily at some fronds of weed that overhung the ring, showing me that he didn't care. Tomas was right: it was I who had been rude.

'I didn't mean to insult you, Othon,' I whispered. 'I am grateful that you allow me to ride you, truly.'

For an answer, Othon straddled his legs and let out a fountain of hot piss, which splashed on my boots. Tomas laughed again.

'I think Othon is ready to take me again,' I remarked. 'Please help to mount me.'

Tomas kept me in the ring another week for hours each day, circling, turning quickly from a canter, taking a small hurdle at first, and then taller ones until I was jumping fences higher than my small self.

'A pretty sight you look, Isabelle,' huffed Agnes.

'I think the Lady Isabelle is ready to walk out, madame,' Tomas said with encouragement.

Agnes fussed and admonished, making me promise over and over to be careful, and to protect my face from the sun and mind my gown. Tomas heard her out, reassuring her that if I grew tired he would take me before him and lead my horse; all the time I could feel Othon tensing beneath me in anticipation. I had to hold him tight as we trotted down the road. Tomas led us through the meadows and over the bridge, his own horse grabbing saucily mouthfuls of high-summer mallow grass, until we turned through the trees and came out into a tight, steep-sided valley. Only the towers of Lusignan were visible now.

'Get down, my lady.'

'Why, Tomas? I want to ride.'

He grinned, showing brown stumps of teeth. Tomas was very old, at least fifty years. Bandy and bent like the reed in a thrush trap, his skin tanned to leather armour, yet he was the strongest man at Lusignan. Only he was allowed the exercise of Lord Hugh's great warhorses.

'I thought you might be wanting this.' He had a sack on his back.

'I'm not hungry, Tomas. I want to ride!'

'Quarrelsome little thing, aren't you? Get down now.' He scooped me up in his arm, the smell of him musky and deep like cumin, somehow familiar. I was on the ground in seconds. The sack did not contain provisions, but a saddle.

'Oh, Tomas!'

'Didn't think you'd have much use for that silly thing.' He swiftly unstrapped the high-pommelled lady's side-saddle that Lord Hugh had had made for me, its wood prettily painted yellow, and replaced it with a real saddle. 'Reckon you can ride astride?'

'But Tomas, it's wicked.'

Queen Eleanor of England, the mother of King John, had ridden astride when she raised her sons and their men in rebel-lion against their own father, and tried to gallop away like a man before old King Henry captured her and locked her up for years and years. Hearing my mother and the maids whisper about it, it seemed that sitting astride was a worse sin than encouraging men to steal their own father's lands.

'There's no one but the trees to see you, my lady. I won't be telling.'

'But Tomas, you might get into trouble. I don't want you to be punished.'

'Never mind about that. You may need it, one day, my lady. You may need to ride fast and hard, like a man so's you can give little lord Hal a run for his money, eh?' Tomas gave a wheezy laugh, delighted with his own impertinence. I threw him a con–spiratorial grin.

I bunched up my gown behind me and Tomas jumped me over the saddle. 'Promise you won't get into trouble, Tomas?'

'I promise. There's an army's worth of saddles in the stable house and I have the key. Are you ready, then?'

I nodded. I couldn't speak I was so excited.

'Wait, now.' Tomas had a little clay crock in his hand. He scooped a handful of paste from it and knelt to rub it into Othon's forelegs. 'Hold out your hands.' The paste was black and smelled of iron and fat. 'This will make you go faster. Let him go.'

I had no spurs, but I barely needed to touch my heels to Othon's side before we were off. I gave myself up to the air.

It did not seem as though Othon's hooves even touched the ground. All I felt was the rush of the wind on my face and my heart opening inside me to suck it in. For a few moments I froze, clinging like a beetle to his back. I would be thrown again, and his hooves would crush my skull like a nut. I had not thought such speed possible. It terrified me, and I tried weakly to pull him back, knowing that my strength was no more to him than a fly's. He wouldn't stop, and I couldn't stop him. Slowly, I felt myself meld with the thud of Othon's huge heart between my legs and we became one creature, weightless and sure as an arrow, just as I had dreamed, so that I felt nothing but his blood in mine and mine in his, not riding but swooping through the wind like a kite until the valley closed and I had to come back to myself, reminding him with the lightest tug on the bit to pull up short before he plunged us both over the hill's edge. Indeed, I nearly flew over his head like a windfall, but I had ridden through my fear. I was gasping and laughing, senseless, yet never had I felt more vividly alive. As I bent over Othon's dampened neck, my own face was wet with tears.

'Thank you,' I murmured. 'Thank you, thank you.'

Tomas cantered up behind us, I had forgotten all about him.

'I knew you could do it!'

I grinned at him, proud and fierce, my hair tumbling into my eyes and my face burning with pleasure. 'I did, too.'

We galloped, over and over again, until Tomas saw that the sun was low and made us turn back. He let out a leading rein for Othon and settled me against his chest, my legs demurely to one

52

side, and I fell asleep against him, my nose full of leather and horse sweat and the strange blood-like tinge of the balm, rocking slowly through the green lanes back to Lusignan.

All that summer and into the autumn until the weather turned and the rain came, I rode out on Othon each day. I was diligent with my prayers and my sewing, my music and deportment so that Agnes could have no cause to forbid me the release I waited for each afternoon. Tomas found a plate coat that had been made for Hal when he was about my age and persuaded Agnes to let me wear it over my gown, saying it should protect my back if I fell. He also gave me a pair of Hal's leather britches, which I slipped on under my gown, and which we didn't mention to Agnes at all. Lord Hugh seemed delighted with my new accomplishment and presented me with a falcon, a delicate merlin with deep blue feathers, a set of silver jesses and a gauntlet traced in silver thread. I was allowed to accompany him, dressed in one of my best silks and nodding along placidly on my side-saddle, when he hunted with his guests. I liked best, though, to go out with Tomas, and better still to leave him to doze and whittle in the shade while I explored the *allées* of the forest alone with Othon. I longed to bathe and comb him myself, but of course Agnes could not allow that, so I begged scraps of parchment from the clerks and twisted them into paper flowers to decorate his stall and made a picture of myself with a finger dipped in soot so that he should not be lonely for me in the night. I gave no thought to Hal, or my marriage, or what was happening in the world beyond the castle. I no longer listened in doorways or heeded the whisperings of the guards. All I wanted was to be alone in the woods with Othon. But then the leaves turned from green to yellow to brown, and when the forest was bare and we had kept the Christmas feast at the castle, a message came that my father was coming, and with him the English king.

CHAPTER FOUR

I WAS BOTH GLAD AND SAD AT THE NEWS OF MY FATHER'S return. Glad because I should see my papa again, and sad because Hal had remained with him, learning the duties of Angouleme, which would one day be his in right of his marriage to me, and their coming would bring the marriage close. I was curious, though, to see John, brother of the great Lionheart, the last of Queen Eleanor's unhappy sons. My father came first, with a long train of men-at-arms to prepare against the king's arrival, and I leaped joyfully into his travel-stained cloak and snuggled my face against his beard. I had grown used to Lord Hugh but now I was struck again by how cold and elegant he looked next to my father, who was rounder and more red-faced than ever. I hopped about Father, asking him where he had been and if he had experienced any adventures, and teasing him for presents.

'I hear you've become a fine rider,' he smiled. 'So I thought you might want this.' He gave me a thin parcel wrapped in vellum. Inside was a whip, an ivory whip tooled in silver with a scarlet tassel on the grip.

'Thank you, oh thank you, Papa!' I hoped he couldn't hear the disappointment in my voice. It was a beautiful gift, but it was a lady's tool, far too small and delicate for Othon. I suddenly felt very sad. Why did things change? Why did people go away and when they came back everything was different? Now that I looked, I could see my papa was older, the lines on his face deepened into little runnels, with streaks of grey in his beard. I was ashamed of my ingratitude and determined to behave beautifully, to make him proud of my accomplishments. His hand felt the same, though, so big and rough around my palm. In that moment I never wanted to let it go.

Hal had grown upwards, not outwards, and I had to think that he looked fine, broader through his shoulders, but still with that same sullen air. We greeted one another coolly, playing at grown-ups, but he barely spoke to me again as we sat over a simple supper of bread, cheese and dried fruit. The kitchens were already swarming with King John's purveyors, who had commandeered every deer and game bird for miles around.

'They're making entremets of marchpane,' I couldn't help whispering excitedly to Hal. 'We can save some for my horse, Othon. He loves sugar.'

'What do I care about your horse?' he hissed back rudely. So he was just as stupid as ever.

Agnes wanted to put me to bed after we had eaten, but I begged to be allowed to sit a little, first mixing the men's wine so that my papa smiled at my grave new manners, and then leaning against him on the settle. The hall at Lusignan had a new fireplace, a huge stone chamber that could take a whole

56

tree, and the heat from the flames made me doze. I slipped in and out of dreams until I was roused by one of my father's mastiffs licking my hand, but something made me keep my eyes closed and let my head drop more heavily against his shoulder.

'Do you think he will really do it?' my father was asking.

'Of course. Look at her. He's known for it, after all,' replied Lord Hugh.

My father's rough hand stroked my cheek, I muttered something and twitched my face away as though he had disturbed my sleep. 'Look at her, though. She's such a little maid.'

'You thought her old enough for my boy.'

'Indeed.'

'And afterwards?'

'We'll wait a while. And then, Duke Arthur knows what we wish.'

Why were they talking about me like this? And why Duke Arthur? Behind my eyelids the firelight glowed red. I was wide awake now, but I kept my breathing soft and regular. For a while there was no sound except the horn beakers on the trestle as the men drank their wine.

'I regret La Marche. Sincerely I do,' Father began.

'No matter. There will be other lands.'

What was my father talking about? La Marche was his county, our county. It had been ever since he had sworn loyalty to King John. La Marche was the reason I was betrothed, was it not? The county that had been contested between Lusignans and Taillefers for generations? When Hal married me, the Lusignan lands, Angouleme and La Marche, would be joined together, creating one apanage for our children.

'I think,' Lord Hugh was speaking now, 'that she has been happy here. I hope she will be obedient.'

'She is my daughter.'

And then the steward came to speak to Lord Hugh and my father picked me up in his arms and carried me to Agnes. He had not done such a thing since I was a tiny child. It had always been my mother who kissed me goodnight.

*

'Oh, Lady Isabelle! Look! What are we to do?' Anges was distraught.

I had stopped my secret snipping when Othon came, indeed forgotten all about what I had done to my betrothal gown, and now here it was in tatters on my chamber floor.

'There must have been mice,' said one of the maids.

'I hated it anyway,' I said stubbornly. I was bad tempered because Agnes had made me have a bath, even though it was bright outside and the ground solid and I could have been riding.

'Shame on you to speak like that of your mother's gift. And what are you to wear? You were to have new clothes at your birthday, all your other gowns are too short,' Agnes scolded.

'You can't blame me for growing.'

Agnes put her hands on her hips. 'Lady Isabelle. Today of all days, I will not have you being insolent. I will not have it, do you hear?'

'What's so special about today?'

'Never you mind. Now go and have your hair combed, you look like a beggar.'

I was sitting on a stool, muttering as the maid wrenched my stinging scalp this way and that, when Lord Hugh appeared. The maids were shocked to see him in my chamber. They leaped up, curtseying and blushing and apologizing all at once, whisking a napkin over the chamber pot and patting their half-pinned hair.

'For you, Lady Isabelle. Excuse me, *mesdames*.' And he handed me a canvas parcel. Inside was a plain white dress, light silk, with no embroidery or ornament, and a pale fur mantle with a deep hood lined in green satin. They were pretty, but I did not think them very fine. 'Dress her.'

The maids shuffled me behind the bed curtains and tugged on the gown.

'Undo her hair,' Lord Hugh demanded. The maids did as they were told, looking puzzled. What was a man doing telling them how to dress me? 'And this is for you, also, Lady Isabelle. You may go into the garden to play with Agnes when you are prepared.' He bowed to the girls, which made them blush all the more, and withdrew.

I looked at what he had handed me. It was a ball. A cloth ball of red and blue patches with silly brass bells on it, like a jongleur's cap. Why had he given me such a stupid toy? I had a horse and a falcon, what did I want with balls? I was mortified to think that Hal might see me with it when I had been plotting to astound him with my riding.

'Come along,' said Agnes, in a voice that I knew meant no argument. I trailed after her along the passage, the fur mantle bunched around me. 'Now we can have a lovely game.' Her voice was high and artificial, as though I was a strange child she didn't much like.

I thought that everyone at Lusignan had run mad that day. Lord Hugh in the wardrobe and my father babbling about Duke Arthur and now Agnes, who disapproved of any game where I didn't sit still, capering about on the lawn with a ball.

The low January sun was captured within the garden walls and dutifully chasing Agnes's throws I grew warm and dropped the new mantle on the ground. I threw the ball back and the bells jingled as she caught it. She tossed it straight up as high as she could as I hovered underneath, catching it and hurling it higher again. I stopped minding the childishness and thought only of the spinning colours against the blue sky. We were both laughing now. It felt so good to play together again in the air, and for once Agnes wasn't telling me not to get dirty. Higher and higher the ball flew, until I threw it so hard I thought it must have got stuck on the chapel roof. We craned our necks at the gutter, until a voice spoke behind me.

'Is this yours, Lady Isabelle?'

The man holding my ball spoke French, but with an odd accent, not the clear, light tempo of the langue d'oc. He was short, hardly taller than Agnes, and his face was sallow and thin, though I could see a paunchy belly poking through his stained travel cloak. He wore riding gloves and a heavy fur cape, which he had pulled about him, though it was noon and really quite warm.

'Where are the guards?' Agnes was anxious.

'Excuse me, madame. I am a guest of the Count of Angouleme. I assumed this must be his charming daughter.' He bowed, and I curtseyed back diffidently.

'Ask the gentleman if he would like to join our game,' prompted Agnes.

I stared at her, but her face was urgent, her eyes wide and expectant, so I held out my hands for a throw. And we carried on like that for a little while, Agnes and the gentleman and I, though Agnes's laughter no longer sounded real and her tread had grown lumbering. When the gentleman dropped the ball and bent to the ground I saw a bald spot shining with grease in the middle of his muddy hair. Perhaps he was a priest.

'What other games do you care for, sir?' I asked politely. Agnes would be pleased if I showed fine manners to a priest.

'I like to play dice.' He reached into his pocket and took out a small ivory box. 'In fact I have a fine set here. Shall we play?'

I was sure that playing dice was sinful, like the Roman soldiers beneath the Holy Cross, but he must know better. Agnes gave me a consenting nod and the gentleman spread his fur wrap on the ground for us to sit on, pulling the wool cloak tighter around him.

'Here sir,' I took my own discarded fur and placed it over his shoulder. 'You will be cold.'

'How kind you are, Lady Isabelle.' He shook the box as a cup and threw, but fur wasn't very good to play on, as the dice got tangled in the hairs and couldn't roll. We tried a few times, but it was no good, the gentleman looked foolish.

'Perhaps we might go in, sir?' I asked gently. 'I too am rather cold, now.'

'Thank you, I am quite comfortable.'

There was a silence. I wondered what my mother would do. She would speak of some pleasing topic to make the guest feel comfortable. So I told the gentleman all about Othon, and how I liked falconry, and then somehow I remembered the marchpane entremets, so I began to tell about the king's visit and wonder what he would be like, and I grew rather bumptious, repeating some of the stories I had overheard in the stables, that the Lionheart's brother was going to war with the king of France, and that perhaps he would lose his lands and have to return to England, which was a horrid place full of fog and blue haired barbarians. Agnes was glaring at me, but I was carried away with the idea of myself as the gracious hostess of Lusignan, there on the lawn in my smudged gown, and I told that the English king was famous for his terrible rages, where he hurled the crockery and chewed the hangings, frothing at the mouth like a mad dog so no one dared go near him. I didn't stop until Agnes jumped to her feet muttering about dinner.

'But we've had our dinner, Agnes. And I was just telling the gentleman—'

'I'm sure the gentleman has heard quite enough of your prattling,' she answered grimly, grabbing me hard on my arm to haul me up.

The gentleman jumped to his feet as we stood and bowed again. 'Thank you for our game, Lady Isabelle. And for such a delightful conversation.'

Agnes marched me silently up the staircase to my chamber, shooed away the maids and closed the door. She was not angry; she looked frightened.

'What's the matter, Agnes? I'm sorry if I was forward. I was only trying to entertain the gentleman.'

'Your father and Lord Hugh will be furious.'

'Why? He was only some old priest. Why should they care? He was lucky I spoke to him at all.' Agnes sank down on the settle and wrapped her arms round me. 'Oh, little one. I forget sometimes. Tha-that gentleman … he is to be your husband.'

'What?' I was in shock. 'What about Hal? You mean he's not a priest?'

'No, Isabelle. He is the king of England.'

If I had been a lady in a poem I would have swooned away, but all I could do was goggle at her like a simpleton.

'His Majesty wished to meet you for the first time this way. So as not to alarm you. It is an honour, Isabelle, a great honour. Your father has agreed to it.'

I recalled what I had heard in the hall, my papa saying that I would be obedient, as I was his daughter.

'Won't Lord Hugh be angry? I don't understand.'

'Speak softly. We could be overheard.' Her voice was very low and clear. I could feel her breath on my hair. 'Lord Hugh will be angry. But he will be pretending, like a play. When the king leaves, we will be with him. Your mother will join us at Bordeaux in a few months' time. Everything is agreed.'

'But I am betrothed to Hal.' We had said the words. I knew that in the law of the Church we were as good as married already.

63

Agnes softened her tone. 'Well, you never cared for Hal much, did you? And think, Isabelle, you shall be a queen! I shall have to kneel to you.'

So would Hal, I thought. Queen. Queen Eleanor had followed her husband on Crusade, had she not? She had ridden through the Holy Land and watched a great battle at Mount Cadmos. Queen. I would see the sea, I would be crowned, I could have as many horses and Venetian silks as I wished.

'What about Othon and Tomas? They have to come too.'

'Good girl, Isabelle. Of course Othon shall come, and old Tomas too if you wish it. I will go to your father now.'

She left me and I climbed into the windowsill, looking down at the forest where I had been so happy, where I had believed I would live forever. No more sewing, I thought, no more prayers. I would be able to do exactly as I pleased, go riding and hawking every day. Queens were not scolded or told not to gobble their custard, and they certainly didn't have to endure silly ill-mannered boys. I remembered the dream I had conjured over a dish of raspberry marmalade, of my mother and I in an Eastern palace full of fountains and Hal locked up in a dungeon full of snakes, at my pleasure. I would not be sorry to leave Lusignan, not when a queen could see the whole world. So I lost myself in my imaginings as I used to do so that it was not until the next summer, when I stood before the altar of the cathedral at Bordeaux, that I thought of John, the gentleman, at all. But before we could leave, I had to act a little longer. While I remained at Lusignan, I was Hal's betrothed, the heiress of Angouleme. I had learned by now that dissembling was easy for women. So long as we stayed silent and waited passively for men to move us like quoits, we were invisible. Only by watching could we learn what was to become of us.

CHAPTER FIVE

THE NEXT DAY, MY FATHER AND LORD HUGH WERE TO swear their fealty to King John. All the magnates of the surrounding counties rode in to witness the ceremony, and I stood quietly among their ladies with Agnes and made my face as smooth as milk. After Mass, we trooped into the hall, which had been scrubbed and freshly laid with clean rushes, though the weather had turned again and fingers of icy wind clawed through the casements, tweaking at the fire and filling the room with wraiths of smoke, as though the ghosts of Lusignan ancestors were among us. Lord Hugh was wearing the serpent brooch, as usual; I wondered if Melusina had twined her way along the battlements to watch a Lusignan swear his fealty to an English king.

John looked more like a king today. He wore a gold circlet on his brow and a red velvet mantle with a huge gold chain hanging from his chest, and as he passed through the hall with his chamberlain bearing his sceptre the company sank to their knees and bowed their heads. I peeped out under my loosened hair and watched him as he passed, swaddled in his furs. Lord Hugh and Hal walked behind him, followed by my father, and knelt as he took his seat under his royal canopy. I thought that I should have a cloth of state too, when I was queen, and hid a tiny smile. Lord Hugh and Hal kissed John's hand and gave him their homage for the Lusignan lands and the county of La Marche, declaring themselves his vassals, bound to fight for him in honour, as my father had already done for Angouleme. They were King John's men, now. The ladies withdrew while the men dined and took wine, and as they dipped manchet bread into cups of sweet liqueur and munched little almond cakes they chattered of the king, how he had put aside his English wife, Hadwise, who had given him no children, and now sought the hand of a princess of Portugal.

'And when may we expect your marriage, Lady Isabelle?' A fat lady with a red face and a sharply pointed nose was questioning me. She was the wife of one of Lord Hugh's men and obliged to curtsey to me, though I could see she did not care for that. Her fashionably tight gown strained its laces as she reached forward to stuff in another cake. I decided I should have only pretty ladies to attend me, when I was queen.

Agnes answered for me, 'We leave tonight for the convent at Langoiran. Until the treaty concerning Duke Arthur is agreed my lord considers it safer for the Lady Isabelle to remain there, where she may complete her education with the holy sisters.'

I didn't like the sound of that at all, but I had the sense to keep quiet.

'And the wedding?' pressed the lady, spilling crumbs into the drooping folds of her coif. My mother would never eat so inelegantly.

'In time. My lady is very young.'

'Humph,' snorted the lady. 'I had my first boy when I was twelve. Fourteen children since, and all of them living. You can't begin too early.'

'You are blessed, madame,' I acknowledged courteously.

We were escorted back to the hall as the dessert course was served. Trestles of candied fruit, each board carried between two men, were set down, then dishes of custard flavoured with bay and vanilla, garnished with dried flowers, then the entremets of which I had boasted, a castle in sugar that was supposed to look like Lusignan, and a leopard with a cockerel between its paws that represented the two kings of France and England lying peacefully side by side. The leopard was a strange bright orange colour and the castle turrets were crooked and shaky; I could see that Lord Hugh was displeased. We stood as the dessert was carried round to polite exclamations and King John reached forward and broke the tail from the leopard and handed it to a server. The boy appeared soon after with the tail in a napkin, sweating and confused to be speaking to someone of such high rank as me.

'His Majesty asked that this be brought to you, my lady. For Othon, his Majesty said.'

'Thank him, Agnes,' I said airily, even as I snapped off the tip and felt the delicious sweetness dissolve on my tongue.

Eventually the ladies withdrew to the quarters that had been prepared for them, in a flurry of flouncing trains and instructions

68

to their maids, and the men were left to their drinking. Agnes took me to my chamber, and as evening fell, I looked out of the window, taking a last survey of the Lusignan forest. I had always liked to watch the woods at night, when the birds were silent and the leaves rustled their secrets. It made my room seem so safe and cosy knowing that the boar and wolves were running out there in the dark. I had believed that I would make my home here at Lusignan. That I too would become one of Melusina's kin, even that I would play with my own babies in the gardens where I had fought with Hal and tossed a coloured ball for a king. And now everything was to change again, and I had barely even seen my father.

'Must we leave in the morning, Agnes?'

'In haste, my lady. If your father's plans are to work, Lord Hugh will send men after you on the road.' I thought of Tomas telling me I would need one day to ride like a man. This was exciting.

'Will they chase us? Shall I ride Othon?'

'Certainly not! You will travel in a litter, as is fitting.'

She saw my disappointed face and came close to me at the casement, wrapping me in her arm as we both looked out over the treetops, deep purple in the twilight.

'You will travel as a future queen, Isabelle. And your maman and papa will be so proud of you, I know they will.

*

'Tell me, Lady Isabelle, did Othon approve of his dessert?' King John had brought his horse up level with the litter, walking slowly as we jerked along the road.

Lusignan was behind us, we had a few hours of dun-coloured daylight left before we reached our lodging. Lord Hugh's leave-taking had betrayed no trace of his conversation with my papa, nor of what he must now know I had learned from Agnes, except perhaps that he had been more cold and correct than in the last months when he had petted and indulged me. Hal had bid me farewell as cheerlessly as he had first greeted me, while my father had whispered as we embraced, 'I am proud of you, Isabelle.'

Looking now into the king's face, I saw that he too thought he had dissembled. It was indeed a play, a comedy of disguises within disguises, with each man believing he had stolen something from the other. 'More, perhaps, than my lord of Lusignan did, Majesty,' I replied.

The king leaned in closer. His beard was pushing through his skin, I could see grey hairs sprouting among the darker ones and his breath smelt sourly of wine. 'Come, Lady Isabelle. We have played at ball together. You need not be so formal.'

'I am sorry, I didn't know …'

'I did not wish you to know. I hope we shall be friends, you and I.'

'It's an honour of which I am unworthy, Majesty.' Agnes had heard me practise that. I too had my lines to get in this strange drama. A sudden ripple of irritation crossed the king's face, quick as a winter cloud. He spurred his horse. 'You shall attend me after I have dined, madame.'

'Agnes,' I whispered, 'why does the king want to marry me and not the Portuguese princess? And why is Lord Hugh pretending not to know of it?'

Agnes drew the curtains of the litter together so that we swayed along in cold half-darkness. 'It's men's business, little one. Just do as you are told, and don't fret.'

I thought suddenly of the silk man, setting out on his journey north about now, from the mysterious flower-covered plains he had told me of. I would not see him this year at Angouleme. It made me sad. I felt like one of the bundles in his pack, trundled about the country to be unrolled and inspected, first to Lusignan and now away into the winter's night to another place I had never seen. I thought of my white bed in the castle and my mother coming to kiss me goodnight and began to snuffle.

'I don't want to be a queen, I think, Agnes. I just want to go home.'

'I know, little one. I know. But you must please him. You must.'

I cheered up when we reached our lodging place, a moated manor house on the Bordeaux track. The lord and his household were waiting with torches to greet us. They knelt on the frozen ground as the king dismounted, barely acknowledging their carefully prepared greetings as he rushed inside to the fire. The king was given the chamber. The family would sleep that night among the rushes with their own servants, while the royal household had been dispersed among smaller houses and even barns nearby. Othon and Tomas would sleep in a field; I hoped they would not be too chilly. The mistress escorted Agnes and me to a small chamber in the roof, well lit with her best wax candles and smelling of lavender. 'I know that it's not what the lady must be used to,' she murmured anxiously, 'but we have done our best. An honour, such an honour.'

The maids, accustomed to the size of Lusignan, were giving themselves airs, grumpily unrolling sleeping pallets and commenting rudely on the wooden shutters. I would dismiss the lot of them when I was queen, the gaggle of sillies.

'I should be flattered if you would dine with me, madame,' I said loudly, so that they should see I at least knew how to behave. I left them to stand while the lady and I ate stewed partridge on a settle by the fire and then sent them down to collect their pottage from the kitchens, so that they could see I would not tolerate poor manners.

Later that evening, I had Agnes comb out my hair and I washed my face before descending to the hall where King John sat alone before the fire pit, the householder and his men standing at a respectful distance in the draughty shadows.

'You did not find the journey too fatiguing, Lady Isabelle?'

'Not at all, Majesty. I am very comfortable.'

'Good. Will you take wine?'

He motioned to one of his liverymen who stepped forward with two tiny gold cups, like the halves of the ball we had played with. The veins of their mother-of-pearl lining showed through the yellow wine.

'I would give you something to remember me, my lady.'

'Thank you, Majesty,' I began to say but I recalled his little cloud of displeasure I had seen on the road. The king liked me to be childish, as we had been together in the garden. I clapped my hands and made my eyes big. 'What is it, what is it?'

He chuckled, pleased, and I saw that I had guessed him right. 'This.'

A tiny gold ring, with a huge pearl, as big as a quail's egg. He slipped it onto my finger, where it drew the light from the fire. It was like wearing a little moon. 'Does it please you? Will you remember me?' he asked eagerly.

I pouted, looking up into his eyes and hoping that the heat had made my cheeks flush. 'It's very pretty, Majesty.' Again the shadow of anger. Had I gone too far?

'Would you have something else?'

'Maybe.'

'Tell me. Tell me what you wish,' John enquired.

I thought quickly. 'May I have a lock of your hair? See, I have my knife.'

'Is that really what you want, Isabelle?'

'If it pleases you to give it me.'

He leaned forward and I cut a little piece from the end of one of the straggles that hung from his thin locks. His eyes shone, he covered my hand with his fingers for a moment.

'It is you who have given me the gift. I thank you.' He put the fingers to his lips in a gesture that reminded me of the way Lord Hugh used to play at kissing my hand, but it did not look so graceful. I kept the hair between my fingers as I backed out of his presence, but on the staircase I let it fall, strand by greasy strand.

The next day King John rode north, towards Le Goulet, within the French king's lands of the Ile de France, where he would do homage to King Philip for his duchy of Normandy, for Aquitaine, which he was to inherit from old Queen Eleanor, and for Brittany, where young Duke Arthur had finally given up his father's claim and conceded his uncle's right. The peace was celebrated with a royal marriage, between John's niece, Blanche of Castile, and King Philip's son, Louis. My mother would be there, attending on the queen; it seemed incredible to me that in time I should be a royal lady of even higher rank than the new princess of France. At twelve, Blanche was just a few years older than me, but while she was riding and dancing her way through the spring residence of her new home, I was bundled off to Langoiran.

The convent stood high on a cliff above the river Garonne, where it flowed wide and lazy on the last stage of its journey to the port at Bordeaux and the sea. It did not look much different from Lusignan, rearing up starkly through the low winter sky on its crag, but where Lusignan had been a place of men, of guards and dogs and horses, the bustle of Lord Hugh's household running to attend him, the smell of meat and sweat and leather always present in the air, the walls of Langoiran contained only women. A sister house of the royal abbey at Fontevraud, near Chinon, where Queen Eleanor had finally retired after delivering her granddaughter Blanche to the French court, Langoiran was a refuge for the well-born women of the south, who dedicated their days to the Holy Virgin. In sending me here, I saw Lord Hugh had been very clever.

I had plenty of time to consider why. I begged Agnes to allow me to ride each day, claiming that the fresh air would be good for my health, but the nuns were so strictly segregated that the abbess, Mother Helene, would only permit me to walk him round the courtyard. Tomas delivered him to the gate, but a lay sister helped me mount and watched me as we plodded in circles. I didn't need to whisper between his ears, I could feel the rebellion in his blood mounting at this unaccustomed constriction, as I knew that he could feel mine, but I chattered to him anyway, murmuring all the things we would do together after I was married. How I would take him on a ship and we should have years of glorious gallops in the hot lands of the East, rather than this dreary trudging through the Garonne mists. Aside from my daily outing, I had to spend hours in the chapel listening to the nuns sing their interminable offices, hours of shifting my aching knees on the unforgiving stone, feeling its dampness creep into my bones, and hours again stitching and stitching at altar cloths and priests' surplices, my fingers clumsy with the chill and my stomach gurgling, for the nuns kept to a plain fast diet of bread, cheese and herbs, with only a muddy-fleshed and bony river fish on holidays, with no sweetmeats at all. Still, I had all those hours to think.

I was sure that Lord Hugh intended to break his vow to the English king, and that my revoked betrothal would be the means of his doing so. That was the meaning of his talk with my father. And Duke Arthur, now John's liegeman? He knew what they wished … but what could that be? Lord Hugh had apparently consented to my being brought to the convent, yet the connection with Fontevraud placed me here under the protection of the English. Lord Hugh had been so confident that the king would offer for me, but what was it that John was 'known for'? And what of my parents? Did they wish me to be queen, or did they have something else in mind for me? As the fat lady at Lusignan had observed, I was old enough to be married, and should soon be able to become a mother. Why then was I kept so ignorant of what I should become? Had all those months at Lusignan been an act, my betrothal to Hal the beginning of a scheme that had begun in Lord Hugh's supple mind the day that the messenger arrived at Angouleme with the news of the Lionheart's death?

I sorted the questions in my mind like beads on a clerk's abacus, yet no matter how I arranged them they still gave me no clear solution. Each day in the convent I was reminded of the trust, the patience, the faith of the Holy Virgin. 'I am the handmaid of the Lord' – was that the precept I was to follow, to accept with glad submission whatever fate my father and Lord Hugh decided for me? And if the convent was a prison, were they not handing me the key? As queen, I should be subject to no man but the king, and it occurred to me that I knew how to manage him, as surely as I had known what to do when Tomas first set me on Othon's back. So I let my questioning grow idle, minded my manners and my needle once more, and waited like any princess in a romance for the time when a man should come to release me from my tower.

*

It was not until mid July that Mother Helene summoned me to her closet. The sky outside was white with heat, and below us the river was crowded with flimsy fishing boats, bobbing sleepily in the summer tide. The abbess had rarely spoken to me, indeed

she rarely spoke at all, preferring to keep to her pious medita-
tions and communicate through her deputy, but today she sat
beneath the statue of Our Lady with a parchment in her lap.
Mother Helene was very learned: she could read, in both French
and Latin, and she was reputed to compose her own prayers,
which she dictated to her writing clerk through the grille in the
convent's visiting room.

'I hope you have been content here with us, Lady Isabelle.'

'Most content, Reverend Mother.'

'I have had a letter from your father, the count. He instructs
me that you are to go to Bordeaux to prepare for your wedding.
The marriage is set for Lammas day.'

The first of August, just a few weeks away.

'My marriage?' I asked cautiously. I had been so long alone
with my thoughts that I wondered, wildly, if my father had
changed his mind again, and that I was to be married to someone
else.

'To the king, Lady Isabelle. You are greatly favoured.'

'Indeed, Reverend Mother.' I kept my eyes on the patient
face of the Virgin, pushing down the joyful skip of my heart.
Just a few more weeks and I should be free.

'But Lady Isabelle, there is something I wish to ask you.'

'Certainly, Reverend Mother.'

'Do you feel, that is, do you wish to be married?'

'Have I a choice? I am my father's heiress, I must do as he
bids me.'

Mother Helene had the same face as all the nuns I had seen,
the pale skin smoothed as though with a pumice until nearly

all vestige of expression had been polished away, like the oldest statues in the cathedral at Angouleme. But her eyes were bright blue, alert and gentle, and now she fixed them on me with an expression that seemed almost pitying.

'You are very young. You have not felt, perhaps, in the time you have spent here, that you might have a ... vocation?'

My mother had told me a story of a Scots queen, a descendant of the royal house of England before the time when the Duke of Normandy conquered England, who had been kept in a convent by a wicked aunt. When the king of England, the first Henry, had wished to marry her, the bishops said that she might not accept, as she was already the bride of Christ, but this princess had torn off her veil and trampled it on the ground, and she was permitted to marry and be crowned since she had been put in the convent against her will. At first I could not understand what Mother Helene was asking of me, but then I saw that she was offering me a choice. I did not have to marry. I could stay in the convent and shave my head and take my vows and spend my days here, locked away from the world in its sacred peacefulness. I did not hesitate. 'Reverend Mother, I confess I have felt no vocation. And I feel I must do the sacred duty which my father requires of me.'

Mother Helene looked at me for a long moment, then got to her feet, smoothing down her black habit.

'Very well. I hope the Holy Virgin will bless your marriage. Let us kneel.'

As I prayed next to her, in that scrubbed, spare room, I felt almost sad that my answer had been so sincere. I had never been

78

offered a choice before. Ever afterwards, when I saw a statue of Our Lady, I remembered Mother Helene's eyes, the same colour as the folds of the Virgin's mantle, and I do not believe I ever saw it again without thinking that she had tried to save me, and that I might have chosen differently had she been able to tell me the truth.

CHAPTER SIX

A LONG WITH MY FATHER'S INSTRUCTIONS CAME LADY
Maude de Braose. She was the wife, as she made sure to
tell me very soon, of William de Braose, one of the king's most
trusted magnates. She was a strong, thick-armed woman with
the carriage of a peasant and a complexion roughened by years
of travel on important royal business. She talked a great deal
about important royal business. She swept into my chamber
during the recreation hour before dinner while I was playing
at cat's cradle with Agnes, clapped her hands to shoo away
the maids and dropped a perfunctory curtsey. She wore men's
riding boots under her gown and her upper lip was shadowed
with a moustache.

'Lady Isabelle, we have not much time.'

'But the Reverend Mother told me I was not to depart for a
fortnight. At least allow me to call for some refreshment for you.
And then our things ...'

'I'm not going anywhere, Lady Isabelle. I meant we have not
much time for you. Now, say goodbye to your nurse.'

'What?'

'Your nurse. I am to be your chaperone now. The queen of England cannot have her old nursemaid about her.'

I was astonished. In all my dreams of being queen I had thought on only pleasant things, of how I should have my mother and Othon and Agnes always near me and have marmalade for supper and do just as I liked. I looked at Agnes. To my horror she had moved to the corner of the room where she kept her chest.

'Come along. Your father's men are waiting. They will accompany her back to Angouleme.'

I ignored her.

'Agnes, did you know about this?'

She nodded, her eyes gleaming with tears. 'It had to come, my lady. You will be travelling to England, and I ... I cannot accompany you.'

'No! No, Agnes! I want you to stay. I ... I order you to stay.'

Agnes was silent, merely placing a few objects in her box, her horn comb and her silver spoon with my father's arms on it that she had had as a New Year's gift the year I was born. The cat's cradle strings still trailed about her wrist. I forgot that I had learned to be a lady, now, I forgot the rules of silence and order which had constrained me in the convent and I rushed at Lady Maude, trying to push her out of the door. 'Go away! I don't want you! Agnes is not leaving! I will tell my papa, just you see!'

Her hand snapped out to cover my mouth and she gripped me tightly behind my head, so that I stifled and spluttered against her.

'Hush. You know you are not to speak of your marriage here. You will do as I bid you, on King John's orders. Now, if I release you, will you be quiet?'

I nodded.

'Very well.'

As soon as she loosed her grip, I screamed for Mother Helene, for the maids, for anyone who could help me. I kicked as hard as I could and bruised my toe in its thin slipper against her sturdy boot. I beat my fists against her brawny arms and howled at the top of my voice.

'Stop this! Stop this at once!' I could hear footsteps in the passage. The maids must have had their ears to the hole of the latch. She grabbed at me again and I writhed in her arms. 'Stop it. You willful, wicked child!'

'I am not a child!'

But something stopped me. I had not thought of myself as a child for a long time. I was a woman; I was betrothed. But then I saw the gentleman as I played ball in the garden, with my hair unpinned like a little girl, I saw his face, eager in the fire-light as I cut the lock from his hair, I saw Lord Hugh smiling indulgently as I played in his lap. I knew how to manage them, did I not? Just as I knew how to conceal my listening back at Lusignan, and my wild forest flights with Othon. I held out my hand, where the king's fat pearl glowed against the faint blush of my skin. I made my eyes wide, and spoke in my most innocent voice.

'Forgive me, Lady Maude. I should not like you to get into trouble. You see, this is the king's gift. When he gave it me, he said I should have anything I wanted, anything that my heart desired. Anything. I should be very unhappy if Agnes is sent away. Very unhappy. And the king might not like that.'

Once again, her grip relaxed. I could see her struggling and in her face, which was so much more intelligible to me than Lord Hugh's smooth mask, I saw many things. I saw her ambition and I saw her fear. I saw that she would use me as my father and Lord Hugh planned to, and that she would take everything I loved from me if I allowed it. And I saw that I had never had an enemy except for Hal, and that he had been more of an idea than a foe. And I thought I might enjoy having an enemy, very much.

'Well, Lady Maude?' I crossed the room, standing as erect and gracious as ever my mother had taught me, and laid a hand on Agnes's sleeve.

'The nurse may stay,' she muttered. 'But you will obey me. I am here to instruct you, as his Majesty wishes.'

'Quite. Just as his Majesty wishes.'

We ate supper together that evening in Mother Helene's chamber. A sheet had been nailed up over the table to accustom me to the cloth of state, which I had imagined back at Lusignan. Lady Maude played the role of server, showing me when she would kneel, when the dish and napkin would be handed, when I must stand if I dined in state with the king. We went through the ceremony of assay – as I would be royalty, it seemed I might also be the victim of poison. Each dish had to be dipped with bread three times, then flourished over the head of the server, then put to the lips of the chief officer, Lady Maude explained, before a queen might eat. I could see that Mother Helene did not think much of English manners, for all that Lady Maude considered herself so refined. Lady Maude boasted of the size of the king's palace at a place called Westminster, of the richness of the English pasture land and fisheries, of the abundance of the forests and the wealth of the magnates, not to mention the knowledge and learning of the king.

'His Majesty owns twenty books, you know,' she announced.

I did not care very much for books myself, I liked stories better, but I knew that the library at Langoiran contained ten times that number, which Mother Helene had collected from all over France and the wild Arab lands of Spain. On and on she flitted, impressing the honour that had been bestowed on me, but her linen was grubby and she moved like a carthorse: compared with my mother, she looked like a kitchen woman. If Lady Maude was the example of English womanhood to which I was to aspire, I thought I should have no difficulty surpassing it.

*

There was no procession to my wedding such as Blanche of Castile had enjoyed. No thousand liveried servants to escort me on the road, no palfrey with jewelled trappings or white-silk litter lined with cloth of gold. Yet again, I was bundled away, with only Agnes and Tomas from Lusignan, Lady Maude and the ignorant maids for my ladies. There was to be no proclamation of the marriage until the contract was indelibly sealed, so I travelled to Bordeaux through a hot milky summer night with the clouds churning above me like curds in a butter pail, on a flat bottomed barge hauled by carthorses and only a troop of silent guards, who rode next to us on the riverbank with their helmets lowered, as though we only happened to find ourselves travelling the same watery road by chance. And still, I was too excited to sleep as I lay among the cushions, the scents of orange flower and summer jasmine and tar from the boat's seams clear and pure in the night air. I should see the sea, and I should see my mother again, and I don't know which made me happier.

We were lodged at the archbishop's house on the evening before I was to be married, the last day of July. My mother was waiting for us. She too had travelled quietly, as a private lady, and I was taken to her chamber without ceremony in my plain tan travelling cloak. When I saw her all the sadness of our last meeting came over me, all the boredom and aloneness of the months at Lusignan and in the convent, and I went to jump into her arms and drink in her beloved smell, but she checked me, sinking gracefully to her knees before the astonished goggling of the maids, and addressed me as 'Madame'.

I felt my face crumple like a jelly. 'Maman?' I ventured.

She gently shook her head. I swallowed hard, biting the inside of my mouth to keep my lips from trembling and extended my hand. 'You may rise, Lady Mother.'

I was not married as a queen. Just as there had been no wedding procession, so there could be no great ceremonial Mass for a stolen bride. My mother and Agnes hurried me through the streets of Bordeaux just after dawn; I stumbled on

85

the hem of the pale blue gown my mother had lent me, one of her own that I was till not tall enough to wear. Until we came to the open space where the great façade of the cathedral reared up at us, no one could have known that this shuffling child would in a few moments be England's queen, but the cathedral square was full of grim-faced guards, positioned ready in case the Lusignans had news of the ceremony and tried to steal me back. That, at least, made me feel important. John awaited me at the door, plainly dressed also, only the white fur of his mantle and the gold circlet on his head indicating that he was no ordinary bridegroom.

My father stood next to him, and it was all I could do not to fling myself into my papa's arms for joy. When he took my arm to give me away, he bent down and whispered, 'See, Isabelle. I have even combed out my beard, now that you shall be such a great lady.' I tried to smile at him, but even the sight of his grey-red beard, coloured like a partridge's wing, all tamed and groomed with oil so it shone like Othon's mane could not cheer me. Papa was delighted at our success, I could see that, and I tried to make my thoughts dutiful. Marriages such as mine brought peace, did they not? Surely my father, who had fought so powerfully and so bravely for his liege lords, for Angouleme, should be allowed peace, now that his sword arm grew weary? But the herald who announced John's titles did so in a hushed voice, as though this were a shameful thing, and I could not share my papa's evident joy.

I repeated the words the archbishop said to me, as I had done to Hal at Lusignan, and then John took my hand, and we were married. Such a small moment. There was no *Te Deum* sung, no coins cast to cheering crowds of townsfolk, no chorus of silver trumpets to hail the queen of England down the nave. It was Lady Maude, not my mother, who carried the grubby train of my dress as we left the church, and that was my marriage done.

*

Our wedding feast, too, was kept quietly. We dined together in the archbishop's garden, and it was not so very different from the time when we had sat beside the fire together after leaving Lusignan. Even in the high-summer heat, the king kept his mantle about him. Lady Maude and my mother attended us. It was so strange to see them kneeling silently side by side, like novices in the convent, as I played with a dish of peaches and a chilled lemon posset. The king hardly ate, just drank cup after cup of sweet white wine, his eyes never leaving me, avid. Then it was time to go to bed. The archbishop led us to his own chamber and blessed the sheets, my mother handed me my shift and my father the king's, his face stern and impassive. The bed was so high he had to lift me into it. The archbishop was still muttering away in Latin as my new husband bared one pale and skinny leg, whorled with dark hair and placed it between the sheets. Then he set a kiss on my brow and the men withdrew, leaving me alone with my mother in the mauve twilight.

'Am I married now?' I asked. I felt hectic and bewildered, drained yet wakeful.

'Almost,' she replied. 'There is something else to be done.'

She said it grimly, but I thought I knew what I should have to endure. I had not been afraid. I knew what happened between married people. Agnes had told me what would be expected when I was bedded with the king, while over the years I had heard enough of the maids' gossip to know how babies came. But the king had not removed my nightgown or lain on top of me, so how could it happen?

My mother combed out my hair again and braided it. Her hands shook.

'Don't you want me to be married, Maman?'

'Of course I do. It is a wonderful match for you and for Angouleme. You are a queen, my little love.'

'Then I command you to stop pulling those knots,' I said over my shoulder.

She smiled, a tired, gentle smile, and put away her comb.

'Very well, Majesty. Try to rest now, Isabelle. Come. You must be very tired, little one,' whispered my mother.

She climbed into bed beside me and for a while I knew again the scent of my mother's skin, the caress of her smooth hair, the gentle hum of her heart. We lay twined together like a kernel in a nutshell, fitting smoothly, as once I had lain inside her body. I was awakened by a scratching at the door, as though a rat were scrabbling under the lintel. I opened my eyes, but all I saw was blackness.

'Maman?'

'Shhh.'

I felt her move beside me and heard the floorboards give as she made her way lightly across the room. The door opened silently, a servant perhaps. I shifted and clutched the bolster to me, drift-ing off into the warmth my mother had left on the pillow.

'He sleeps?' Her voice was low, apprehensive.

'He will not wake soon,' the low burr of a man's tone.

'Come, then.'

The blurred yellow light of a tallow lamp lit the room. I half sat up, pushing the hair from my eyes. A tall figure in black stood over my mother. As he turned, with a finger to his lips, I saw it was Lord Hugh. How could he be in the palace? My wedding was supposed to be a secret, kept from the Lusignans as part of whatever charade my father was playing out. How could he have got past the guards? Had he come to kill my papa? Or my mother and me? I gasped and pulled myself to a corner of the mattress, gathering the coverlet about me as a shield. Lord Hugh approached the bed. 'Don't be afraid, Isabelle.'

'How did you get here? I don't understand.'

He smiled teasingly, 'I flew, of course.' I caught the glint of the serpent brooch at his throat. Had he whisked through the night on a fairy dragon's tale?

'Sit up, Isabelle.' I obeyed dumbly. My mother reached and unlaced my shift, puffing my hair over my naked shoulders. Her fingers moved to my back and found the tiny mark there, the scar from the night of my dream that I thought I had forgotten. It throbbed at the touch of her hot fingers. 'Turn her.'

Just a push and I toppled like a rag doll, my face buried in the bed linen. Just before she blew out the lamp, I saw there was a shadow on the wall before me, a rearing, pointed shape: the horned man. I wanted to scream but my mother's fist was between my teeth. The sheet was lifted from my bared body, a draught fingered across my flesh. The bed gave as the creature moved over me, and then Lord Hugh did what he had come to do, and all I can say for him is that he did it quickly.

CHAPTER SEVEN

S O WHEN AT LAST I SAW THE SEA, IT LOOKED TO MY EYES
as dank and sour as a stagnant millpond. I wished I could be
blinkered like Othon and the other horses. I wished that I could
stuff my nose and ears with wax so as not to smell the salt mist
or hear the waves. To Agnes's puzzlement I asked to be taken
below deck as soon as we stepped onto the ship and I did not
stir from my bed all the time it took to make the crossing. Lady
Maude ordered basins, and screens around my face, for it would
never do for the queen of England to be seen puking, but I had
no need of them, I was dry and hard within, and I lay on my
couch as still as my own effigy. Lady Maude tried to rouse me,
thinking that I was so overwhelmed by my new station that I
was afraid to speak, and Agnes, more sensitive, merely sat by me
and stroked my hand, but my throat seemed full of the feathers
from the bolster where my face had been pressed. If I tried to
speak I knew that my voice would grate my tongue to shreds. A
day and a night I lay there, and when we docked at Portsmouth,
the first town of my strange new country, I suffered myself to

be sponged and scented and dressed in silence. The king had travelled on an earlier tide, it was bad luck for us to sail together, and I was to join him at his capital at London, where I would make my entry as queen.

We journeyed along high narrow roads, the horses picking their way carefully through the flint-strewn soil. I watched endless green hedgerows through the curtains of the litter, so that England seemed to me a country of green shade and grey stone, a damp mossy hollow where I had been rolled like a pebble. Perhaps if I had moved even slightly I should have seen the leafy pelt of the trees rippling against the sky, the spires of churches or even the faces of the people who Agnes and Lady Maude assured me had travelled for miles to glimpse their new queen, but I did not look up. I turned my head away from the food offered me, which smelt coarse and rancid. I accepted only a few sips of a brown drink called ale. I closed my eyes when I was lifted for the litter at night and carried to my bed in the township of tents erected for the queen's passing and let Lady Maude give out that I was ill, overwrought by the journey. I could see that she and Agnes had formed an unlikely alliance, each praying for her own reasons that I should survive, and they changed roles, Agnes scolding and Lady Maude awkwardly coaxing, but I could not eat even when I heard the pain in the feigned sharpness of Agnes's tone. As the days passed, I grew dizzy, fuddled by the shifting green shadows creeping into the litter, sometimes sobbing silently into my fists, often drifting and dreaming and waking in a moment that had lasted a morning.

To say that I did not care if I lived or died would suggest I had thoughts of either. Rather, I thought nothing, felt nothing. I paid no mind to my wedding, to my arrival in London, or the coronation that would be expected of me. I had no wish, as I grew daily weaker and Agnes and Lady Maude more frantic, beyond the green shadows of the roadside, the calls of the birds and the shuffle of the shifting leaves, that I might eventually slip away painlessly to meld with them and simply be no more. Until we broke our journey one evening in a clearing where there was a half-ruined chapel, its rounded arches recalling to me the lines of the old cathedral at Angouleme, whose bones were built into the newer apse erected in my grandfather's time. Dully, I thought that it must be very old.

'See, Majesty, what a charming place,' remarked Lady Maude brightly. I took no pleasure in the new title, with not one moment's joy of it. Two guards helped me from the litter and my maids fussed to arrange cushions that I might sit while my tent was set up. Below us in the forest, I could hear the grunts of the men as they hauled the baggage carts into a ring for the night. The deep forests of England were haunted by wolves, and the men lit fires in a circle each night to keep them off.

I was seated next to a little well, no more than a heap of stones with a cracked leather pitcher set into a ledge, and the thought of the cool water made me suddenly thirsty. I motioned to one of the maids to fetch me to drink and saw Agnes and Lady Maude exchange a meaningful look. It was the first time I had expressed any wish since we had been on the road. I swallowed the clean, flinty water, first sipping, then gulping. I could feel

93

it flowing through me, reviving and cooling me from within. I sat straighter, and something in the doorway of the chapel caught my eye. Slowly, with my legs trembling with effort, I pushed myself to my feet. The maids leaped forward to support me, but I saw Agnes hold up a quick hand to still them. A few faltering steps brought me across the thick summer grass to the deep shade of the chapel porch. Set into the stone lintel was a carving, a poor thing, the kind of drawing I might once have made for Othon, not the skilled work of a mason, and newer than the chapel, its planes still raw bright stone among the moss and ivy of the walls. A face with two horns surrounded by a few crudely shaped leaves above, with a line on its forehead and another flickering leaf-shape above that, like a candle's flame. It did not frighten me – what could frighten me now? The beauty and peace of the glade seemed to cup my puny body in its greenness, sheltering. This was a holy place. I pushed at the rough wooden door. Within, the chapel was dark and surprisingly cold, its only light a round window pushed through the wall where an altar had once been. The floor was littered with the desiccated corpses of songbirds, poor things, who had flown through and died in their dim prison, battering their fragile bodies against the walls. And there was something else. A heap of rags in one corner, curled over a stick. As I looked, I saw it move, very slightly.

'Lady Maude!' I had been right, I had lost my old voice. This was a new tone, clear and commanding, with an edge in it like the flint in the water I had swallowed. Lady Maude rushed up, followed by the guards. 'There is a person here.'

94

I waited outside, exhausted on my cushions, while the figure was dragged into the light. An old woman, though the thick grey hair on her wrinkled berry of a face made her seem as sexless as the figure carved into the door. One pathetically thin hand clutched a broomstick, and when she moved her layers of skirts they gave off a thick, dirty barnyard scent, high and pungent like a chicken run.

'Only a beggar, Majesty. I shall pack her off?' gasped Lady Maude, struggling between fear that I should be angry at being privately disturbed and delight that I had at last spoken.

'No. Ask her if she is hungry. I am hungry. Bring us some food.' No one moved. 'Lady Maude, you heard me. Bring us some food. And the woman may sit.'

I wondered later if the poor old lady knew that she had shared her meal with the queen of England. We were both ravenous. She nibbled swiftly and furtively at her food like an animal, mumbling chunks of bread into her toothless mouth as fast as she could swallow, and I tried to smile at her to show she should not be afraid, while I stuffed down cold fowl and cold baked eggs until my astonished stomach bulged and twitched with pain. I washed my hands and myself handed the creature a napkin to wipe the crumbs from her mouth.

'Now. Ask her what this place is,' I instructed Lady Maude.

'Majesty, I cannot think—'

'I said, ask her.'

Lady Maude spoke to the woman in the English tongue. I was surprised to find that a few of the words already sounded familiar.

'It is an old chapel, Majesty. This … person lives in a hut nearby. She sweeps it to keep it tidy. Sometimes a pilgrim will sleep or pray here. That is all.'

'Ask about that.' I pointed to the face in the porch.

'It is nothing, Majesty. The common people call it a "green man". A sort of …' Lady Maude trailed, 'woodland sprite. Just an old superstition.'

'Ask her. Tell her she has no reason to fear, if she will answer. Ask her politely, Lady Maude.'

The old woman paused then began to roll up her sleeve, exposing a withered arm much weaker looking than her broomstick. It was hard not to recoil in disgust at her stench. She held it out to me and I bent forward eagerly, ignoring Lady Maude's disapproving glare. The flesh was bluish white where the sun had not reached it. It was easy to see the tiny purpled coil, a raised scar. It could be a repulsive cyst, or it could be a serpent. Such as the one hidden beneath my own heavy linen gown. I looked into the old woman's darting, birdlike eyes, and placed one finger slowly on the mark. 'Ask her how she came by this?'

Lady Maude reluctantly translated the question. The woman's answer was short, as though she thought Lady Maude ought already to know it.

'The black man, Majesty. She says the black man put it there.' Lady Maude crossed herself and the ninny maids piously imitated her. I was desperate to ask more, but there was one word I was fearful of hearing.

'Please thank the woman. You may give her enough food for

another meal, and some pennies. Not too many, she might get into trouble for stealing. Take her away, now. I am tired.'

I smiled at the woman, trying to reassure her, but she made no gesture of thanks, as I had been accustomed to see poor folks use. She scrabbled together her rags as decently as she could and stepped away from us with a surprising agility, like an old proud doe. One of the maids gingerly handed her some provisions wrapped in a cloth, and then she was gone, calmly, vanishing along an invisible path through the trees.

'Now I would bathe. Have the bath set up, Lady Maude. And then I will dine. How many more days until London?'

'Three, Majesty. Perhaps four.'

'Very well. I will not use the litter, the air is too close. That is what has made me ill. Tomorrow, you shall have my horse prepared, and I will ride.' As the maids bustled to fetch out the tub and the screens, the soaps and the sheets, I looked around for Agnes, holding her face in my gaze until she returned it. 'Dear Agnes, see, I am well. You shall help me bathe.'

I rested as the water was boiled in cauldrons over the fire until it steamed, watching while the maids added cold from the well and Agnes the herbs and soap she carried in her travelling bag. My bath was a gift from my husband, who Lady Maude said liked to bathe every few days in the southern style, a polished cedar tub with thick handles carved with mermaids. I was rather tired of women with tails. The guards formed a ring around the glade, their backs turned, to protect the queen's modesty, and the maids held the sailcloth screens around the bath. I wrapped myself in the sheet that Agnes held for me and she unlaced my dress and I sank into the water, the wet folds clinging to my skin. My ribs stuck out and my stomach was distended between them with the food I had gobbled, the ankle bones of my floating feet poking out like hinges. Agnes combed and bound up my hair, humming to herself as she had always done when she washed me.

'It wasn't a dream, was it?' I asked as she bent to rub the olive oil soap into my back.

'No, Lady Isabelle,' she whispered sadly.

'And in Bordeaux, the night of the wedding … you knew of that?'

'I knew that he would come. Nothing more.'

'Yet you burned the bed linen?'

'I did as I was told.'

'I know you did. You would never hurt me.'

'Never, never!' Agnes cried.

'Hush,' I whispered. One of the maids had looked behind her.

'I was so sorry. I had no idea. But your mother …'

'You must tell me now. You have to. If the king should see?' I felt her fingers trace the mark on my shoulder, as my hand had traced the line on the old woman's flesh.

'He won't. Not for a long while, little one. Your mother made him promise.'

'What do you think of my mother's care for me, Agnes? What should I feel about my mother's promises?'

'You will understand, you will. Please, please be patient.'

'When? When will you tell me?'

'When you are crowned, Isabelle. When you are safe.'

I stood up and peeled the sheet from my wet body. Agnes held the towel and I allowed her to lift me from the tub against her hip as I had done since I was tiny, as I had always done. I couldn't be angry with her, she had not known how to protect me, how could she? There was no statue in that ruined chapel, only the green man, gloating at me. I thought of the Virgin in Mother Helene's closet, of the nun's serene face, tranquil in her assurance that the Holy Mother would protect her. But I had come alive again with the cool water of the forest, just like the king in the story of Melusina. There were other things than bits of painted wood to believe in. I would not commend myself to an ornament. My mind shied from the word but I forced myself to think it. Agnes could not protect me because she had been bewitched. And if my mother would not, and Agnes could not, then there would be nobody to protect me now I was in England – except myself.

CHAPTER EIGHT

I WAS A COURTENAY, AND A TAILLEFER, AND THEN, IN THE first week of October in the first year of the new century, and the twelfth of my own life, I became a queen. The king's heralds announced my ancestry over the blaring of trumpets in the cathedral at Westminster: Isabelle, Countess of Angouleme, great-granddaughter of Louis VI of France, niece to the Emperor of Contantinople, kin to the royal houses of Hungary, Aragon, Castile, Jerusalem and Cyprus, to the counts of Champagne, Hainault, Forez, Namur, Nevers, anointed with the common consent and agreement of the archbishops, bishops, counts, barons and people of the realm of England, by the grace of God, Duchess of Aquitaine and Normandy, Countess of Anjou and Maine. So many titles, so many great names. Names that were recorded on parchments in the monasteries of Europe and howled on battlefields; names that were muttered around peasants' hearths and cried in the lists of tournaments. And they all belonged to me. I felt too small to carry them.

king took me on progress across the country to the border of the wild lands of Wales, north to Lincoln and south once more to Guildford, where we kept Christmas and I gave out bright silk shirts with my own hands to his knights. Then north again, as far as the Scots march, across a range of hills where we heard the wolves howling across the snow-streaked moors and back to the holy city of Canterbury where we wore our crowns at the Easter Mass.

I looked on graciously as the burghers of each town we visited came out beyond the walls to make their bumbling and lengthy speeches of welcome, I listened gravely to the reports of my clerk of the revenues, I hawked with the king on the road and knelt at prayer and dined beneath my gold canopy of state and distributed alms and grants, but as I went about in my new guise, as gentle and docile as even Lady Maude could have wished, I thought of little but the stories Agnes told me, when she crept from her pallet at the foot of my bed to whisper to me in the candlelight.

At Angouleme, and then at Lusignan and Langoiran, I had been left a great deal to myself, and I had scarcely noticed, much less minded. Only now that I knew what it was never to be alone did I recall the long hours in the forest with Othon or my games in the garden with disbelief. Queens, it seemed, might never be alone. Agnes had said that my marriage would be like a play, but I had not expected that I should be constantly on the stage. From the moment Lady Maude drew the tester curtains in the morning, to the time my maids undressed me when I retired, I had to act my part. I was rarely private with the king. Since he could not yet share my bed, he would summon me after supper to sit on his lap and chatter in his ear, and I did not much mind his hands stroking my neck or the length of my thigh over my gown, though I did dislike the wet, wine-soaked kisses I had to accept from his mouth. That he doted on me was the only satisfaction of this new life, and even that was for the pleasure of tormenting Lady Maude. At first, I thought of extravagant trifles it would plague her to fetch me, fresh figs in November, a pure white kitten, winter roses to scatter on my sheets, but quickly these things seemed as childish and stupid as my half forgotten dreams of monkeys and silver sherbet bowls, and though the king begged me to think of anything he could procure that would delight me, I ceased to find pleasure in Lady Maude's disapproval. I did not care for jewels nor for silks any longer, nor even for the discomfiting of my enemy.

The kitten developed disgusting pus in its eyes and I told one of the guards to drown it. I found I no longer liked marmalade, much. I rode Othon each day that we travelled and made Tomas the master of my horse, but even that was not what I had expected. I was no longer ill. I ate and laughed, and found I could delight the king by teasing him, but all my thoughts were on that black night at the riverside in Lusignan, because the mark was on me.

The serpent on my shoulder twisted deep in my flesh, as deep as Lord Hugh had done. I scratched and worried at it, until the scar broke out in a weeping sore, then I raked my nails across it, knowing I could never smooth it out, unable to leave it be. Agnes made a plaster and told me that I should have to sleep in mittens if I did not leave myself alone. But it disgusted me, even as I made my own blood run down my back, the thin red trail a rope that bound me to the Lusignans across the sea. The mark trapped me, and at night I hated everyone who had conspired to put it there. It was a slave's brand, for all that I was queen, and like a slave, my thoughts were filled with futile schemes against my despised masters. The only thread of hope in that watery, ferrous skein was Agnes, because Agnes knew what I did not, and I believed that if I could only know too, I might understand. Not forgive, yet, but understand.

*

It came out slowly. Just a few snatched moments each night. I could not hear too much, Agnes said, since it made me nervous and unable to sleep, and it would displease the king if he saw me white and hollow eyed. Lady Maude supervised my food carefully, trying to stuff me with white bread and cream, because the king wanted me to grow plump and ready to become his true wife, but after hearing Agnes's story I pushed my dishes away and ate only a little fruit and meat, since I had no desire to grow at all. My mother had told me of a Saracen princess who saved her own life each night by inventing a new tale to divert her husband the sultan, and as Agnes faltered out what knowledge she had it seemed that I too was wrapped in a skein of stories except that each night I grew a little closer to my own end.

Agnes's family had always served the Courtenays. Back in Poitou she had sisters in service to my aunts and her uncles had gone as grooms or men-at-arms to the Holy Land. As a child she had been taken by her own mother to the summoning of the horned man, and watched the Courtenay ladies draw off their gowns and dance with him under the moon. It was the old faith, she said, much older than the Church, and all the men of Poitou, the Taillefers and the Lusignans and even the Aquitaine dukes included, knew that in their veins ran the blood of sky-clad women with unbound hair who knew of a religion deeper and more ancient than that of Christ. King Richard had known of it through his mother old Queen Eleanor, and when he was dying of the arrow wound in his shoulder had said bitterly that his family had come from the Devil and would return to him, but he was wrong, Agnes whispered, close in the dark. He was wrong because the Devil was an invention of the priests in Rome, who wished the people to adhere to the new faith, and tried to frighten them with stories of demons. The horned god was the spirit of all that kept the earth alive, and no more wicked than a tree or a sheep.

It was women's business, Agnes said. The men, the lords like my father, held themselves apart from it, for the Church and its bishops were what kept the world in balance. So long as the Holy Land was disputed, the Church supporting the system of lordship and vassalage, its wealth could be drawn upon, and in return there was great power to be obtained for the Crusader princes of Outremer. If the Holy Land was fully conquered, Agnes said, and I felt her stout shoulders shrug against me under the bedclothes, then perhaps there would be less need of popes and prelates.

I had never been so enthralled by any of the stories my mother told me, nor so appalled. Was this not wickedness, I asked, great wickedness? Certainly what was done to me could not be good. And what about sin, and minding my missal like a Christian child? All my life, Agnes had heard Mass alongside me each day, it was her voice that had taught me the 'Ave' and the 'Our Father', her hands which had folded my own small fingers in prayer. Agnes shrugged again and I could sense her struggling to find the words. The Lord was good, she sighed at last. What the Church taught – kindness, compassion, charity – were good things, and it was right to be mindful of them, especially for great people. But the old faith made no distinction between good and evil, it simply, it simply was. And many of the festivals we kept – Christmas and Easter and Lammastide, my marriage night – were the feasts of the old faith, covered up and made new, like, she struggled, again, like a plaster wall painted over, where the old patterns worked their way through the lime.

I could not believe it. All the people at Lusignan – the half-recognizable village folk, even my mother's maids – they all knew of this? And what about Lord Hugh? If this religion was women's business, then what was Lord Hugh doing wearing a stag's head and dancing about on the riverbank at night? I could not mention the other thing, though it was there between us, solid as a warming pan beneath the sheet. Instead I tried to make it sound foolish, a matter for muttering peasants like the old woman we had seen in the woods.

'It was not him,' Agnes insisted.

'Agnes, I *saw* him. I saw the brooch, the Lusignan serpent. The same shape as the mark he put upon me, a serpent, like Melusina. Why?'

Agnes couldn't say. At least, she tried, but she was not learned, and she could not make words to fit what was inside her.

'It might have looked like Lord Hugh, but it was something else, in Lord Hugh's body. Like the body of Christ, at Mass.'

'Lord Hugh is not a god, Agnes. Do not speak so sinfully! Whether you believe it or not, the thing I saw on May Eve was Lord Hugh. And I know that as surely as I know he was in my chamber on my wedding eve. You know it too. Don't lie!' I was so angry I thought of having her whipped, of having John's guard pull off her shift and shame her, of weals cut across her poor old back with a burning leather brand. But how could I think such things? I was wicked, the mark was making me as wicked as Lord Hugh. So I tried to be patient, to listen and to believe that she had acted because she thought it right.

All Agnes was able to explain clearly was that she had taken me to the *sabbat*, the meeting of the old faith, on my mother's instructions, just as her own mother had carried her.

'It was Tomas who took me, wasn't it?'

'He flew with you, yes.'

'Flew?'

'That's what we call it, when we are summoned. Flying.'

I recalled the thick grease Tomas had smeared on Othon's hooves the first time I had galloped him. It had felt as though we were flying.

Agnes explained that those who worshipped the horned man believed that they could take the form of animals, swift and light as foxes, strong as horses, fleet as hares.

'What else? What else do they believe?' I was insatiable now.

'That there is no death.'

'Like Christians, then?'

Agnes puzzled again over her words. 'Not like that. There is no death, because it is the same as life, just a different ... stage. When we eat bread, we are eating the death of the wheat that made it, but it becomes part of us, of our life. And when we die, we become part of the fields.'

'Like the bread at Mass.'

Agnes smiled, quite the scholar, 'That is where the Mass comes from, little one, from the old ways.'

'And my mother? She wanted to make me part of this?'

'Your mother loves you, little one. You are a queen now. Surely you see that?'

'Then why—'

'I cannot say.'

'Did it happen to you too?'

'Once. It happens to all of us. We have to become one with the horned man.'

I was bewildered. Agnes was an old maid, a spinster who had never had a husband. Had she ... done that? I could not picture it.

'And now? Why did Lord Hugh want me to marry Hal and then change his mind? Why did he treat me so kindly, and then ...' I could not say it. I bit my lip and took a deep breath. 'Why did he pretend that the king had tricked him, if he didn't care?'

'I have only told you what I was bid, little one. But your mother said she would send you a messenger, someone who will explain, when the time is right. I was not to tell you, except for what happened in the woods that day, and you so ill, and I so afraid.'

I reached out and touched Agnes's face. Her cheeks were wet. 'I will not be without you for anything, Agnes. Don't worry. You did what you were told. Don't cry.'

But somehow that made her cry the harder.

*

I wished then that I had learned to write during those quiet days in the convent. I could read quite well, in both French languages, but like any lady, I had clerks to make out the grants and charters I was expected to witness as queen, and though I could dictate a letter, as Queen Eleanor had done to the Pope himself when her son the Lionheart was a hostage in Austria, I could hardly ask a nervous young priest to take down words about stag's heads and midnight sabbats. And to whom should I send it? Did my mother intend to send me a letter? Or Lord Hugh?

I doubted that, too, because my marriage with the king had brought rebellion to Poitou. My flight with King John had made war, not peace. At first, Lord Hugh had feinted, asking John to offer him some recompense for the loss of his son's bride. Instead, my husband sent his seneschal in Normandy to seize the castle of the Count of Eu there, who was Lord Hugh's brother, and demanded that the vassals of La Marche, which he had granted to the Lusignans, pay homage direct to the English crown. Lord Hugh's response was to throw off his allegiance to John and declare once more for the French king, sending his men to attack the garrisons held in John's name. Each time my husband held a council, I questioned him, claiming that I wished to know the workings of his government, that I might be a better wife to him, but often he would play with my hair and tell me not to mind, that this was men's business, and that I should not meddle in it as his own mother Eleanor had done. He preferred me to play with toys, or eat cakes with my ladies, or practise my dancing, to think on pretty things, he said, since I was so pretty myself. But sometimes, he would indulge me, and I discovered all I could of the Lusignans' plottings, all the time feeling the throb of the mark on my shoulder and recalling the coldness inside me, which meant I belonged to them.

In May, a priest in Essex was summoned to a court of bishops to answer for himself after reports that he had led dancing in his churchyard on Easter Day wearing ram's horns on his head. My husband took me to Portsmouth to meet with his barons and plan an attack on the rebels. We were to go to Normandy, and then, at the invitation of the French king, to visit him in Paris. I ordered a new wardrobe, more for the pleasure of hearing Lady Maude grumble at the expense than for any delight I took in it, and a scarlet velvet caparison for Othon, for when I rode him at our entry. So we crossed the sea once more, and once more, I could not rejoice in it, for all that water was surely my element now, as one of Melusina's kin.

We lodged the first night at the Louvre, the fortress built over the river Seine, facing out towards the Norman strong-holds of the English kings. The royal palace, the Cité was on an island in the middle of that river. King Philip had given it over for our use, and we would ride there in procession the next day. I was in my chamber with Agnes and the maids, looking over my cloth of silver gown, when a page skittered in with a message. I had sent a pair of beautiful gloves, gold-chased doeskin, to Princess Blanche, whom I was very curious to see, and she had returned a parcel of delicate lace to me. I thought carelessly that it must be another gift, and told the boy he might send the bearer in.

Outside, the spring night was clear, but the Louvre was a gloomy place, the walls vastly thick, with forbidding round towers at each corner and just two narrow gates to the south and east, barely wide enough for a mounted man to pass. I should be glad to lodge at the Cité, I thought, this place felt more like a prison than a palace. Still, the casements were shut against the stink of the river mud, and the room was bright with candles so that the maids could see about their stitching. When he came in, it was as though all their light danced to his face, so that for a moment, we sat in darkness. I thought two things: I thought that I might be looking into my own countenance, and that I had never seen a beautiful man before.

His hair, like mine, was ashy gold, with a sheen like new corn. His eyes, like mine, were the brightest turquoise, his skin, like mine, the colour of new cream. He was tall, and broad shouldered, and his waist was narrow. In fact, from the titters from the maids I could see he possessed all the features of a knight in a romance, and somehow that made me cross.

I greeted him coolly, leaving him a long time on his knees, had water brought for his hands, fruit and wine, though I did not rise, and when we had accomplished the courtesies I asked him his name.

'Pierre de Joigny, Majesty. Sent by your lady mother, the Countess of Angouleme.'

I shot a quick glance at Agnes, seated quietly in a corner busying herself with the lacings on my slippers. Her head moved very slightly, though she did not look up.

'Leave us,' I ordered the maids. 'Now!'

As the girls made a languid show of gathering up their needles, for the chance of a few more seconds' ogling. I could hear them giggling along the passageway after they had curtsied their way out. Agnes went quietly to the door and locked it before returning to her place.

'Will it please you to sit, sir?'

'Majesty, do you know who I am?' asked Pierre.

'I should think you are my brother, sir,' I smiled. 'I am very glad to see you, at last.'

Before my mother's marriage to my father, she had been the wife of the Comte de Joigny, until the marriage was dissolved by the church as the two were found to be too closely related. I had never known anything of my brother except his existence, and that he was the king of France's man. Had my mother sent him to make amends? I could not help being delighted to see him. We had the same blood, after all.

'You are most welcome, Brother. I believe you were with King Philip in the Holy Land.'

He assented with a modest nod.

'Then you will have much to tell me. I long to hear of your adventures.'

'Indeed, Majesty. I hope we shall become good friends, if Majesty will do me the honour.'

'Perhaps.'

'Though perhaps it is too much to aspire to, the friendship of such a beautiful lady as Majesty.'

'You flatter me, sir. And perhaps yourself too, since a looking glass would show our countenances so alike.'

'Impossible, Majesty. I could only ever hope to be a shadow to your sun.'

I had come a long way, I thought, from my hoyden days at Lusignan. I could keep up this kind of flirtatious patter for hours, charming, feinting, the idlest of conversation, designed with nothing more than mutual smugness and the whiling away of an evening. 'But sir, you must forgive me. It grows late and I am rather fatigued by our journey. You say you bear a message from our lady mother?'

'Just so, Majesty.'

I wondered what it could be. A letter, perhaps? But watching his face, I saw a tiny shadow cross it, like a cloud's silhouette on the surface of a calm and sparkling sea. I tried to tell myself that this visit was a kindness, that Pierre had taken the chance to meet me while I was in his master's city, or perhaps ask me some favour, a grant or a place, but I knew it was none of those things, and I felt cold again inside.

'Then you will trust what I have to tell you?'

'Why should I need to trust you, sir?'

'It is a … delicate matter, Majesty.'

'Then how might I know to trust you? You bring a letter, maybe? Or some token?'

'I bring proof.' His face in the candlelight now looked hard, marble-planed, and I knew that despite his pleasantries, he wished me ill.

'As I said, sir, I am rather tired. Perhaps you will be so good as to find me once more at the Cité, once the ceremonies tomorrow are concluded. Agnes, would you be so good as to show the gentleman out?'

I turned but Agnes had not stirred.

'Agnes!' I rapped sharply. 'I asked you to show my guest out.'

She shook her head dumbly. 'Agnes! What can you mean by disobeying me?' I glared at her, but she only shook her head and mumbled something.

'What? What are you saying?'

'That you need to hear what your brother has to say.'

I could not be angry with her. She looked so cowed and fearful. I thought wearily that I could summon the guard and order Pierre away from my presence in King John's name, but then all my state, my commands, had done nothing to protect me so far. I might as well hear it, I thought, drawing myself up straight.

'Very well. But do not tarry. What is this "proof" you speak of?'

'This.' He took a small package of black watered-silk from the pocket on his mantle. 'Our mother sent it.'

He revealed a square of linen with a dark, red-brown stain. Inside, a little piece of parchment with a crude drawing in charcoal, slightly smudged, seven lines making a stag's antlered skull, and beside it, a coiled shape that might have been another smudge had it not looked so very like another mark that I knew well.

I looked at the things, put out a hand to touch them, withdrew it, my fingers hovering over the pulse of their horrible power. I felt my composure fracture, dug my nails into the soft palms of my hands, bit down hard on my lower lip. I could not give way, yet my exclamation was a child's, not a queen's.

'Agnes! Agnes, why? You said you burned it—'

'I cut away a piece, as the Countess instructed me.'

'I am come from court,' said Pierre. 'Our mother is there, as you perceive. You will see her tomorrow.'

'I do not wish to see her. I will not.'

'But you will listen?' he asked.

'Have I a choice?'

'Where is the king?'

'At supper with his men of Normandy. He will not come for a long time.'

'Sister, please believe me. I know how strange this must have been for you, how lonely and hard. But I am here now.' Pierre's voice was so gentle, it made me want to weep. 'You have been very good, and very brave, and I can help you, now.'

Perhaps it was the struggle to keep back my tears, or the irritation I had felt when the maids looked at him, but I could not hold on to my temper. And by God, I was bored of weeping. I threw the disgusting little bundle to the floor and hissed at him.

'I am weary, do you hear me? I am tired to death of all these whispers and plotting. I am queen of England! I have no need of your protection, or my mother's interference. You are nothing to me, and I will not have you make mischief in my life any more. And these,' I kicked contemptuously at the scribble and the scrap of cloth. 'These are wicked tokens. A priest would call them the Devil's work and I will not have them near me. So you can tell our lady mother that. Now get out before I call the guard.'

And then I spoiled all my injured dignity by bursting into sobs after all, stifling them reproachfully in the hem of my gown, hunching myself smaller and smaller into a snail shell of pain. In a moment, I felt his hand gently stroking my back, and his touch felt like my mother's, and I cried all the harder, until I lost my breath and began to gasp for air.

'Here.' Agnes took me firmly in her arms and gave me a little shake before pressing my wet face to her bosom. 'Calm yourself, little one, there now, there now.'

Pierre knelt, as gracefully as if he were dancing, or handing a lady to her horse in a tapestry, to gather his foul tokens.

'Sister, I cannot leave until I have spoken with you. Please, calm yourself, as your nurse says. Here, sit.'

They fussed about me, sponging my face and fetching a cup of wine, Pierre's voice murmuring that all would be well. 'You are recovered, Sister? I am so sorry for your distress. Now, here are the things you must consider. You are queen, indeed, but you are in danger. Your husband is weak, he will not hold his lands if the king of France moves against him.'

'My husband loves me. He will protect me, whatever happens.'

'Will he love you so much, Majesty, when he knows you are not a maid?' He let it hang there, and then his voice continued, supple and sinuous. 'You know he will not. Perhaps he would let you retire to a convent. But you know the penalty for adultery in a queen? It is treachery, after all, what you did.'

'I didn't do anything! It wasn't my fault, I was forced—' I stopped myself. The dumb sickness that had come upon me after my wedding had been a blessing, I saw. I had shrivelled away in shock, like a snail caught in sunlight, and stopped my mouth. I might have cried out on Lord Hugh, proclaimed what he had done to me and asked my husband to avenge me. But John would not have wished to avenge me, as I had been spoiled, and in so spoiling me, Lord Hugh had made me party to the most heinous crime of all.

'You could tell him that, Sister. Perhaps he will be merciful. But you have had a show of his temper, I think. He is not always a reasonable man, you must concede. *Lèse majesté* is a burning offence for a woman, know you that. Besides, John will not long be king. Lord Hugh never intended to be John's man. Why do you think your betrothal was arranged to Angouleme's old enemy as soon as the Lionheart died? Why did you think the king came to Lusignan to hear his fealty?'

'I thought, I thought it was an alliance. To join their lands, as is usual. To bring peace.'

He snorted. 'Are you such a child still, Sister, that you believe that? No one wished for peace. They wished for power, as all men do. And the lord of Angouleme with them.'

Papa. But my papa was a good man.

'Lord Hugh knew that King John had certain ... tastes,' Pierre continued, 'and certain ... incapacities. Why do you think there are no children of his marriage with Lady Hadwisa?'

'The king has bastards, like his brothers. Like all kings.'

'Perhaps, but he is older now. And has no legitimate child. Lord Hugh knew that he would want you, knew that in taking you he would give the Lusignans a legitimate grievance to rebel against him. So he arranged it with your Lord Aymer, the betrothal, then the betrayal. The Count of Angouleme thought of nothing except that his daughter would be queen.'

'As I am.' I would not let him see how the thought of my father using me hurt.

'Or not ... the king has not known your bed. It would be an interesting case for a church court, would it not, Sister?'

'And now?'

'Lord Hugh will rise against John, and the men of Normandy will support him. The next heir is Duke Arthur.'

'What of it?'

'You, my dear Sister, are England's queen. You have been shown to the people, shopped about like a pedlar's bundle over the countryside, we hear. You will be useful to Arthur's claim, when you marry him. So you will still be queen of England,

and Duchess of Normandy and Aquitaine. And perhaps queen of France, too.'

My mouth was bubbling with questions, but he held up a hand. His voice was growing colder and colder. 'I will finish. Now, as you know, the kings of France are related to the Courtenays, as well as the dukes of Brittany. Lord Hugh considers that if Louis of France should … die, then Arthur, as King of England and Duke of Brittany, would have a strong claim.'

'This is madness. I will not hear it.'

'I think you will. You see, Lord Hugh is an adherent of the old religion.'

At the words, I felt the throb of the scar on my shoulder. I tried to turn away from the images that tumbled into my mind, the horned figure on the rock at Lusignan, the dark man in my wedding bed, the leering face in the green chapel in the wilds of England. I thought I might scream with it, scream and never stop, run mad and they would take me away and lock me up and drug me and I could be done with this, done with this spider's web of vileness. I could feel it swell and billow inside me like a great wave, all the horror and rage I had quenched inside me during the time of my quietness. I opened my mouth to release it, but no sound came, only a weak little gasp. I breathed, swallowed, tried again, putting as much dismissive contempt into my voice as I could muster. 'Yes, I know of that. Nonsense. Superstition for peasants. Ungodly and disgusting.'

'No, not nonsense. You know it. Whatever you believe, Isabelle, Sister, Majesty, it has a powerful hold on the people. And you belong, too.'

'I do not! I will not!'

Pierre turned up his sleeve, the skin of his arm even smoother and paler than that of his face. Our face. I suddenly saw the old woman in the glade, rolling up her foetid rags. The mark was clear on his forearm, just below the elbow.

'The serpent. What of it?' I was confused.

'Because we are Courtenay, and we are Lusignan. Sister.'

I wanted to laugh. Finally, I could see what had been plain before my eyes for so long. Not for a moment could I question him. My mother, Lord Hugh, that last time at Lusignan. It had always been like that with them, and I had always known it, I saw now. I had simply chosen not to see.

'But you … we are so fair,' was all I could manage, absurdly. 'The Lusignan men are black.'

'Indeed. And the Courtenays are fair. And you are very lovely, Sister.'

'And so are you, Brother,' I managed to add, scornfully, though I felt faint.

My mother, my mother … my beautiful, elegant, Maman. And my papa. My round, red-bearded Papa. I was not Taillefer, I was Lusignan, not the warrior's daughter descended from the enemies of the Norsemen, but a *cambion*, the offspring of a human and a demon. Melusina's tail was twined in my veins, too, and for all that Agnes told me there was no such thing as the Devil, how could I believe that when he stood before me, so gentle, so courteous, so handsome? Demons and goblins may have been tales to frighten children, but Pierre and Lord Hugh, fine gentlemen both, one black, the other white, had their dealings with Him. The church forbids it; it is the wickedest sin, incest. That is why marriages in great houses are dissolved, if they are found within the prohibited degrees of the Church.

'But we are not ... not?' I blurted.

'Monsters, Sister? No, we are not. The blood can turn different ways, in the Lusignans. Do you not recall the story of Melusina and Geoffrey Spike-Tooth from your nursery? The blood went another path, there.'

Why was this man babbling of fairytales? I was distraught, could only think of getting him out of my sight, that I might think.

'What is it that you want from me?' I asked quietly.

'As I said, Sister. We wish you to marry Duke Arthur, and be queen again, of England and of France, too. Are you not grateful?'

'Grateful? Grateful? This is wickedness, madness! I will not do it. I will not betray my husband.'

'He is not your husband, truly. And you have betrayed him. And think, Sister, think! Not just France and England, Normandy and Brittany, but the Holy Land, too! Our uncle, Peter de Courtenay, will be the next emperor in Constantinople. And you shall be his heiress. And then—'

'You are out of your wits. Or you are a simpleton. You are a puppet to Lord Hugh ... a-a dog. He cannot believe such a thing is possible.'

'No, Sister.' I hated the sibillant slide of that word, in his mouth. 'I am no puppet. But you? What is it St Paul says, as your priests teach you? "Better to marry than to burn"? You shall marry where Lord Hugh chooses, or you shall burn. You are marked. And now I shall take my leave, Majesty. I am honoured to have been granted a visit with such a gracious queen. My profound thanks.'

He was bowing himself out, once, twice, three times, and then he rapped on the door for the guard, and was gone.

How could I not have seen it, when my mother told me the tale of Melusina? How could I have missed it, when she left me at Lusignan? Saturday, the day the witches held their sabbat, the day that Melusina could not be seen … The burning of the abbey … Lord Hugh training me like a blinded hawk, teaching me the pretty ways that would ensnare the king, showing me how to lead and tease him, even as I was myself ensnared. And to have done such things as he had done with his own daughter. His daughter! I think I groaned aloud, for Agnes came to me and placed a nervous hand on my shoulder. I could not bear for her to watch me as I contemplated my mother's shame. Without raising my head, I motioned her wearily away.

'I will stay alone, tonight, Agnes, do you understand? Send to King John and tell him that I cannot come down, that I am resting before the entry tomorrow. Go, please. Go!'

When I heard the door close I went to my bed and lay down, my face flat against the linens. I forced myself to follow it through, what my mother had done with Lord Hugh, how they had conspired to cheat my father, and me, and John. What they planned … I did not know I had wept again until I lifted my head, seeing that the room had grown dark, and saw the soaked shadow of my face on the pillow. I dragged myself to the window and pushed the casement open to the stench of the river mud. Just a push and a step, I thought, nothing to me. I could release myself and fall to the stinking ooze and be lost, and surely God would not punish me, for He knew what had been done to me, and that His world would be better without me. Or perhaps we were fiends already, me and my mother and Pierre, gold and white outside and rotten corruption within, like Lucifer's fallen servants? I had nothing to live for, no child, no real husband, as Pierre had observed, only Agnes's mute and stupid love, as fond and useless as a lapdog's.

I hopped up to the narrow sill, my limbs moving as easily under my gown as if I climbed an apple tree in the garden at Angouleme. One push. One push and I would fly, briefly, as swift and sure as I had once flown with Othon, long ago in the woods at Lusignan. Even that word made me writhe with shame now. My palms smarted where I had buried my nails, I clenched them on the wood of the casement, closed my eyes for the last time, clenched my arm muscles—

'Isabelle!' The clatter of the door, John's face, flushed with wine, his squat body swaying in the doorway clutching at the lintel for support. Behind him, the shocked faces of my maids. The sight of me had shocked the drunkenness from him, 'Isabelle! They told me you were ill! Here,' he stepped firmly across the floor and reached for me. I allowed my body to fall softly against his chest and he buried his face in my hair. The gold Courtenay hair.

'Forgive me, my lord. The room was so close. I just wanted a little … a little air.'

'Open the casements! Bring herbs to sweeten the room. Can you not see that your mistress is unwell?'

'Was I in danger, sir?' I murmured prettily. 'Have you rescued me?'

'Oh Isabelle.' Now it was passed I could smell the wine in his pores, and he stumbled as he set me on the bed.

'Forgive me, my lord. I should never wish to alarm you.' It made me sick to do it, but I twined my arms around his neck, in full sight of the bustling maids.

'You are very naughty,' he muttered, delightedly. To my disgust, I could feel his excitement as he held me against him.

'Then naughty girls should sleep,' I said, making a penitent moue at him, turning up my face for a kiss.

'Indeed. Sleep,' he slurred, and rolled sideways onto the bed. The maids had not even lit the incense bowls before he was snoring. I was shamed for him.

'Summon the king's valet and his guard. He will rest here tonight. Look sharp!'

When, finally, we were alone, I curled myself around my husband's back, my eyes raw in the thick darkness. There was some comfort in the warmth of him. I tried to match my breaths to the sound of his heart and sought refuge in the sour fumes of his mantle. In a while, I slept, and so we shared our first night as man and wife, in one bed.

As John and I processed in clouds of incense and ermine the *Laudes*, the ancient hymn of the Norman dukes, was sung, proclaiming me party to my husband's empire. At the banquet beneath the great beams of Westminster Hall the queen's champion, William Marshal, the finest of the Lionheart's knights, walked his destrier three times among the trestles, challenging any man who disputed my title to single combat. The Royal Exchequer released thirty pounds for my coronation regalia, and my crown of thick and ancient English gold had been worn by the Danish queens long before England passed to the Normans.

My queenship was recorded by stiff fingered monks in freezing northern abbeys and Arab scribes beyond the Pyrenees; I was one of God's elect, and would be the mother of kings. The most powerful vassals of my husband's lands, from my own father to the king of Scots, would kneel before me. My revenues included lands in Saintes and Niort, Saumur, La Flèche, Beaufort-en-Vallée, Baugé and Châteaux de Loir, manors in Devon, Ilchester, Wilton, Malmesbury, Wiltshire, Rutland, Berkhamsted, Falaise and Domfront and Bonneville-sur-Touque, all solemnly granted in the king's name. I had a household of my own, and the rights of a bridge and a dock in London. I had a chaplain and a mistress of the robes and, for what it mattered, a silver chamber pot.

The men I had known as a child had only travelled in order to make war, at the summons of their king. Mules and carts were for pedlars. But my new husband could not get enough of moving, that strange restless energy which possessed him only being assuaged by constant journeying. As the leaves turned, the

CHAPTER NINE

THE NEXT DAY, WE RODE IN PROCESSION ACROSS THE new bridge of St Michel, to the island palace of the kings of France. I rode behind my husband in a litter hung with crimson silk, my hair unbound and flowing down the shoulders of the silver dress, my small crown tight on my brow. I had asked Agnes for some rouge to disguise the paleness of my cheeks, and I hoped the shadow of my hair would disguise the hollows beneath my eyes.

The bells of the great cathedral of Notre Dame were pealing as we came into the courtyard before the palace where, as a great honour, the French king's seneschal held John's horse as he dismounted onto a tree stump, traditionally the first step for the kings of France to take upon their homecoming. I thought how absurd it was, the significance men gave to such symbols, as though this tree stump was anything more than a lump of firewood, but I could see from John's face that he deemed it a tribute to his power, and I pitied him, in his ignorance and his pride. When the men had passed into the hall, Princess Blanche and her ladies came forward to welcome me. As the toes of my slippers touched the ground, we both made deep curtseys, precisely timed so that neither of us should appear to be giving precedence to the other, and then Blanche stepped forward and offered me her hand.

'You are most welcome to the Cité, esteemed Aunt,' for Blanche was John's niece, the daughter of his sister Eleanor of England and her Spanish husband, so I was her senior relative, though she was perhaps two years older than me. Her face was round, plain and placid. I had heard the story of how the old, indomitable English queen, John's mother, had made the last of her long journeys across the mountains to personally select which of her granddaughters should be the next queen of France, and how Blanche's sister, Urracca, had been passed over in favour of her sibling. I wondered why. Perhaps Blanche was more ... biddable? But I could not think of obedience, not today. I complimented Blanche on her elegant white silk mantle, which fell over her blue dress beneath her crown. In turn, she praised my own cloth of silver, and we passed through among our kneeling women exchanging pleasantries, just as I had so often heard my mother do.

Our husbands were presently held bond by a truce; soon, no doubt, they would once again be at war, as they had been so often, but this was not our business. We were to admire, to praise one another's girdles and cloaks, to speak of the sweetness of the music and the elegance of the banquet, to arrange our sleeves and trill and coo like so many ornamental birds in an aviary. To be light and gracious and charming and never let it be seen that beneath our elaborate trains, a mere yard of which would have kept a merchant man's family for a year, lay the blood and muscle and bone that would decide more surely than our husband's armies what the future of their lands would be. Would Blanche's son rule one day in the south, or mine? It was unbecoming of me to wonder it, though I wondered whether she thought about it, too.

As we progressed into the palace, I saw that the conduits in the outer court had been filled with wine so that the people of Paris could celebrate the meeting of the two kings. We passed through a pleasant garden with vines trellised along the walls and plantings of willow, pear and fig trees.

'My grandmother planted those,' remarked Blanche. 'They are very fragrant, in season, here in the shelter.'

I acknowledged her politely, thinking of old Queen Eleanor, of how she had come here when she was a girl of an age with us, to be queen of France before her divorce and marriage to John's father. The fig branches were crooked and gnarled now, as she must be. Had she planted them to remind her of her lost home in Aquitaine?

We heard Mass in the chapel of St Nicholas, which looked more like a dragon's lair than a church, so piled was it with gold ornaments. It seemed hard to believe, among the solidity of such wealth, in the fumes of the incense, and the low murmuring of King Philip's chaplains in their beautifully embroidered vestments, that my brother believed such things could be easily swept away. I prayed fervently, asking forgiveness for my wickedness at the Louvre the previous evening, asking God for grace and guidance, yet I did not feel any less alone as we rose from our knees and followed the sound of blaring trumpets into the *grande salle* of the Cité.

The room was lit with candles, for though the casements with their wooden shutters were open, they were narrow, designed for arrows rather than light and air. The Bourges tapestries shimmered as we took our seats, as though the figures they depicted were real and likely to step down and dance among us. King Philip sat on his throne in the centre of the dais, with my husband to his right and, on a slightly lower throne, the French heir, Blanche's husband, Louis. We were conducted to our seats, I to the right of the prince, Blanche to the left of John. *Lower your eyes as the grace is said, Isabelle, raise them respectfully to your husband when the trumpets sound, lean forward appreciatively as the first course is carried in, to show your pleasure to your host.* The hours dragged by, and I passed them by playing myself as a model lady, imagining myself into my role so hard that for some of that endless time I even convinced myself.

As the first course of venison in verjuice, gingered beef and a flight of roast egrets and herons, their feathers gilded with saffron and their wings sheltering tiny gold cups of camel-ine sauce, was carried in, I watched the room discreetly. My mother and Pierre were seated at the first table below the royal dais where the most high-ranking magnates of the two kings had taken their places. My mother caught my gaze, rose and made me a low curtsey, which I acknowledged with a dip of my head, no more. If I looked longer at my maman, I knew I should weep. Pierre was seated a little further along, among the French lords, his hair a blazon in the candlelight, his fine profile attracting admiring glances from the women nearby. The servers staggered in with the entremet, a cockatrice, a pig and a capon sewn together, stuffed with bread, egg and suet, surrounded by tiny quails with piglets' snouts to represent its litter. I smiled at the praises of the guests, but the thing made me sick, I thought it crude and ugly. The cockatrice was followed by peacocks and swan, a huge side of ox carried by four men, dishes of wild duck in tarragon and cream seated on nests of pastry. I had to force myself to eat. The pungent spices were overwhelming and the mouths of the men, dripping with fat as they gnawed and swilled, appeared grotesque, a carnival of feasting demons. John was drinking hard, but I noticed that the French king took only a little watered wine as his restless eyes spidered around the room.

Before the dessert course, it was time for the gift giving. I saw King Philip give a tiny smirk into his beard, knowing what was to come. The doors of the salle were thrown wide, and though, of course, I might not rise from my seat to peer eagerly like the other guests, I could glimpse the crowd at the outer gate and hear the murmurs of surprise and admiration as a troop of acrobats, wearing nothing but wide blue-and-gold-striped pantaloons and outlandish silk turbans pinned to their heads, their faces and torsos blackened with cork, came flipping and tumbling over the rushes. When they reached us, they formed themselves into a tower, five men at the base, four more grasping their shoulders and turning a long, full circle to grasp the elbows of the first, with three more climbing up to balance, shaking with effort, on their upturned feet. Then two more, topsy-turvy, then the last one, who shimmied like a monkey along the flanks of his fellows, a gold scroll clasped between his teeth. When he had attained the precarious summit, he unrolled the scroll and feigned to read, the sweat pouring through his makeup all the while, 'Majesties: an envoy from the East.'

The musicians played a strange, wandering, keening tune, and as the tower of men collapsed itself, each of them rolling to a corner of the salle, heads tucked into knees like jewelled scarabs, a monster was led through the doors. Twice as high as the tallest destrier, with short legs, a pendulous body covered in sagging, grey hide, the beast had huge flapping ears and a monstrous snout that waved before it, thicker than a man's arm. On its back was a litter with a pointed roof, upon which perched a skinny boy, with fat lips, a squashed nose and skin the colour of a bruised plum, truly, not painted, with only a white cloth wound around his limbs. The room fell silent, for as it moved, it was clear the monster was real, not a wooden construction with hidden wheels, but a living thing. Many of the ladies crossed themselves, and though the men kept their right hands on the table, for manners' sake, I watched their eyes slide to their daggers. Closer and closer the thing plodded. The French king caught my eye, looking perhaps for a sign of fear, but I met his gaze clearly. I saw far worse monsters in my dreams.

Slowly, the murmurs rose again, everyone exclaiming as to what the thing could be and where it had come from. A few brave souls even reached out to brush its wrinkled skin. As it approached, the mounted boy, whose head nearly touched the rafters of the salle, produced a long ebony pole and touched the thing behind one of its drooping ears. Slowly, effortfully, the creature knelt down on its forelegs, the little silk house bucking crazily on its back, and lowered its head in obeisance. I stood up, clapping my hands with delight, and Blanche followed my example.

'See, ladies,' called the king. 'Their Majesties are not afraid. This is an elephant!' The word rolled through the room, people milling the sound around their tongues like an unusual sweetmeat. 'Sent from Persia, a gift from the Sultan,' the king continued. 'And now, a gift from me to my brother of England.'

I flashed a glance at John, whose face was mangled with drink and irritation. What were we to do with such a thing? What would it eat? How much would it cost? I knew my husband's mean-minded suspiciousness, his quickness to imagine a slight, and fearful that he would give offence, I moved forward, curtsied gratefully to King Philip, and approached the beast myself. Nearby on the table was a dish of baked apples, their skin gilded with saffron and cinnamon. I picked one up and held it towards the creature, keeping my palm flat as though I was feeding Othon, but unsure where its mouth might be.

'Be careful, madame!' gasped Princess Blanche.

I didn't care whether it ate me or not. I could disappear into its maw with my hose sticking out behind like a soul in Hell being swallowed by a demon for all I minded.

'Here you are, Elephant,' I whispered.

I recoiled as the huge snout swayed towards me, and then the creature picked up the apple with the end of its nose, and popped it underneath, to where I could see a surprisingly small opening. This time my delight was genuine.

'Look!' I cried. 'It eats apples with its nose!'

The room erupted with relieved laughter, quickly followed by applause. I could hear the remarks 'How brave she is!', 'How charming!', 'How lovely!'

Four horses, ridden by young squires in pale blue surcoats showing the French *fleur-de-lys*, now rode down the salle towards the creature. Ladders were brought, and the 'knights' mounted them as though the poor animal was a castle they were besieging, grasped the supporting poles of the structure on its back and brought it to the ground. As the elephant was led away by its tiny rider, the four opened the litter, which, I could see now, seemed to be made all of silver, and began to pull out gifts: saddles with gilt trappings, mail coats which swam from their hands like fish scales, *cotte* of heavy linen faced with silver, axes with thick ivory handles, knives in curious curved sheaths. One by one, the men stepped up to receive their gifts, making their obeisance towards the dais as they did so. Among them knelt my brother, but I kept my eyes on the elephant and a gentle smile curving at the corners of my lips.

When all the men had received their prizes, the doors of the salle swung wide again, and two pages ran along the length of the hall, laying down a dark blue cloth between them. I could hear more gasps of delight from the crowd outside. John scowled – another unwanted present? Along the waves of cloth came a low cart, bearing a narrow black boat, its prow viciously pointed and mounted with a shining steel horn, close and neat as a coffin.

'It is one of the boats they use at Venice,' whispered Louis.

'How original,' I managed to whisper back.

The thing sailed towards us on its watery carpet, the cart's rope drawn by unseen hands. When it reached the dais, I saw that it was loaded with canvas bales, and a figure lying between them. I gasped with surprise as he rose and bowed, swaying a little, for all the world as though he hovered on a real boat on a real Venetian canal, for though his face was lowered, I caught the watery flash of his pale eyes, the colour of the lagoons in my maman's lost stories. The silk man.

My fingers strayed to the cloth of my gown. It had begun with him, that day when the messenger had overtaken him on the Angouleme Road. Was he part of it, too, his silks stretching about like a net, drawing us closer and closer to the madness that waited at Lusignan? Princess Blanche clapped her hands delightedly, and now the ladies came forward, exclaiming over the bales of airy fabric being unpacked from the boat. The silk man flung them about him like a conjuror so that the space around him became a meadow of improbable silk blooms, turquoise and scarlet, leaf green and dull gold. My mother approached, and as she made her curtsey towards the thrones, I saw her eyes slide to meet the silk man's subtly expectant gaze. He reached into the boat and handed her two small parcels of white linen. One she offered, with another deep curtsey, to Blanche, and then she turned to me.

'Majesty.'

'Lady Mother.'

Our words were hidden under the gasps of the swarming women. The men on the dais looked on, indulgent and slightly bored.

'I trust you are well, my daughter.'

'Quite well, thank God.'

'Would it please you to accept a gift?'

'Gladly, Mother.'

It astonishes me still, how much suffering the heart can accommodate. Like a swelling muslin bag of cheese in a dairy, it bellies out with pain, bulging and dripping, yet always there is space for more. The cold formality of my mother's words, the familiar sight of her smooth, lovely face, felt more than I could bear. And yet, I did. As she stretched her hand towards mine, our fingers brushed, and all I wanted to do was hurl myself into her arms and sob out my pain as I had done as a child until she soothed me against her breast and the world was restored to sense. I took the parcel, and a small, mean pleasure, too, in turning my head away, dismissing her.

'Isabelle!' she gasped.

Through my teeth, the bright, easy smile still clamped to my face. 'What is it, Lady Mother? What can you possibly have to say to me?'

'I sent Pierre to you,' she tried to reason.

'Indeed.'

'And you understood?'

'Quite clearly. It is so kind of you. My thanks,' my sarcasm palpable.

'And your answer?'

One of Blanche's women stood nearby, holding a length of buttercup sarsenet. I reached out to touch it, murmured something about how pretty it was.

'I have no answer, Lady Mother. You see, I have nothing to say to you at all.' I laughed gaily, at nothing, and she returned it so that for a moment our voices rang above the murmur in the salle, lost and bitter and shrill as the voice of a banshee, screaming round a battlement. Then King Philip stood, scattering the ladies before him, and offered me his hand to lead me out to dance.

Only later, when we left the men to their drinking, and I had bidden a courteous farewell to Blanche, after I had been handed into the king's barge and returned under the curious eyes of the citizens to the Louvre, after I prayed, and had my face washed and my hair combed out and was finally, finally, alone in my chamber with Agnes, did I ask for the parcel to be opened. Under the linen lay a thin red cord, such as I had seen my mother wearing, bound about her leg on the day she went from Lusignan.

'You must wear it, little one,' said Agnes tentatively. 'It is what they wish.'

'Burn it.'

Agnes's face worked painfully, she was afraid.

'Agnes, it is nothing. See?' I held it up and cast it onto the brazier, where it curled and charred like a cast-off snake skin. 'It is nothing to do with us. Please don't be afraid, now. We will have nothing to do with their folly, with their ... wickedness. I am queen, and I will keep you safe. Look. It is quite gone.'

'We should throw away the ashes.'

'Why, Agnes? In case a witch comes in the night, to take them for a charm?' One look at her poor old trusting face showed me that this was precisely what she feared. I sighed, 'Very well. Empty the brazier into the river, then go to your chamber and rest. We go south tomorrow.'

I had kept my countenance. I had survived this interminable day. I did not believe what I had said to Agnes, that I could protect her, but I saw that I had, at least, to try. To protect Agnes, and John, and that way, myself. The sun was setting over the city. Glancing up at the casement, I saw a red streak across the sky, in the direction of Normandy, spooling through the clouds like a skein of red silk. I called for a maid, and had her close the window tight.

CHAPTER TEN

THE GATES OF PARIS HAD BARELY CLOSED BEHIND THE
last of our baggage trains when we saw the first signs of
the Lusignan rebellion. Leaving the royal demesnes of France
near Orleans, John planned to traverse the county of Blois
towards his own lands in Maine, moving west towards Chinon
and then south to Poitiers, where his mother Queen Eleanor
had kept her capital. Encumbered as we were by mule carts
bearing our furnishings and provisions, our tents where we
slept, our kitchens, our regalia, moving at the pace of the foot
guards who surrounded my ladies' litters, we travelled far more
slowly than King Philip's marshals, who paused to pay their
respects to John as they passed us on the road. It was only as we
approached Le Mans that the captain of my husband's garrison
rode out to explain, fearfully, to John, that Lord Hugh and his
brother, Ralph of Eu, had taken their complaint to the French
king, demanding the county of La Marche as recompense for
my betrothal, and that Philip had declared John's holdings in
France forfeit. The English standard flew alone above the Le

Mans keep, fluttering high over the green July country, showing that my husband was in breach of his obligation to his liege lord. If the Lusignans attempted his dominions, the empty space next to the standard declared, Philip was not bound to defend his oath. Philip, who knew nothing more of the Lusignans' plans than my poor husband, was quite content in his greed for Angevin fields and castles. If the Lusignans made war on John, there would be ample spoils for the French king if he supported them.

I instructed the maids that we would dine quietly in our quarters that day, but even from the distance of my chambers in the tower I could hear my husband screaming, ranting out his fury at the treachery of the Lusignans and the French king. He came reeling and stinking to my bed that night, and vomited in the rushes before falling into a muttering sleep from which I could not rouse him until long after the rest of the household had heard Mass. For days, he continued so, summoning his captains each morning, issuing orders to his seneschals for funds to raise troops, then drinking away all his plans through the afternoon and snoring hopelessly late each morning, clutching me to his sour-smelling body, mumbling of traitors and vengeance. I had the maids lay fresh linen and rushes each day, keep the windows wide to the summer air and burned sweet herbs in my rooms, but nothing could drive the stench of him away, so it seemed as though my own skin was polluted with his folly and helplessness. I tried to be meek and gentle, to speak only soft, encouraging words, and asked Agnes to discreetly command his servers to water the king's wine, but the longer John tarried, the more fearful I became. Was he intending to let his lands, and me, slip away in his drunken lassitude? As I passed to the chapel or the gardens among my women, I felt the same uncertainty and discontent among the garrison, and I saw in their disgusted glances that they felt I was to blame. What kind of a king was this, whom, when his holdings were challenged by his enemies, preferred to stay swilling and lolling in bed with a woman who was no more than a child?

Each day, messengers poured into Le Mans with news from the south. I was shamed to see them waiting anxiously in the hall as my husband rolled and grunted through his drunken dreams in the tower. Duke Arthur raised his standard in Brittany, calling on his men to defend his title to the English throne, and my husband did nothing. Duke Arthur was at Tours, where the Lusignans declared for him, and my husband did nothing. The lands of the south were in open rebellion, with the peasants leaving their fields before the harvest to join the Lusignan host, and my husband did nothing.

July turned towards August, and, finally, John ordered that we move on towards Chinon. It was a joy, at least, to be riding in the clear air, among the scents of the grass and the hedgerows, but if the king's household thought they might at last be riding to confront the rebels, they were wrong. John drank all day in the saddle, swigging from a gold-chased horn, and when we pitched camp each evening he had to be helped from his horse. He then staggered around, barking and countermanding orders until his tent was pitched and he tumbled onto his bed in his boots. I followed his swaying progress along the white roads, decorously mounted on a side-saddle, ashamed even to lift my face to the bands of grubby farmers who paused in their work, incurious as cattle, to watch their king pass by.

William Marshal, one of the greatest of my husband's English magnates, took charge of our progress, sending out the purveyors and working with the clerks, as John was barely capable of speech by noon. He treated me with great courtesy, as though he alone knew that John's unmanly doting on me was none of my doing, and though I was grateful for his attempts at kindness, my pride throbbed at what he might imagine the king did to me when the curtains of our bed were drawn. For John insisted that I lie with him each night now, as I had done since Paris, and I was torn between revulsion at his clammy, clumsy fumblings beneath my shift, and the hope that he might make me truly his wife now, and save me at least from Pierre's threat that our marriage was invalid. My only comfort on the journey was Othon's body, plodding dutifully beneath me, but I felt his frustration, his need for flight, and so many times I came close to throwing my legs astride, touching him with my heels and letting him run us both far away, leaping the white-flowered hedges, until we had fled this moving prison and could be alone again in the forest.

With a day's ride left before we reached Chinon came the news that Lord Hugh had made his move. Eleanor, the old queen, had left her retired doting at the abbey of Fontevraud and bravely ridden south, towards Poitiers, to do what her lineage as Duchess of Aquitaine still could for the English cause there. The post rider who brought the message to our camp might have been as soused as his king, so dazed and reeling was he after the effort of his flight; his horse was fit for dog meat. He was too exhausted to rise from his knees, coughing through the dust of the road in his throat as he gasped out his news. Lord Hugh and Duke Arthur had approached Queen Eleanor at Mirebeau, near Poitiers, and aimed, it seemed, to take her hostage. The cunning old queen had managed to stay them several days with courtesies, but now she was imprisoned in the keep, and Mirebeau was besieged.

Before my eyes, I watched John transfigure himself. As the poor man croaked out his message, John was calling for his coat of mail and his men-at-arms fastened on their swords. The whole camp was swarming like a beehive, fires being kicked out, horses saddled, my own tent vanishing into a cart like a kerchief in a jongleur's sleeve. For once, John ignored me. I had to hover at his elbow as he shouted commands to Marshal to send to the garrison at Chinon to muster. I trotted between them, trying to make them listen to me, but they paid me no mind. I knew why Lord Hugh was trying to take the old queen. It would have been a clumsy feint had we been playing at chess.

'Please, my lord.'

'Not now, Isabelle.'

'Please, don't go. It's a trap. They are using your mother as bait,' I warned.

'She is my mother. I have no choice. Go to your ladies now, I will be quite safe.'

'It's you they want to capture, my lord, not her. Your lady mother is a lure.'

'Isabelle! I said, not now. What can you know of this? Go!' He had never spoken so harshly to me, and as soon as the words passed his lips, I saw his face soften with remorse. I scrunched my dust-rimed eyelids together to try to force out a few tears, and gave him my most loving look. Gently, I slipped my palm into his, letting him feel how small and soft it was.

'Then I want to go with you.'

He dropped a kiss on my brow. I hated my own anxious countenance then, even as I feigned, hated myself for arousing his tenderness. 'My love, you cannot.' He looked away down the road, calculating. 'As it is, we'll have to ride like the Devil.'

'I can ride as fast as any man.'

'Isabelle, I forbid you.'

'If I am alone with my ladies, who will defend me? The king of France might have an army on the road in pursuit of me right now. It could be part of their plan, I will be safer at least with you, my lord.'

He hesitated, still calculating. I showed him the face I wore when I played with his hair in the firelight, the face that made him groan and press me to him and scramble at my flesh in the dark. 'Do not forbid me, my dear lord. I have not asked anything of you for so long. Please.'

I didn't wait for his answer. I ran away, back to where my tent had been moments before. Agnes was hustling the maids into a cart, all of them fretting and squeaking as usual. 'Find Tomas,' I ordered. 'Then you will accompany the maids to Chinon.' I held up my hand, the pearl the king had given me on our betrothal warm on my finger. 'Any messenger who comes to you must bear this. Pay no mind otherwise. Promise me, Agnes. Now, find Tomas.'

I couldn't help feeling joyful. As Tomas threw me up onto Othon's back, my gown indecently hitched up behind, I inhaled the scent of his impatience and buried my face in his neck. 'See, I promised you, didn't I? We will have our dream, at last.'

There was no time for the scuttling priest to bless us. The king's household knights were already hidden in a dust cloud at the far point of the horizon. I had no whip, no spurs, no sword, no flat helm, I might have been a little girl again, playing at Crusaders, but Othon sprang forward at the gentlest touch of my heels, and for eighty miles of delirious flight, we were warriors. I might not be Taillefer, true, but I would ride at my lord's side, and we would take Queen Eleanor, and I should be safe.

For each of those miles, I knew the happiness and purity of purpose of being a man. There was no thought except the movements of Othon's flanks beneath me, the steam of his sweat, the dust of the white road in my eyes, fixed between the rein and his hooves, scouring always for the stone that could throw us to our death, until my fingers and thighs were reduced to one function, tensed only to ride, careless of what we should find at Mirebeau so long as, by miracle, we arrived in time. Action cancelled out thought, cancelled out everything except the drum of hoof beats and the occasional warning cries of the riders ahead. I was transported, fevered with the chase, and when we paused, during those eight and forty hours of hard riding, it was only to gulp ecstatically from a canteen, to splash my face with water, to cover myself in a cloak and slump deliciously against Othon's heaving flank for an hour or two of black sleep before I turned my screaming body once again into the saddle. If the men of my husband's *familia* were astonished to see their queen filthy and dishevelled, riding astride and alone and as swift as the best of them, they only showed it in curt nods of appreciation. I was a queen, was I not? And queens are magical. It was glorious. I felt equal among them, me, Isabelle, and if I ever truly loved John it was in those hours, when he forged ahead in the vanguard, high on his mount's shoulder, looking every bit the king his brother the Lionheart had been.

Queen Eleanor had just enough time to dispatch the messenger to her son before immuring herself in the keep at Mirebeau. The Lusignan troops, two hundred and fifty knights and their sergeants, had pursued her first to Fontevraud, and then, finding she had fled, sped to the little walled town below the castle. They were encamped beneath the curtain with Duke Arthur, Lord Hugh and my old fiancé Hal among them. Queen Eleanor, eighty years old and shut up with a few ladies, could do nothing but pray. I wondered to what.

It was early evening on the last day of July when we reined in, the citadel in sight. There was barely time for speech, let alone ceremony. My husband's regalia were far back in the train from Le Mans, so he pulled his own light crown from his saddlebag and stumped it on his head like a baker at a bread oven before he had even dismounted. I slipped down, handed Othon to Tomas and walked bandy-legged to his side, silently twining my hand into his own. He squeezed it gently but was already calling for William des Roches to come forward. Des Roches, the seneschal of Anjou, had been Arthur's man, but had declared for my husband earlier in the summer. The two men washed their hands

144

perfunctorily and then squatted on the ground, sucking at tepid wine, waving away hastily gathered platters of dried meat and cheese. Since John did not dismiss me, I sat down too, though my backside was so sore that I too scrambled into a delighted squat, keeping my eyes low lest they notice me. The Poitevins were confident of taking Eleanor, des Roches explained, sketching quickly with a stick in the ground how they had stopped all the gates of Mirebeau but one with earthworks.

'Can we get in?'

'I can lead you, Majesty, yes. But I have a request, if you would be so gracious as to hear it.'

I could feel John's temper on edge, the closed-in tension of the flight building to explode. I laid a calming hand on his dusty sleeve, hard with mail beneath the stained linen.

'My mother is within, and you speak to me of requests, man?'

'I must. Duke Arthur is with the Lusignans. I will lead your men into the citadel, but in return I ask that I be given charge of him if he is taken. I was his man, once.'

I held my breath.

'Very well, you shall have keeping of this foolish boy,' John agreed. 'When?'

'In the morning.'

My husband rose slowly, des Roches waiting on his knees.

'Have you a man to take charge of the queen?'

'The queen, Majesty?'

Des Roches had simply not noticed me. I watched his face change as he observed the filthy urchin in her stained, ragged gown clutching his master's hand.

'Majesty, forgive me.' He scrambled an obeisance, but I waved him off.

'There is no need to waste a man on me, Lord des Roches. The Lusignans will not harm me. I will be safe next my husband.'

John turned to me, astonished. 'Isabelle, it is impossible. You cannot.'

I lowered my voice, 'My lord, you need every man we have. I cannot wait alone; there are no women with us. If I am captured, who shall answer for me? You said I could not ride with you, and yet here I am. I will not be an impediment, I shall stay quiet behind until it is done. And I will be company for your lady mother, if it should fail.' I smiled up at him, and added, 'I am certain that they will not harm me. And I am a Taillefer, am I not? I will be quite safe.'

'You are my wife.'

I played my last card, leaning close to him so that no one else could hear. 'And I have borne you no child, yet. You can take more wives. I am not afraid.'

'Bless you then, Isabelle.'

I left them, and went to find Tomas.

*

At dawn the next morning, we were ready. It was Lammas day, the second anniversary of my wedding. I was nearly fourteen. Grumbling and sceptical, Tomas had found me a page's hauberk which dangled heavily to my ankles, a barrel helmet and a grubby surcoat with the royal arms. I used his knife to slash a tear in my ruined gown and rip the skirt around the

146

hem, enough to protect me as a woman, but close enough to ride in the fray. I remembered what I had done to my betrothal gown and imagined Agnes's horrified face if she could see me. Though she could not scold me now for behaving like a hoyden. We decided I should leave my hair down for safety, too, and only close the helm to protect my face if I was close to the fighting. Othon was given a mail cotte and even a *champron*, with winged steel to protect his cheeks. I told him he looked splendid. I was giddy with joy. If I met Hal, we'd see who was the stupid girl, now, at last. For once, I brushed Othon down myself, as merry as a stable lad, and curled up next to him to pass the short night between exhausted drowsing and quick shocks of anticipation. We had no fires, lest they be seen from the citadel, but the summer night was hot, and I was weary and comfortable, one hand on Othon's belly, the other never leaving my precious helmet.

It was not until we rode out in the first yellow-grey light that I saw what it meant to fight. Even at first, I still believed it a sort of magnificent game. The king had given Tomas instructions to keep close, we were to make straight for the citadel once we were inside the walls, and if we could, make our way to Queen Eleanor. We walked our horses slowly across a bridge and around the white walls of the little town. The king's bowmen fired on the scouts on the walls; some of them toppled, but they were far away, as insignificant to my eyes as thrushes tumbled in a merlin's claws. For those moments, the hum of the bows seemed to be the only sound in the world, the arrows' flight stretching arcs of silvery silence between the men within and those without. The eerie stillness was shattered by a crash as though the cloudless summer sky had cracked in half.

The king's infantry had improvised a battering ram from a poplar trunk; they had been hacking at it all night. Twenty of them ran it up and began beating at the unstopped gate. I thought of the knights mustering in readiness behind the walls. Othon was desperately flighty, pawing and twisting under me, for the first time I had to struggle to keep him in check. Des Roches's earth map had showed a narrow street beyond the gate, opening into a square. The men were divided into three groups. The van, with John at its head, would make directly for the citadel, straight up through the lanes of the town. Two flanks would divide and circle the castle, fighting their way round to the rear of the keep. Tomas and I were to ride in the van. The infantry heaved and strained, relaying their strength around the trunk, aware that their king's eyes were on them. Each blow on the gate was a taunt to Lord Hugh's men inside.

And then, in a horrible surge, it began. The gates splintered, trembled, gave. In one explosion of steel, the knights unsheathed their swords, as one they brought up their horses singly and ran at the opening, tight as a tournament list. Othon was wild, tripping on the scattered planks, plunging, struggling between the heavier, well-trained destriers of the household. I tucked my head into my chest and gave him the rein, making no attempt to guide him, allowing him to steer us between two of his mailed and blinkered fellows. And we were in. Slithering, the horses hurtled over the rough paving of the little street, checked as they flew into the square, coming up four abreast and divided.

The Lusignan troops were waiting, and the king's men fell upon them. I saw des Roches at the head go down, his horse's belly sliced, scrambling through the steaming entrails as his squire brought a second mount, then the squire fell under an axe blow as des Roches and the king screamed the men onwards. The helmet fell over my eyes, I could barely see through the cross-slit in the aperture. My hands were sliding on the reins. I held Othon between my knees with all my strength and managed to pull the thing off, just as a whiplash of air passed my face and I threw myself sideways, almost falling, and the sword took Othon on his foreleg. He howled and reared. I looked round frantically for Tomas, a little ahead, swinging his sword as sure as if he had been born to it, brought Othon behind him and saw him point to the standard wobbling up the hill before us.

'This way, this way, push through!' he yelled, but I couldn't move. I watched Tomas vanish into a roiling pool of bodies and horseflesh, Lusignan green and royal scarlet blurring into a por-ridge of gore, the screams of falling men rising in a hideous music that would suddenly arrest, so that in the silence I could hear only the scrape of steel and the kites calling, far above us in that cloudless sky. I don't know how long we remained there, men and horses pushing one another to their death, and I could not count how many fell, except that in a while the ground was sick-eningly soft with trampled corpses. Ahead, the standard seemed petrified, I knew that the king would be in the fighting beneath it, and tried to push Othon up, but his poor chest was heaving and wheezing, he was losing blood, and then a Lusignan man-at-arms was before us, swinging his axe and I flattened myself into the saddle as the blow came down on Othon's neck and we were tipped into the writhing mire. There was no time to bid my poor darling goodbye. I felt a hand on my arm, wrenching it almost from the socket, and I was up behind Tomas, making for a break in the line. We came up behind the standard, now surging forward.

'No! Tomas! Othon, no!'

He had me gripped round the waist, riding with his legs to keep his sword arm free. I did what I could to kick out at the men as they came up alongside us, forced ahead by their own cavalry, the weight of the great Lusignan destriers sending them down the steep hill in an avalanche of bloodied green. Then Tomas's weight thudded against me and I felt him slump and lose his grip on the reins. He had been struck. I grabbed the reins and turned the horse. Tomas's face was blank steel, but as I watched the helmet slipped sideways and a great gout of blood spurted over me, hot and stinking, and Tomas's head peeled slowly from his neck as his body slid to the ground. *Tomas* ... The horse tripped over his corpse, stumbled, righted itself and cantered on with me splayed over its wide back, unable to do anything but shield my head with my arm. 'This way! Go! Go!'

Des Roches was rallying the men for the charge on the citadel, but as I was carried forward among them I saw that the yard was empty. The frenzied horses were gradually walked down. We circled aimlessly until one of the squires called, 'Over here!' I was shaking too much now to control my mount, but he came up quietly and nosed at des Roches's third, or fourth, horse, I had lost count, as placidly as if they were nibbling at a hedge.

'Majesty?'

I raised my head, my eyes still burning with Tomas's blood.

'You are injured?'

I managed to shake it, no.

'Come then, come quickly. The king is already inside.'

I followed him through a doorway, my legs like water, my throat heaving at the scent of blood. The hall was sweet with wood smoke and rosemary and summer dust. Within, a group of sergeants stood with drawn swords around a tableau on the dais. The trestle was covered with the remains of a breakfast, grapes, bread, a half-eaten pigeon pie. Hal, Lord Hugh and another lad were frozen, blenched, their hand at their sword hilts. Hal had a spot of grease by his mouth. Lord Hugh's face was as cool and still as ever, the serpent at his collar polished and gleaming.

'Isabelle?' Hal was gasping, his surprise at seeing me wiping the fear momentarily from his features.

I didn't care to look at him. I felt no triumph, only nausea.

'Take them,' my husband's voice from somewhere above us. He was already climbing the inner staircase to the second floor of the keep. Shuffling, holding the drooping hem of my drenched hauberk over what was left of my gown, I began to follow him. I could feel Lord Hugh's eyes on my back, measuring, as he had once appraised me in the hall at Lusignan when I came to my betrothal. In his look, I sensed that he did not believe it was finished, not even now, when he was the king's prisoner. I knew the madness that glittered in the black depths of those eyes, and I would not return his glance. Still, I could wish myself back at Lusignan, I could have wished even that I had been married to Hal and safely at home in Poitou if I could have been spared what I had seen in the last hour. I forced myself to turn and find the eyes of the other boy. Arthur.

A flash of blue in the darkness of the hall. Deep blue, the blue of a halcyon's feathers. His gaze held mine, and while I tried to dip my reddened lashes, I could not. Turquoise and sapphire, our eyes' light the ink of a lapidary. He inclined his head courteously, his bright hair the sun to my bloodied moon. Madly, I thought of the poets' stories so beloved of my mother's maids. In the songs of the troubadours, love strikes like an arrow, like a blade in the heart. But perhaps that is because poets seldom see battle. When I looked at Arthur, the world was still. Just that, a tiny, plenteous moment, a question silently asked and its answer silently given. In that flash of illumination between us, I saw what I had to do, and beneath the exhaustion of the journey's sleepless nights and the as yet unbroken storm cloud of my grief for Tomas and Othon, I felt another great weariness. There was only one way to end it, I thought, only one way to defeat the Lusignan demon. A sacrifice. Then my legs buckled under me like willow wands, and I fainted like a woman.

CHAPTER ELEVEN

OVER TWO HUNDRED LUSIGNAN KNIGHTS WERE TAKEN at Mirebeau that day. Many were sent to Corfe, my husband's favourite English castle, where he had spent a thousand pounds on fortifications. The king had Hal, Lord Hugh and Duke Arthur manacled and sent north by cart, the most disparaging and humiliating spectacle that could be made of a warrior. Arthur and Hal were sent to Falaise in Normandy and Lord Hugh was to be confined alone at Caen. With the king, I travelled first to Fontevraud, so that the people of the countryside saw two queens of England riding side by side in the same litter, though I might have been Queen Eleanor's great-great-grandchild. I had been so curious to meet this legendary woman, queen in turn of France and England, Crusader, rebel and, many said, adulteress, but what I found was a bent-backed, crack-voiced old crone, her eyes milky with cataracts, barely in her wits long enough to thank the son who had delivered her. After leaving her in the care of the nuns, we, too, made for Normandy.

If I had felt love for John, briefly, at Mirebeau, that feeling was extinguished forever by the time the Christmas feast at Caen was over. I had reason enough to hate Lord Hugh, but I knew that it was ignominious to show him thus to the peasants, trussed up in a farm cart, and while I was glad that he should be so stripped of his dignity I knew that the magnates would dislike it. But the Angevin spirit which had called my husband to win the greatest victory for the English since his brother the Lionheart had relieved the garrison at Jaffa in the Holy Land before I was born, had simmered and curdled in him, making him swaggering and arrogant. He flitted about the victory, drinking more and more wine each night as he recounted it over and over. The lords said nothing, but I could see their looks.

Worse, the king still insisted that I join him in his bed each night, and kept me there until noon each day. The fumbling attempts he had made since Paris were repeated, but this time, when he failed, he would turn furiously away from me, and it was only by endless caresses and promises of my love that I could keep him gentle. I hated the way the men at court looked at me, the lewd whisperings that followed me to dinner. At Mirebeau, I had felt magnificent, but now, in the veiled contempt in their eyes as they knelt to me, I could see that they thought again that I was a little slut, who had infatuated their king and forced him to leave the business of governing to them while he wallowed in my bed. And while it suited me to have them think this, just as it suited me that each night my husband grew more frustrated by his inability to make me his true wife, I was disgusted, and despised them.

I had sent my pearl ring to Agnes at Chinon, and she joined us at Caen with my women. I could not begin my plan until her arrival, and between John's repulsive caresses and the endless feasting, time stopped once more. I might have ridden, there were plentiful horses for me to choose from, but after losing Othon I no longer wished to ride. I mourned Tomas, my friend and my saviour, but I was a warrior's child, one way or the other, and I was not so sad for him. He had died bravely, at a great age, and I knew that he would have been glad to do so, glad to die like the men he had armed and trained all his life, gloriously, instead of keeling over in the stable yard with a bunch of keys for company. The Lusignan lands were now forfeit and my husband would tax the tenants heavily but I wheedled a grant out of him that would keep Tomas's family in Poitou comfortable for many years. I tried to tell myself that Othon had died as a warrior, too, that he would have wished it so, but when John was finally snoring beside me in the darkness I saw his eyes, rolling and terrified, heard the great heaves of his ebbing heart, saw him fall, again and again, into that mess of bodies, and I knew that I had wronged him with my pride, with my wish to act out my childish game instead of staying safe at Chinon where I belonged. When Agnes came she said that perhaps the household would not have fought so hard had they not known their queen was among them, that perhaps it was my presence which had inspired the victory, and that Othon had not been slaughtered for nothing. It was kind, but I knew it wasn't true, and besides, she had never liked him.

As the year turned, we received news from Angouleme that my father had died. John asked me, quite gently, if I should like to go south to join my mother, but I refused. I never wanted to see her, or my brother Pierre, again. It was a wise choice, for William des Roches, to whom the king had promised the care of Duke Arthur after Mirebeau, was infuriated when the prince was locked up at Falaise without his consent, and turned his coat once more to the king of France. And with him went Aimery de Thouars, a great magnate, and together they began attacking the borders of Anjou. We heard of a plan to kidnap me at Chinon, when it was given out that I would be travelling to my grieving mother, and John laughed it off, saying he had mercenaries enough to defend his wife without troubling his treacherous vassals, and was the queen herself not a match for any knight? Just a few months before I should have thrilled at such a compliment, and I tried to smile prettily as he chucked me under the chin and praised my bravery at Mirebeau, but I could see, as he could not in his arrogance, that his men were turning against him, and that while I had no child and Arthur lived, I should never be safe from the Lusignans.

And did I grieve for my papa despite now knowing the truth? I could not think of him that way, could not think of him as anything other than my rough-bearded father who had seemed the grandest man in the world to me when I knew nothing beyond the walls of our home at Angouleme. His presence had filled that little world, his dogs and his horses and his weapons, his hunting boots and hauberks, his huge gentle hands that swung me up on his shoulders as my mother laughed and looked on. Yet that father had given me to Lord Hugh and then plotted to make me queen twice over. I could not blame him for his ambition, for at least it was clear and honest, after his fashion. He had never known of the Lusignan plan to make an empire, or of how my mother had made him a cuckold with a creature who wore horns of a different kind. I sorrowed, and ordered Masses for his soul, but I could not grieve, not truly. I was glad that he had been spared what was to come. Still, in some way, I wished that he had lived, for perhaps he could have advised my husband, have made him listen as I, a woman, could not. John had never lived in the south, he was English born and bred. As I had heard in his voice the first time I heard him speak, and he did not understand as my father had done the ways of the men there; men whose strength came from a darker source than the crosses blazoned on their surcoats.

With des Roches and de Thouars gone to France, my husband judged it politic to release the Lusignans, thinking that their gratitude would bind them to obedience. But as soon as Lord Hugh and his son were free, they ignored the noble promises they had made him in Normandy and took their knights to Poitou to make war yet again. The English strongholds in the Anjou were falling, one by one, and now the Lusignans were raising Aquitaine. Daily, there were reports of pillage and burning, and as my husband sought to strengthen his fortresses by filling them with mercenaries, those same hired troops took to plundering the towns and the abbeys. It was said that the peasants shut themselves in their homes, too fearful to work the fields, and if the crops were not planted then in a year my husband's people would begin to starve. And still, he did nothing. He drank and boasted and spent more and more of the taxes raised from the grudging English barons on masterless foreign soldiers, while the knights he had imprisoned after Mirebeau escaped from Corfe and starved themselves to death in the English hills rather than kneel to their king.

Perhaps it was his inability to do more than shove impotently at me in our bedchamber that prompted John's first and stupidest cruelty to Duke Arthur. If I could not be got with child, then Arthur must not be able to get one. In defying his promise to des Roches, my husband had entrusted Arthur's custody at Falaise to Hubert de Burgh, who was now ordered to blind and castrate his prisoner. De Burgh could not bring himself to such wickedness, but mindful of my husband's rage when he was disobeyed, the foolish man gave out that the Duke was dead. For a few days, I gratefully believed it, but then came news that the men of Brittany had risen against John in defence of their lost Duke, and de Burgh was obliged to confess that Arthur lived, and was whole. And while I submitted to John's hopeless lust, trying not to let my disgust show as his flabby belly spilled against my body, the Count of Alençon declared for Philip, and Anjou and Maine and Touraine were lost as the French battered at the borders of Normandy like the sergeants with the poplar trunk at the gate of Mirebeau. Queen Eleanor was too fragile and confused to do more than totter to Mass; she could no longer rouse the men of her duchy against the Lusignans. My brother had been right: the crazed glare of Lord Hugh's black eyes at Mirebeau kept their promise. But I thought I knew how I could save myself, at least.

*

'I think we should go to Rouen, my love.' John was drunk, but not yet so lost in his wine that he was bitter. I wriggled into his lap and played with his sparse hair in the way he loved. 'I am unhappy here.'

'I have moved Arthur to Rouen, damn him.'

'I was thinking, perhaps this is the time to make overtures to the Duke? He is a boy, barely sixteen, I think? Perhaps he is not clever, like you, my love. He has been confused and pushed every way by the French and the Lusignans. And he is your nephew. Perhaps he will be glad to make peace now you have shown your strength.'

I kissed him along his jawline, a fluttering path to the corner of his mouth, though the stench of his breath made me want to retch. And then I talked of the new gown I wished for Easter, and let the idea flower in him, so that he should believe it was his own.

We went to Rouen, though we had now to travel by night with a mercenary guard as my husband was no longer safe even in his own duchy. Arthur was fetched from his dungeon, bathed, and provided with fresh clothes so that we might dine together the morning of our arrival. He was thin, and his eyes were sunken, the flesh drawn tightly over his cheekbones, but the hair that had been dulled a little with dust at Mirebeau now blazed its red-gold, the blue eyes were still as sharp as the glitter of a halcyon's wing, and I thought, sadly of how handsome he was, and how it would have been if I had been betrothed to him rightly.

John was sullen but civil. I had Lady Maude order plenty of strong wine and delicate foods, despite it being Lent, that might please an invalid, lest rich meat after a prison diet make Arthur ill. Lady Maude's husband, William, had replaced de Burgh as Arthur's keeper and I had them join us at dinner, to show that all was agreeable. I spoke little to Arthur, making sure to defer to my husband as we talked of hawking, the preparations for the Easter crown, the mission of ambassadors my husband planned to send to the African coast, quite as though it were a family dinner. But I made sure to glance often at Arthur, to allow our fingers to touch for a second as he served me, enquired as to whether the fire in his chamber was well made – pleasant courtesies, modest smiles. Lady Maude watched me with approval. I knew she would be glad of her husband's being relieved of Arthur's care, so that they would be able to return to their lands on the Welsh March.

Afterwards, I asked Arthur if he should care to hear some music. One of the many indulgences that my husband had granted me was an Occitan *trouvère*, such as I had known at Angouleme and Lusignan. The man began one of Bernart de Ventadorn's lyrics in a light style, softly accompanying himself on a harp. I waited until the old people were dozing and then whispered to Arthur, 'It is a great comfort to me to receive you like this, Duke. My dearest hope is that this strife should finish peacefully.'

'And mine, Majesty.'

I leaned my head to one side and looked into his eyes. 'Is that so? I wonder.'

'What else could I wish for, Majesty?'

'Oh, many things, Duke. You have suffered a great deal, since we last met.'

'Majesty is even more beautiful now than she was that day.'

Slowly, I thought, slowly. 'You flatter me. How could any *man*,' I was careful to stress the word, 'find a woman beautiful in such circumstances? But then,' I cast a wistful glance towards the slumped form of my husband, 'it is pleasant, a little flattery, now and then.'

'You need no flattery, Majesty. You are peerless, a-a pearl.'

I wanted to giggle. True, the poor boy had been locked in an airless cell for two seasons, but surely he had learned more elegant manners than that. But then they had no real poets in Brittany.

'But untouched pearls lose their lustre, Duke.' Had I gone too far? Had I alarmed him? No. He thought me willing, and would have smiled had he not been struggling for a compliment.

'And they also require a setting, Majesty. They look so well … in crowns,' he managed at last.

'Indeed. But you need not give me my title. I think I am your aunt, isn't that funny! *Tante* Isabelle, you may call me.'

He blushed like the boy he still was and I wondered how long it would take him to get word to Lord Hugh in Poitou that I was ready.

To John, I said that there could be no impropriety in my riding out next day with my own nephew. Arthur had been treated too harshly, I wheedled, he was not so clever as my husband and needed only a little kindness to bring him round. I told Lady Maude that she need not accompany us through the chilly Norman fields, that my guard would be enough, and that she must spare her strength for the journey she would soon be making to Wales. And I told Agnes to be ready. So I spent each afternoon of those last Lenten weeks outdoors with Arthur, and learned what had been waiting inside me since Mirebeau – that I had fallen in love.

In all those songs and poems I had heard, love was described as a pain, an exquisite sickness, a freezing fire, the most elegant of impossible contradictions. Yet I wondered if any pair of lovers held quite such hypocrisies in their burning hearts as Arthur and I did. At first, I let him see only by accepting his compliments that I wanted him. I made sure to have my hair beautifully arranged and scented so that its perfume would fall across his face as he held the reins for me to mount. The merest touches, the feather brush of my fingers against the soft inner skin of his wrist when I unfastened a glove for him, the slightest pressure of my hand on his arm as he escorted me to the stables, were enough to bring colour to the poor lad's cheeks. I listened to him describe the wild coasts of his home in Brittany, the tumbling cliffs and the storms that raised the seas to a nest of thrashing dragons, and made my eyes wide with wonder at his stories. I should like to go there, I told him, to see that mist-silvered country, and of course he promised me that one day we should ride together on the wide Brittany beaches. Arthur rode beautifully, rejoicing as the strength came back to his limbs, and it was easy for us to race our mounts along the lanes, leaving my guard a little further behind each day.

In the evenings, we could have no dancing, since it was Lent, but once John had slurped and belched his way into a stupor, we could play at chess or cards in the warm firelight as my harpist strummed and our fingers touched and clung, twined and touched again over the pieces. John was calmer now, believing that Arthur had finally rescinded his claim, and I noticed with wry admiration how the young Duke flattered him, talking at supper in the hall of the great campaign to be mounted in the south once the Easter ceremonies were concluded. They would pay for their treachery, des Roches, de Thouars, the Lusignans, their castles would be burned and their lands attaindered. John even hinted that once I had a child, if it proved a daughter, she might be betrothed to her cousin of Brittany. I smiled sweetly at that, and made sure, again, that Arthur would see a little spasm of distaste pass my lips, as though I could not help my fear of where that child would come from.

Arthur began to give me little presents. It became a custom with us, when we met to ride each day after dinner, that he would present me with some small delight: a turquoise-handled whip, a pair of pink silk roses for my slippers, an ivory comb for my hair. Was Lord Hugh supplying them, I wondered, as he had once sent for marmalade and a child's ball? I let him fasten the comb, his fingers straying over the fine skin of my scalp as he fixed it, trembling, in place. And though I knew I must stay cold inside if I were to accomplish my purpose, I could not help a rush of pleasure, deep within me, at the touch of those speaking fingers.

With fresh air and good food, Arthur was growing more handsome by the day, his shoulders so neat and strong under his coat, his waist so supple and tight. As we sat by the firelight in the evening, I could not help but wonder how his naked skin would look in that red glow, smooth and pale as my ivory comb, I thought. How would it be to run my fingers along his collarbone, trace the muscles of his flank, even, even to let my tongue linger in the hollow of his arm, his navel? Something was happening to my body, too. My breasts stretched at the bodice of my gown, my skin felt creamy and sensitive, my lips fuller, my belly softer. It could not be the wretched Lenten fare of fish and herbs that was causing it. Two weeks before Easter I had my first flowers, and though I instructed Agnes to boil the bloodied rags secretly, and soothed the cramps with a posset of hyssop and comfrey, so that John should not learn I was ready for breeding, his ardour for me only increased with the new fullness of my figure, so that one night I almost thought he would succeed in taking me. I could not let it happen, I had to remain a maid a little longer if my plan was to work. So I had to tell him, whispering shyly in his ear, and begging the indulgence of sleeping a few nights alone. He was almost as pleased as if I had told him I was with child, ordering extra braziers for my chamber and a sable quilt.

'Next month, my darling,' he told me, 'next month, I will get a son on you.'

*

On Palm Sunday, the king whispered to me at dinner that he would come to my bed that evening. I giggled and lowered my eyes and reminded him that it was still Lent, and that it would be sinful for him to do so. 'Wait another week, my love,' I wheedled him, 'and then you shall pay my bride-price.'

On Easter Sunday, when men were once more allowed to come to their wives, it was royal custom that the king should surprise the queen in her chamber with her ladies, and hand them a purse of money as a fee to be left alone. John smirked and patted the soft little pad of fat on my belly. 'You are growing so plump, Isabelle. My beautiful little wife. It is so hard to wait.'

'I am glad that I please you,' I answered modestly. His hand dipped beneath the sheet and squeezed my thigh.

'You are growing fat as a partridge. I want to be here,' he pinched again, more roughly, truly dribbling with desire; it was all I could do not to kick the hand away, I hated him so.

'I want you there too, my dear lord,' I whispered, feeling my flesh tighten with disgust. I said that I should ride out, so as not to tempt him, and he turned gladly back to his wine.

I had excused Agnes from the Palm Sunday procession, as she had other business to be about for me. Once John was settled comfortably by the fire, I sent to Arthur to request that he would ride with me as usual. He appeared, his face glowing with hot water and his lovely hair freshly combed, but his manner was sullen, and when he helped me to mount he turned his face away. He had brought no gift for me. I was perturbed, in part because this was not what I wished to happen, and truly because

I hated to see him unhappy. Once we were beyond the city gates, I asked him if he should like a gallop, but instead of flashing a white grin at me and kicking his horse into flight, he trotted forward a little, beyond the guards, then slowed to a walk. 'Are you unwell?' I asked gently.

'Forgive me. Perhaps a little. I may turn back, Majesty, if you will permit me.'

'Of course I shall permit you. But what troubles you?'

He sank his chin on his chest and plodded grimly along. I waited. After another mile in silence, he burst out, 'I thought that you cared for me! But you don't! You care for the king. I saw him, at the Easter game, touching you. You liked it.'

'I am his wife. His queen.'

'Majesty will forgive my impertinence.'

'Please, do not be sour. Listen, I have something to tell you.'

The hope in his face was unbearable. I could not think of it. Just for today, for tonight, I would not think of it.

'I wish, that is … I would ask, to be alone with you, a little. Tonight.'

'But the king—'

'Will be sleeping. Come.'

I moved to a canter, and this time he did follow me. I turned from the road and took us up a ridge, with a view into a narrow valley, wooded at the rim and falling to a bowl where a broad stream ran beside a tiny chapel and a fat round tower, older than the trees that sheltered it. I glanced quickly behind us; the guards were labouring up the hill. 'There. It will be safe. Come after supper, bring no light. I will wait for you.'

Always plans, always excuses, always contrivances. I recalled my delight when I had learned I should be queen, how I had imagined that I should order everything to my liking and never be scolded any more, but indeed I was no more free now than I had been as a child. Any milkmaid going to meet her beau had more liberty than I. The hours stalled, then raced as Agnes drew my bath and combed out my hair, stalled again, agonizingly, as I waited through supper, assiduously serving the king's wine with my own hands, reaching to caress his cheek and run my fingers delicately up his arm, until between the sweet liquid and my attention he was well sotted, and I called discreetly for his valet to help him to his chamber. I was so accustomed to my husband's drunkenness that I barely felt shame any more at having to issue this regular command; this night, I felt I could not breathe until he was safely abed.

I had been over and over the plan with Agnes. I could see plainly that she disliked it, but I reminded her of what Pierre had told me in Paris. That Lord Hugh wanted John gone, and me married to Arthur, and to rule through the boy, to displace the heir to France and make Arthur king there too, to take an empire in his serpent's coils. I asked Agnes if she had a better scheme than mine. John's throne would never be safe while Arthur lived. Poor Agnes had nothing to say, except that she would do as she was bid. I did not tell her that this part, this night, was to be my gift to myself. It helped that the garrison at Rouen had grown slack under my husband's neglect. He may have believed himself well protected, but in fact I could have walked to his rooms and slit his throat myself: his guards were too occupied with their drinking and dicing, for all that it was Lent, to pay any mind to a serving maid.

I put on a fine lawn shift over my clean body then threw on the greasy woollen gown Agnes had bought for me at the market. It was like nothing I had ever worn before, barely a skirt and bodice, more like a loose cloak with a leather thong to belt the waist. The wool scratched at my wrists and legs, and the gown smelt evilly of old sheep. I smiled to myself. I had had no wedding dress, and now, when I was to meet my lover, I should go stinking of old cloth like a peasant. *My lover.* I loved the word as I thought it.

'Won't you lie down, my lady? Rest a little. There is still some time to pass.'

'I cannot, Agnes. Tell me again.'

'There is a brazier ready. Here is the firebox, see, in the bag.'

I took out the flint and examined it. I had watched it done many times, but I had never lit a fire before.

'And the candles, and the perfume.'

'All here. I left some cakes in a napkin on a plate, and a jug of wine. I left the cloak wrapped in a sheet.' The sable my husband had given me for my bed.

'And you swept it clean, and spread the herbs, as we said?'

'Just as you said. Oh little one, I could wish—'

'Don't, Agnes. Please don't. Not tonight.'

'It is a long walk …'

'I am not afraid of walking. Now, what are you to say should anyone call for me?'

'That you are gone to the king at his request.'

'And if the king should summon me?'

'That you are indisposed and have taken a sleeping draught. That you are not to be disturbed.'

It would have to do.

'Is it time yet, Agnes?' The eagerness in my voice reminded me of Angouleme, when I had begged and pestered Agnes to hurry forward a treat.

'Not yet. We will listen for the abbey bell.'

*

When the hour of compline sounded at last, I hugged Agnes tightly to me, softly closed the door and glided like a spirit through the castle, carrying my riding boots, which were the stoutest shoes I owned. My slippers were all made for rushes and litters and Turkey carpets, tiny embroidered prisons all. Keeping close to the walls, I passed through the inner court-yard, then the outer. The night was cold, most of the men were in the hall or the guardrooms. Instead of going by the gate, which would be manned, I slipped down a paved incline, once used for soldiers to bring their horses up to the keep. At the bottom was a row of privies, a rough wooden hangar covering a long bench with holes over the pit beneath. Holding my breath against the stench of the jakes, I cautiously lifted the latch of the wooden gate used for clearing the night soil. Agnes had oiled it, another of her tasks while her mistress was at Mass. I took a great breath of damp night air and searched the sky above me. There was heavy cloud, only the milkiest flash of star was visible, but below to my left, in the town, I could see a few lanterns, fixed in doorways to deter thieves. Keeping the castle wall at my back, I moved towards the light, which brought me to the bridge to the road. This would be the most dangerous part. There was a dark hood in Agnes's bag, I muffled my face carefully, so that my hair should attract no light, and trotted softly across the bridge, my spine taut with the expectation of a warning shout. But all was silent. I sped over hard cold dirt until I had to catch my breath, then stooped and put on my boots and felt in my pocket for one last thing: a small, dirty soapstone jar with a seal on the lid. It contained a little of the strange grease Tomas had rubbed on Othon's hooves the first day I galloped him. I had begged him for it many times, curiously, fearfully, but always because I had hoped to recover the joy of that first giddy flight. He had pushed the little pot into my hand in the last moments before we rode out to Mirebeau. I had hidden it in my bodice then, and forgotten it, thought it lost in the bloody swamp of the battle, until Agnes handed it back to me, when I reclaimed my pearl ring from her, which now shone again on my hand. Perhaps Tomas had given her some of the ointment too. Perhaps he knew that I would need it, the last thing I had left of him. I closed my eyes and sent a prayer to them, Tomas and Othon, thanking them for those hours in the green allées when I had learned, so briefly, what it was to be free. Then I smeared the paste on the heels of my boots, bent my head to the wind, and began to run.

Perhaps I was fevered with eagerness to reach Arthur, perhaps the fear of discovery gave me strength, or, perhaps, there was some potency beyond dark faith in Tomas's gift, but it seemed that night that I covered those miles in a dream of swiftness, unencumbered by my ugly dress and my clumsy boots, the road clear before my night-blind eyes as though the moon gleamed beneath their lids. Or perhaps something else called to me as I moved through those black miles, the scar on my shoulder throbbing like a new vein, so that I should not have been surprised, or indeed afraid, to find the horned man waiting for me on the road, for I was part of the night then, another twilight-coloured creature who trod softly in its shadows, belonging to the still time between one word and another, belonging to him. Or perhaps that was all my fancy, and I ran towards what I had never known since that time in the forest with Othon. Towards joy.

Arthur was singing, down in the valley by the little tower. I heard the words as I staggered, half-tumbling, down the slope towards the stream. 'He alouete, Joliete, petit t'est de mes maus.' I did not stop running until my head was against his breast and his arms were about me, I cared nothing for my filthy gown nor for the scent I had so carefully packed to disguise it, I needed only the scent of him, his hair, lips, hands, eyes. We did not speak. We did not even make a light. We lay down on the chill ground by the water so that our bodies could find one another, and he conjured all my sorrow from me.

Later, when he had laughed at me as I chipped at the flint and lit the brazier himself, when we had spread out the cloak on Agnes's sweet herbs and taken a little wine, I told him that I had never known the king as a wife, and he fetched icy water from the brook in the cup of his palms, and washed me, and put his mouth there, and stroked me with his tongue until the flame that danced from the coal to the flame in his hair glimmered and twisted deep inside me. And then he came to me again, gently this time, his face resting against mine and his hands tight beneath my body, lifting me onto him, his teeth finding my breast and biting down on the nipple as he moved more urgently so that I cried out with the exquisite pain of it as I felt the flood of him between my thighs.

It seemed that we floated above the world, enclosed in the glowing walls of the abandoned tower, entwined like the curling inks of a monk's writing. I told him the story of the fairy Pressine and the king, and he told me that he knew it too, that he had heard it from his nurse, and that the shores and coves of Brittany were full of fairy-folk. We could not think of sleeping, although we were weary, it took only the touch of a fingertip, the trail of my hair across the lustre of his marble chest, for our bodies to come together again and again, so that we were dizzied with it, so that our selves were mingled like the moonlight and the silver water which murmured beyond the door. Finally, we lay breathing softly, his eyes on mine gently closing, opening to look once more, and smile, and close again, but just as we were drowsing, I heard a tap at the half-broken door, and Agnes appeared, filling that little room with lilac-coloured dawn mist and a sudden cold. Arthur moved to cover himself, blushing so sweetly, but Agnes was as brisk and practical as his own Breton nursemaid might have been.

'Come, my lord, you must dress and leave. I shall accompany my lady to the first hour at church and we shall return afterwards. You will see her Majesty at dinner.'

Arthur started, as though he had only just remembered who I was, and attempted a bow, tripping over the tails of his shift. I went close to him, not caring that Agnes could see me naked before him, pulling the pearl from my finger and closing it into his hand.

'Take this, my love. It will be my token to you, now, to my true love. Come to my chamber tonight. Agnes will make it safe. Go now.'

The cloak John had given me was damp and filled with the scent of us. When Arthur had gone I lay down again on my face and inhaled his smell. I heard Agnes moving about, gathering up the jug, the untouched plate of cakes.

'Leave them, Agnes. We will leave it all. Perhaps some other people might find the things and be glad of them.'

I dressed swiftly in my own things, Agnes quickly braided my tangled hair and covered me with the cloak. She had even remembered our missals. I felt sorry, suddenly, for how frightened she must have been, puffing along that long road in the grey dawn, so anxious and exhausted. 'You are very brave, Agnes,' I told her.

'Perhaps I might have made a Crusader after all, eh, little one,' she smiled at me. 'Come now. You cannot weep. Be glad. You have had your happiness.'

As we walked through the glade I paused at the spot where I had lain with Arthur hours before. I squeezed my finger where I had cut it on the flint, until a drop of blood fell to the ground, a benediction for tonight. I could marry him, I thought wildly. I could let John fall and Lord Hugh make his plots, and perhaps there would be a way, when I was Arthur's wife, to make us safe. We would have beautiful sons, and they would rule ... No. I understood my mother then. I saw how she must have hated what she felt herself obliged to do, however contorted her reasoning. No. The drop of blood was a promise.

*

On the second day of Holy Week, I let out a scream from my chamber. When I opened my mouth to cry out I knew that Agnes would already be rushing through the castle, rousing the guard, beating at the locks of the king's room. It seemed that Arthur had only a moment to look bewildered before my door crashed open and I was throwing myself upon my husband, sheltering myself under his sword arm, yelling that the Duke had tried to force himself upon me. I could not look at Arthur, still naked on my bed, but I heard his words, 'Isabelle! My Isabelle, no!' And then I was flung from the room and rushed away by my women with the sound of my husband bellowing for vengeance on my love in my wicked, wicked ears.

It was no difficulty to feign the tears I needed. I was wracked and breathless with sobbing, heaving and gasping for air, so that the maids caught my panic, and one of them fainted, another had to be slapped back into sense. Their shrieking and confusion drowned the noise of Arthur being dragged away, but not his voice, calling my name over and over, demanding his sword, a messenger to his cousin of France, Isabelle, his Isabelle ...

When John returned to me I was still insensible, howling and lashing out at anyone who approached me, until Agnes spoke to him and told him that I had to rest before I could speak. He tipped the draught down my throat himself, the draught I had begged Agnes to prepare, that I might have a few hours of oblivion before I began the next stage of my lie.

And when I woke his face was above me. As my eyelids fluttered apart, I saw the pain in his countenance, but I could feel no pity for anyone but Arthur.

'Isabelle.' He was white, he had not rested, but he was calm, his rage contained for the present.

'I cannot speak to you, my lord. I am no longer worthy. I beg you, please to let me leave now.'

'My love, what can you mean?' Oh, how I despised him then, for allowing me to deceive him so easily.

'I wish you to permit me to enter a convent. Fontevraud, in memory of your Holy Mother, or Langoiran, where I was … where I was.' I feigned to give way to sobs once more, though my throat and my eyes were quite dry.

'Isabelle! What is this talk? You must tell me, now, what happened? Of course you will not be sent away.'

I sat up effortfully, as though every part of me ached.

'You are too good, my lord. It is my fault. I believe that I … encouraged the Duke. I thought it my duty, to weave peace between you. I hoped that since he had given up his claim that he might help you restore your lands in France. And then he—'

'What did he do, Isabelle?'

I looked around, feigned surprise that the room was full of people. Two of the king's tally clerks were seated on stools, gravely scratching down what I spoke. Several of John's barons lounged against the wall, grim faced, my maids kneeling in a row like St Ursula's virgins.

'Please, I am too ashamed to speak. Agnes can be my witness, if you must have a witness, my lord.'

When the room was empty, I told Agnes to bring the sheet from my bed.

'The Duke came to my chamber while you were resting. He told me that he and the king of France were planning to besiege you, and that when you were their prisoner they would petition to Rome for the Duke's right to the crown of England.'

'Why did you not call for help?'

'I thought, at first, that he was warning me. That his affection for you was giving us time to fly, to reach the coast. And then he told me that when you were no longer king I should be his queen, instead. And then he ...' I buried my face between my hands and spoke through my fingers. 'Show him, Agnes.'

I knew that she would be unfolding the thin Flemish linen, holding up the treacherous butterfly-stain we had made there that morning after we returned from Mass. Fowl's blood from the kitchens. The proof that Arthur had done what in his heart my husband knew he could not. I heard him draw a long, tightly whistling breath.

'There is something more. The Duke will tell you that I lie, that I beguiled him, but it is not so. He has my ring, my pearl betrothal ring. You will find it with him. He tore it from my hand, before ... Before.'

I dared to glance up at John's face. It surprised me that even then I had it in me to feel saddened as I watched his love for me

176

slowly drain away. I reached a hand to his face, but he brushed it aside, not unkindly, but as though the fingers whose touch he had sought and loved to toy with were slightly troublesome, like a summer fly.

'You will tell no one of this, Isabelle. Do you understand? No one is to know of your disgrace. You will never speak his name again. Tell me that you understand.'

I nodded as he rose to leave me. He bent ceremoniously over my hand.

'Take care of her Majesty,' he instructed Agnes. 'She will need to recover from this dreadful assault. And I will have your tongue out, old woman, if you ever speak of this.'

Agnes curtsied, and so the man I loved and the man who loved me died together.

CHAPTER TWELVE

A GNES HAD LAID OUT A PLAIN DARK GOWN FOR THE
Maundy Mass. Alongside my husband, I would have to
wash the feet of twelve poor women of Rouen before distribut-
ing purses of alms to those in want. After the last of the service
was sung in the cathedral, we progressed into the city square
where the paupers were seated facing one another on stools, a
basin of water by each pair of filthy feet. The space was packed
with worshippers, come to gawp at the wonder of a king kneeling to a commoner. The nuns of the abbey flapped like crows in
their black habits as they sang the order.

The April day was leaden and icy, with a thin sharp wind
that fluttered the poor people's rags, so that the stink of their
bodies wafted into my face, a bouquet of sweat and dirt that
revolted me. John neither looked at nor spoke to me. There
was something in his unusually erect bearing that recalled his
face at Mirebeau, entirely determined, taut with authority; yet
instead of feeling proud, as I had done then, I felt only a sick
fear that I had to swallow down in my throat like sour vomit.

As my women looked on, I set my hand on the brow of the first woman and spoke a blessing in as kind and clear a voice as I could muster. I knelt, averting my eyes from the reddened sores on her unhosed legs, dipped the cloth in the basin and began to wipe the heated water around her feet. I was careful to keep it between her skin and mine, but the water in the bowl was soon clouded with filth. From beneath a cracked layer of mud her feet emerged, the flesh white against a grain of dirt worked so deep into their calloused soles that they might have been striped marble. How could people be so disgusting? Had not God sent rain that even the poorest might cleanse themselves? I reproached myself for such prideful thoughts, rose, blessed, knelt and began on the second woman. This time, I kept my eyes closed, saying the Ave under my breath to remind myself to be humble. When I reached the end of the line of stools, my shoulders were shaking under my cloak and my hands were tight, puffed like fresh bread from the water and the freezing wind. I would ask Agnes to make me a balm, or the skin would crack and look ugly, and Arthur – but of course, that did not matter, now. I would never see Arthur again. I glanced around for Lady Maude. It seemed strange to me that I had once thought of her as my enemy, before I knew what real enmity was. I truly hoped that she would be pleased with me, that I had conducted myself so properly, and done credit to her lessons. But Lady Maude was nowhere among my ladies.

Relieved, I cleaned my own hands with a fresh linen cloth and dropped it into a basin held by a waiting page. It would be a year before I knelt again, except at Mass. John turned and took my arm as we walked back between the stools, handing a cloth purse and a few kind words to each of the paupers. Few of them even attempted to thank us. They looked, if not merely bewildered, actively frightened. I had spent so long despising John that I had forgotten what his power really meant. One word from him and any one of these unfortunate people could be whipped, or hanged. And I had conjured his cruelty like a malicious crone squatting over a cauldron. So Arthur was alone, alone in the dark … I staggered and John gripped my arm more tightly, so tightly that I felt the malicious stab of his nails through the wool of my sleeve.

'You are well, my lady?' There was sneering, not solicitousness, in his voice.

'Quite well, my lord.'

'Then come. Let us dine.'

*

'Why did Lady Maude not attend Mass?' I asked Agnes as she laced me into a fresh gown.

'She is gone.'

'Gone? Gone where? It is the crown wearing on Easter Day, she ought to be here. Had she bad news of her family in England?'

'They left this morning, she and her husband. He was some time first with the king.'

'Find out then. Find out why they have left.'

For the first time in several months, I dined that day at Rouen without Arthur. Only in his absence did I notice what a mean, grim place our court had become. So many of my husband's household knights had slunk away, some pleading business on their lands elsewhere, others merely taking horse without leave and riding south to the rebels. I had been so taken up with my game with Arthur that I had barely listened as John fulminated against one weak-minded traitor after another, but now, seeing the empty places in the hall, I said their names over to myself, appalled at how many we had lost. And of course, Arthur's absence glared among those who remained; I could see the speculation in the low murmurings of the men, their watchful glances at the king. I felt as fearful as the paupers in the town square. John barely touched his food, staring dully in front of him and emptying cup after cup of wine, his arm rising steady and regular as a woodsman's axe. I pushed a grey morsel of salt fish around my plate with a lump of bread. At least we would be relieved this dreary diet in two days' time. Abruptly, my husband turned to me.

'Have you dined, my lady?'

'Yes, my lord.' I was agonized by the coldness of his tone, desperate for some softening, something that would absolve me of what I had done. Even now it need not be too late.

'My lord, I would speak with you. Perhaps I might come to your chamber?'

He would never have refused such a request, before.

'Leave us.'

'But my lord…'

'I said, leave us.' The words came out like iron pebbles, spat with disgust.

Though I could not see them, I could feel the shock of his tone in the swift intake of breath among the women kneeling to my right, spreading out along the trestles and down the hall.

Even when foully drunk, John had never spoken to me discourteously. What new scandal was this? Had the little Angouleme baggage lost her charm? I didn't need to look to know that some of the ladies would be preening themselves already, dipping glances beneath their lashes towards the king. Had he not already put aside one childless wife? Had I not reminded him myself that wives could always be got for kings? And there were several of them, I was sure, who would have been content to be less than a wife if there was a chance of getting a royal bastard. 'You chose this, Isabelle,' I told myself. 'You chose this.' I made a beautiful curtsey to John and walked from the hall with my head held proudly erect.

When we reached the antechamber, I turned to them. 'I think it would be fitting if all of us ladies sewed for the poor this afternoon. The maids have an ample supply of coarse linen. I shall work in my chamber, until the king joins me. I will have the cloth sent to the dorter. I intend to fast this evening, in preparation for tomorrow. I suggest that you join me.'

It was a pathetic little show of power, but was that not what they coveted? To receive curtseys, give orders, and spoil other people's pleasure on a spiteful whim? And they would still covet, even if they knew the truth, for what was Lord Hugh not prepared to do for the chance to control a crown?

Although it was just a few hours after noon, Agnes had already lit the lamps in my chamber. The morning's wind had blown in a heavy twilight of dull cloud. How cold Arthur must be, locked away in the dark. But I must not think of him. I could not.

'What news of Lady Maude? Don't tell me Sir William has turned his coat too?' For a moment I tried to believe that this was the reason for John's silent rage, though I knew it could not be so.

'I asked among the maids. Lady Maude's tiring-woman was furious. Off to the coast, and barely a minute to pack the baggage. She had to leave a feather bed behind ...'

'Yes, yes, Agnes, but why? Why so suddenly?'

'Because Sir William had the charge of Duke Arthur. And because after what his Majesty spoke of last night, he felt he could no longer in honour keep his charge.'

'You mean he refused to do what my husband asked?'

'How could I know? How could Lady Maude's tiring-woman know of such a thing? No one knows.'

'Except us,' I said.

'Except us. And perhaps Sir William, now. They will be at Honfleur soon, to take ship for England.'

'So it will happen?'

'As it must.'

'Then we must pray, Agnes. There is nothing else we can do. We must pray for forgiveness. Put out the lamps. We shall not need them.'

I knelt and began to mutter the Pater Noster. In a while, I no longer felt the cold stone beneath me, and in a while longer, stupefied by the low hum of my own frantically repeated words, I felt nothing at all. I must have prayed myself to sleep, for when I woke, Agnes was sleeping beside me, still in her gown, and the sky outside the casement was black. I listened for a few moments, but all was silent. There was no noise from the hall below, the men must have retired to the guardrooms, or be sleeping among the rushes. It took me a few moments to ease my stiffened joints into suppleness, then I stepped quietly to the door. The latch would not lift. It was locked – John's doing. I tapped softly on the wood.

'Is anyone there?'

Silence, and then a stirring, the bang of a scabbard on stone.

'Yes, Majesty.' No voice I recognized, though he was not a Rouen man; his tone, though thick with sleep, carried the light clear accent of the langue d'oc.

'Why is my door locked?'

'The king's orders, Majesty.'

'Open the door.'

'Majesty, I cannot.'

'I said, open the door!' I hissed.

'Forgive me, Majesty. I cannot disobey the king.'

'And I am your queen!' Even to my ears, there was no threat, only shrill petulance. Then I had an idea. What was a man of the south doing here when all of his countrymen had fled? I heard him settle his weight against the door, imagined his hand poised on his sword. 'What is your name?' I whispered.

'Gilbert, Majesty,' he answered reluctantly.

'Then, Gilbert, open the door. Not in the king's name, but for the old ones. I have their mark on me.'

I heard a sharp intake of breath, then nothing. He was shocked, and he was thinking.

'I do not know what you speak of, begging your pardon, Majesty.'

When I spoke again, I did not know where the words came from. They twisted out of me, supple as a serpent's tail.

'Yes you do, Gilbert. Yes you do. And you shall see it too, when Duke Arthur is come into his own again. You shall see it on my naked flesh at the sabbat. It's just … here.' I scrunched my gown against the keyhole so he could hear the rustle of fabric. 'Just here, on my shoulder, where the horned man placed it. Shall you kiss it then, Gilbert? Shall you?'

The bolt slid smoothly open. As I came into the passage, he was on his knees. I bent and allowed my lips to brush his hair. 'Thank you. I shall not forget,' I breathed.

As I skittered down the staircase to the hall, my slippers silent on the stone, I saw a light through one of the arrow slits set into the wall. Rouen was an ancient fortress, built for the first Viking dukes of Normandy. In places the walls of the keep were ten feet thick, with passages cut into them like wedges of cheese to allow bowmen to defend it. I paused, listened, then hauled myself onto the ledge and followed it to the opening. I put my face against the stone, worn smooth with hundreds of years of salt rain, and breathed the cold air off the river. Something was moving on the bank, a humped shape silhouetted by a lantern. Just for a moment, the heavy cloud moved, and I recognized a bending figure in a shard of moonlight. John. I knew him from the white surcoat he had worn to the Maundy service, gleaming briefly until the clouds banked once more. At the same time, it was as though a cloud that had been across my mind since Paris shifted. I had not cared since then, I saw, whether I lived or died. My savage joy at Mirebeau had come from that, my reckless pleasure in Arthur, too. I lived now, and Arthur was dead, so I had stopped Lord Hugh. Even if I was killed by one of the castle guards, I would have stopped Lord Hugh. I had chosen Arthur for my sacrifice, and only God knew how easy it would have been for me to sacrifice myself in his place. I did not pretend to myself that I had been courageous. I had committed a foul, foul sin. I had not always wished to live. Yet when I had prayed to God to end it, when Lord Hugh raped me, when Pierre blackmailed me, all He had shown me was more death. Very well. Let it come now.

Although I had put on flesh during my brief, happy time with Arthur, it was easy enough to work my way through the tall arrow slit and onto the ledge. The drop to the riverbank on this side of the keep was no longer than a tall man, so I peered down into the darkness, trying to spy a shrub or young tree by which I could lower myself. The bank seemed clear below me; John must have had the ground cleared in case of attack. I twisted myself around, worked my body downwards until I was clinging to the ledge with my hands, and allowed myself to drop. I landed heavily, sinking ankle deep in freezing, reeking ooze, yet I was unharmed. My feet would look like a pauper's, now. Cautiously, my hands stretched out before me, I half walked, half slid towards the river's edge, where I had seen the muffled light.

It was John. John and another man, both of them filthy, dragging a bundle between them down to the water's edge. I crouched down, low to the ground. They did not speak, merely grunted occasionally with effort. The second man held the light

186

awkwardly in one hand, using the other to drag at the bundle, while John held the other end. Briefly, in the glow of the lantern, I caught sight of a bare leg. So it was done. I had driven my husband to this. I squinted into the dark, trying to trace the line of Arthur's body beneath John's straining shoulders. Maybe I could catch one last glimpse of his poor innocent face. Then the clouds opened once more, and I wished that I had not looked, for Arthur had no face, any more. John had not even allowed him to die by the sword, like a man.

The two burdened figures were staggering into the shallows now, the Seine flowed swiftly here and the second man was struggling to keep the lantern upright.

'Hold still, curse you,' hissed John. 'Take it in your teeth. We need to swing it.'

As the man raised the lantern to his mouth by its leather strap the light showed more fully. Arthur was naked, as naked as I had last seen him, and all of him so clean and lovely, his limbs marble-bright. The lantern bearer had a purchase on his shoulders now, and together they swung the body, once, twice, three times, releasing it to fall with a low splash into the black water.

'It is done then, Majesty?'

'It is done. You have seen nothing, do you hear? Nothing.'

'Of course. As Majesty wishes.'

His speech was blurred by the lantern still caught between his teeth. John was behind him in the darkness, he had no time to turn around as my husband came up behind him, close, too close. The pale wool of John's sleeve drove up against his back, the last thing I saw before the lantern was quenched, he grunted and toppled, a louder splash here in the shallows, then fell forward. John kicked him savagely … wet thumps, holding his boot, or a knee, on his back as he thrashed like a fish on land, until the waves of his dying ceased to sound.

'Good,' John muttered to himself. 'You saw nothing.'

I rose from the mud, 'Will you kill me, too, my lord?'

'Isabelle?' John shuffled towards me, the marshy bank sucking beneath us. Then his arms were about me, and for a moment my heart clutched inside, a faint wren flutter of fear, which passed before I felt his right arm move, replaced only with a great exhaustion.

'Do it, then, John. Kill me too, if you must.' I closed my eyes and breathed deep. I could feel myself shaking, but it was only the damp cold. I was ready. I did not believe any more that God cared me to make my peace with Him. I had been ready for so very long. But John's arm was about my neck, steadying himself as he pulled me towards him, he was holding me tight against his wet body, his mouth buried in my hair, his throat tight with sobs.

'Isabelle. What have I done? Oh Isabelle, what have I done?'

PART TWO

CHAPTER THIRTEEN

THE FISHERMAN WHO FOUND ARTHUR'S BODY KNEW him by the ring. My betrothal pearl was jammed tight on the stump of his smallest finger, so tight that it had remained when John tried to slice it off, so tight that it stayed embedded in his softening flesh as he floated in the Seine like so much discarded bait. And for a jewel on a dead boy's finger, the castles of Normandy fell at the king of France's touch like a column in a game of tiles. First Conches, then Le Vaudreuil melted at the very sight of his troops as though they were built of sand, while my husband's liegemen scuttled away like white-bellied crabs before the tide. So many of them had sworn to defend their king to the death, but now they preferred the shame of breaking their oath than that of fighting for a murderer.

The fisherman hauled the corpse to the nuns at Notre-Dame-des-Prés, and it was only when the good sisters fearfully cleansed the body that they found the ring. The king and his fellow assassin had done their work well. Arthur's strong Plantagenet features were a mangled lump, his breast a sponge of stab wounds. Had it not been for the ring, they would have buried the body quietly, believing the poor youth a traveller, perhaps, the victim of vicious outlaws. The countryside was swarming with thieves at that time, desperate men driven half-mad with hunger as the lords' wars were burning their crops and starving their children. Yet one of the sisters recognized Queen Isabelle's ring, that pure, priceless pearl, and they sent word to Philip. I had thought to protect John, to provoke him to such enormity only to finish the Lusignans once and for all, I had given my love as a sacrifice, and yet in the time after Arthur's death, as the couriers came and went and the whole of the Angevin lands were raised against John, I saw that I had not escaped Lord Hugh's bond over me. I had taken Arthur as my lover, and had him killed, and the horned man was well pleased.

I feared at first that my husband would revenge himself on the sisters of the abbey, like Geoffrey Spike-Tooth in my mother's long-ago story of Melusina, but the rage I had stoked in him was quenched the night he cast Arthur's body into the Seine, and he moved about his own castle like a ghost, no longer ranting or carousing, no longer even calling for wine, but slumped in a lassitude from which nothing could rouse him, not even the news of the crumbling of his father's empire. Lackland, they had called him once, when he was nothing but the younger son of great Henry, and, it seemed, the name was apt. William Marshal, still the most loyal of my husband's magnates, did what he could to dismiss the news of Arthur's death, calling it a foul calumny, but Philip of France returned calmly that if John of England wanted peace, he had only to produce his living nephew, and that, of course, John could not do.

Brittany was irreparably lost, Poitou, stirred up by the Lusignans, slipped further from John's control by the day, and Philip's men gnawed at the fringes of Normandy like so many rats. When Philip went to receive the fealty of his vassals in the south, he travelled down the Loire by barge, through what had once been the heart of Angevin territory, and there was not a man who came out to challenge his right.

We remained at Rouen from Easter until harvest time, a dragging, grey season. To me, it was as though the sun had been buried in that black water, bound in Arthur's red-gold hair. I had nothing to do but walk, and pray, and mourn, and the only mercy was that John's anger against me had vanished too in that murderous blaze which had consumed my beautiful boy. That time on the riverbank, in his desperation, was the last time my husband called me 'love'. I knew that there were women who lay with men for money, and I knew the name for them, too. Whore. That was what they called a woman who was paid to have a man between her legs. The barons had whispered it of me before, when it seemed that John preferred to loll abed with his bride rather than fight for his lands, and now it was true. I had known that John would never forgive me for shaming him by losing my maidenhead to Arthur, for all he believed it had not been my will, yet this had seemed a tiny loss in comparison to what I knew I must do to Arthur himself. Enduring John was a fit penance, perhaps, for what I had done to Arthur, my love. His manner to me was respectful enough in public, as befitted his own dignity, but when we were alone in his chamber, whence he summoned me each night if he was not too far gone in drink, he adopted a falsely jocular air, treating me as if I was no more than a tavern wench. I cannot speak of the things that he made me do, though his fumblings and his filthy satisfactions left me as much a maid as if Arthur had never touched me, while they seemed to please him well enough. I pitied him. He sought to humiliate me, for the private knowledge of what I was not, yet the insults he wrought on my flesh were nothing to me, I had no more feeling, then, than a corpse.

And even death had abandoned me. To live, it seemed, was my punishment. To live through the dull aching cruelty of every dawn, when I opened my eyes beside John's lumpen form and saw Arthur. Arthur riding next to me, Arthur opening his arms joyfully, Arthur's lips above mine as his body moved inside me, Arthur broken and white, cast endlessly into the freezing river that pumped relentlessly through my veins. I grew thin again, and my husband whispered spitefully that I was a scrawny bitch and when would I get him a child? I cared nothing for him. My heart was no longer made of rushing nerves and taut sinew, alive for Arthur, rather it was dull and ugly as a lump of kitchen tallow. I thought that one day it would just stop beating for despair, and that I would fall to the ground like a log, but I could no longer even hope it. I had done what I had done to prevent more hateful bloodshed, such as I had seen at Mirebeau, but now I knew with a keening grief that I had been wrong, that I could have eloped with Arthur and married him and been duchess and queen at his side and found another way to thwart the Lusignans. It would have brought war, true, but it seemed that all men were insatiable for war.

That knowledge might have driven me mad in time, but it was Angouleme that saved me. Since my Taillefer father's death I had been Countess of Angouleme in my own right, but I never would return to my city while my mother was there. But Lord Hugh was pressing hard, in right of the alliance of my betrothal, and I knew that my mother would not hold the city against her lover, if he was her lover still. As the riders came daily from Poitou, I began to understand why it was that men could fight for land. Why when everything else was gone, it stayed in their blood and their bones, and why they would kill and die for it. I thought of the water meadows, and the swallows' nests under the eaves of the cathedral, of the pure silver air and the sound of the wind in the oak trees, and the memory of those leaves coaxed a flutter of feeling in me. When I heard that my mother was gone to Paris supposedly to seek help from the king, but I knew it was really to leave the gates open for Lord Hugh, I felt the beginning of rage.

I tried to beg John to send troops to relieve the men of Angouleme, but even when I tried my prettiest wiles, gritting my teeth as I caressed him, he merely looked at me scornfully and told me that he had already given up everything for me, and what more did I want that he should send men he could not spare to die for a single county? He dismissed me, saying that if I was no use for getting sons I had better be at my prayers, and went back to his wine, only to call for me again when he had drunk enough to rouse his lust. I wanted to hiss at him that I had had the best man in the world murdered for him, but his anger was of no more use to me. I saw that I needed two things: first gold, and then a son.

I had money of my own, why should I not defend my city? My English lands were worth four hundred pounds a year, a huge sum, I thought, enough to pay an army. But who could lead it? So I sent for my clerks and since I had no chancellor, not even a household of my own at Rouen, I instructed them myself. I wished I had paid better attention to my lessons, for I could make no sense of the figures in the account books they showed me, how so many shillings could belong to this manor in Devonshire, or this mill in Bedfordshire, places I had ridden through, perhaps, but never paid any mind. I was not even certain that I knew what a shilling was. I even missed Lady Maude, who might have assisted me in making it out, but she was gone far away, to her husband's lands on the march of Wales, another place of which I knew nothing.

There was one man who had an interest in defending my abandoned city, one who was wily and slippery enough to persuade the Lusignans to take their soldiers and campaign for other prizes. I gritted my teeth and dictated a most tender letter to my brother Pierre, asking him to be my seneschal in my husband's name, and promising him the men and gold he would need to hold Angouleme against his father. I thought this very cunning, for Pierre would never fight Lord Hugh. Rather, now Arthur was gone, they would come to some accommodation and work out how they could best make use of me. And if I could keep Angouleme safe for a time, then I might have another use for my brother.

So Pierre became John's man, and my husband thanked me grudgingly for what I had contrived. I tried to persuade him to go down to Poitou, and confront the Lusignans, but as almost always, he hesitated, and once again gave the advantage to the French king. Philip of France was mustering to attack the Lionheart's great fortress as Les Andelys, Château Gaillard. I had heard my poor Taillefer father speak of it with awe, this castle raised on a rock within five miles of the French king's keep at Gaillon, the 'Saucy Castle' built as a gesture of defiance when the Lionheart still ruled in the south. Richard had built it in two years, it was perhaps his true love, as his poor rejected Spanish queen had never been, and it had eaten at his coffers like the most jealous of mistresses. My papa said that while the stones of Gaillard rose, blood rained from the skies. Now Philip planned to take it from the English, this last symbol of their martial strength. It was William Marshal who raised the defence, who sent to England for gold to pay the northern mercenaries, who summoned the boats to break the French siege from the river that ran hundreds of feet below Gaillard's walls. And it seemed as if Melusina, the water spirit, swam to the aid of her Lusignan kinsmen, thrashing the currents of the Seine with her tail, so that the oarsmen lost their time and were swept downstream, losing sight of the soldiers on the banks. When the remains of Marshal's flotilla were hauled back to Rouen by horses roped to the barges, their shallow keels were still swimmy and stained with blood. It was the last attempt the English made to recover their own.

Marshal gave out that his lord would remain and fight on through another year, but even as he gave his seal to the clerks, our sad household at Rouen was being broken up. Early in

December, John told me we would soon leave for England. It would be hard riding, he explained to me, we would have to leave before dawn to make our way to Bayeux, and on to Caen on the coast, but then I took pleasure in that, did I not? His little soldier, he had taken to calling me, carelessly, his pretty squire. I produced a rueful smile and bade Agnes to prepare our trunks. I was glad, so very glad to be leaving this cursed place, I prayed that once in England we should be safe, and I could begin again. I prayed that I might have a son, a son who would be an English king, at least, and even more one day. So I took the enamelled box in which I kept the gifts Arthur had given me, and went down to the river at night one last time. I sent them after his body, all those pretty trinkets, for though I had pawed them over and wept, I knew them to be false, gifts from a boy who had never truly known his love. As I raised myself from the bank I promised that I should cry no more for him, sleeping now at the abbey with my pearl ring on his finger. I should be an English queen, I told myself, the mother of English sons, sons who would fight one day for my city of Angouleme. The Lusignans might triumph in my husband's lands, but I should deal with them on my own terms, as a queen.

CHAPTER FOURTEEN

JOHN GAVE A GREAT FEAST AT OUR RETURN TO WESTMINSTER, as though he returned a conquering king rather than the miserable vassal he was. He summoned the barons of England to attend our crowning ceremony, but it seemed that there was much business in the shires of England that winter, for most of them relayed their compliments and their excuses, and did not appear. They were waiting, I knew. If John had no heir soon they thought to offer the crown to France and be done with this half-man who sat on their throne. And what would become of me, then? While I was queen, I had the means to defend Angouleme, but how could I do so if I had no money to pay for it? Lord Hugh would swallow up my city like a comfit.

Pierre joined us at court a week after our arrival in London. I had summoned him in his role as seneschal, and the report he made to John's council declared the walls of Angouleme unbreached. I did not care what arrangement he might have made with Lord Hugh, though the reports from my tittering maids on his lavish spending in the city told me where my gold had gone. It was easy enough to avoid him in that sprawling palace, and he did not seek me out. I had no stomach for another of his conversations, and besides, it was not yet time to employ him. I had a gift of game sent to his lodgings, and another of a pair of spurs, but when he sent to thank me in person I replied only with a message and did not invite him to the queen's chamber.

My husband remained barely a month in his capital before he set off once more to tour his lands, to raise monies and drink and quarrel, which gave him more pleasure than fighting like a king. To my relief, Pierre left too in his lord's retinue. I had business to attend to in the city: there were the levies of the queen's gold to be accounted for; there was my dock at Queenhithe, on the banks of the Thames, to be inspected; there was my wardrobe to order; and my ladies to be chosen. John might care to live like a squire, sleeping in a barn when there was no house to hand on his wanderings, but I should keep a gracious court, I thought, a court worthy of a queen from the south. I had a bathhouse built at Westminster, lined in blue tile from Castile, I ordered a great cleaning of all the rooms in the palace and had their walls freshly limed, I sent to the City merchants for silk cushions and new plate, so that while John had returned from France a disgrace to the name of his father and brother, any ambassador who came to him should see that he was a mighty prince, and make report of it. I did not do this for John, though.

There was something else I did, too. There was a woman spoken of in London then, who had been locked up in the Clink prison at Southwark for the making of poppets. She was a whore, they said, a *pute* from the stews, who had been abandoned by her keeper, a merchant, and she had made small figures of the man, his wife and son, of cloth and wax, and driven pins through them and left them in the churchyard there, where they had been found by the sexton. The woman was locked up against her trial by the bishop's court, and if she was found guilty, she should burn. I ordered that she be brought from her cell and rowed across the river to Westminster stairs, for the queen had a mind to cast her eye on a witch. My chaplain heard of it and came bustling to see me, daring, if I would permit him, to suggest that it might be a danger to my person to see such a creature, though I knew that what he meant was that it was a scandal for such as I to consort with such as she. Besides, my ladies were as curious as I to see the spectacle of a sorceress, and it would amuse us to view her. I did not care that they might gossip, for I had been capricious when I had first come to London, as John's bride, and for all the court at Westminster knew, I was the king's darling still.

The woman was brought to the guardhouse at Westminster in irons. My women clucked and stared, as though she were a wild animal, but beneath the filth of the prison she looked to me like any girl, perhaps of an age with me, and pretty enough, though her teeth were black and her hair was dull with dust and grease. Her name was Susan. As she entered the guardroom she threw herself forward on the ground, crying at the top of her voice that she was innocent, that she had never made any conjurings, and begged me to help her, to speak to the king on her behalf. She had a child, she said, a little baby, who would starve without her. I could not address her myself, but I spoke through my herald, instructing him to tell her that she need not be afraid, that the king was merciful, and that she would not be harmed. I had the irons unlocked, and when the manacles came off the room was filled with the stench of putrid flesh. Her wrists were green under her sorry cloak, where they had lain against the metal. My ladies coughed and stared and held their kerchiefs to their noses.

'Ask her why she made the poppets,' I instructed.

Susan did not deny that she had made the creatures. They were to shame her keeper, she said, who had got her with child and then left her. He was a rich man, but he would give nothing for their provision. She had only wanted to frighten him, she and her babe were hungry, but she was no witch, I heard her babble, she was a good Christian girl who knew her Hail Mary and her Pater Noster. She began to recite the prayers to prove it, until the herald silenced her.

'Who is the man who fathered this woman's child?'

The keeper of the Clink unrolled a parchment, the testament prepared for the church court, and gave a name.

'Have him found. Tell him that unless he agrees to sustain his child, he will find himself in the church courts as an adul–terer. It is a disgrace that he has charged this poor girl with witchcraft.'

Hearing my meaning, my women muttered virtuously that it was a shame and scandal that such things could go on.

'Have her washed and fed and brought to me. We will find a place for her where she can care for her child and live decently.'

Susan began to howl, all the fear she must have lived with pouring from her in a gush of grief and thanks.

Later, I waited for her in my small chamber, Agnes at my side. I did not fear that she would understand our conversation. When the girl returned, she looked quite different, in a decent petticoat, with her hair combed. She had even been found a pair of shoes. I saw her eyes dart around the room, absorbing the thick hangings on the walls, the scent of the apple-wood fire and the perfume in the brazier, the thick curtains of Turkey work at the casement. She would never have seen a room such as this.

'Now Susan, do not be afraid. I am going to find a place for you, far away from London, in a house of good women, where you can take care of your child. Should you like that?'

She nodded, too awed to speak.

'But first I would ask you something. I know of ... how you earned your living, across the river.'

She shook her head as if to deny it, then began to weep.

'I do not mean to distress you, nor to judge you. I only wish to know something you may have learned in your, your trade?'

Her eyes slid towards Agnes.

'She does not speak the English tongue. You may answer freely. What I wish to know is that if there is a way you know to be sure of having a child?'

She hesitated. Such things were the province of midwives and wise women, and to claim such knowledge might see her irons replaced.

'I have a gold piece for you, if you answer me.'

Another nod.

'Well.'

When she spoke, her voice was raw from her tears and exclamations. I had some difficulty in making out her words in English, 'Yes, lady. There is a drink. Not harmful. To be taken before the man fucks you.'

I wanted to giggle. No one had ever spoken that word aloud to me, not even John in the worst of his cups. 'Can you get it for me?'

'Yes.'

I might have asked Agnes, who was an expert in the herbs and medicines of Angouleme, but I thought that things might be different here in England. And besides, I could not tell Agnes what I was thinking. They made a song on it, how Queen Isabelle saved the witch who was a whore that was sung for years about London. It pleased me, that I had power to be kind to the girl. And perhaps it made the people like me a little. I had a new litter, hung with white satin and carried by four greys, with cushions of saffron-coloured silk, and in the streets they cried, 'God save the queen,' as my litter passed through London, when we left the city for the spring.

*

By Lammastide, my court was at Woodstock, not far from the colleges of the city of Oxford. It was one of the oldest of my husband's palaces, built amidst broad rides for hunting, with a fine garden laid out, they said, by old Henry for the pleasure of his mistress, fair Rosalind. The musicians sang ballads of her, how she had been the king's true love, instead of his rebellious Queen Eleanor, and how the queen had poisoned her for spite, and how the roses in her garden hung their heads and wept for her memory. It was a sweet story, and I thought of it as I walked in the thickly scented garden with my maids in the high heat of that summer.

John was restless as ever, vanishing for days on end on hectic rides through the country, leaving me to the company of Agnes and my women, which I minded not at all. Agnes was old now. It tired her to stand while she combed out and put up my hair, and for all my teasing she had still never mastered the English tongue. She said it was too late for her tongue to twine itself around those strange harsh words, and it pleased me to hear the soft sounds of my childhood in her accent still, as we sat peacefully stitching beneath a sky the colour of the Virgin's robe. We would chat until she dozed off, and then I would run to my maids to play at butterfly catching, or to bathe in the river, smiling to think that Agnes could no longer run after me and remind me to be a lady. I could not be happy, not when Arthur's body still stalked my dreams, but since I had to live, I tried to act as though I was.

We rode to Oxford for the feast of the first fruits, to watch as the priest broke a new wheaten loaf into quarters and placed one at each corner of the church for luck. Afterwards we listened solemnly to a long discourse in Latin from one of the university scholars, and I did not chide my maids for ogling and making eyes at the poor young man. I had couriers from John each day, from Westminster, from Rochester, even from Portsmouth, but so long as he stayed away we were peaceful there together, with our music and our games.

On Lammas Eve, I entertained the Bishop of Oxford to dinner in a white silk tent to protect us from the heat, and afterwards, though we had few gentlemen, I permitted my ladies to dance. I even stepped out with the bishop himself, a dear, gentle old man, who giggled to see himself hitching up his cassock in an *estampie*. The bishop was mopping his bald head and helping himself to a large bowl of cream cheese with tiny wild strawberries when I heard whispers and laughter from the doorway of the pavilion, and then the familiar rustle of a crowd of women curtseying. I did not need to turn my head to know that it was Pierre. My brother needed no herald, it was enough to follow the sound of women sighing. I stood to receive him as he walked between the stooping flowerbed of bright gowns, a mail coat slung over a yellow mantle as bright as his hair. As ever, I remarked on Pierre's beauty, and as ever, I hated myself for it.

I greeted him, waited while he washed his hands and was served with cooled sweet wine, blessed by the stammering bishop, asked if he would eat. 'You are come from my lord the king, Brother?'

'Indeed. His Majesty is at Eltham, presently.'

'And so?'

'And so he is well, Majesty. He asked me to send you his blessing.'

'Thank you. You may return my blessing to him.'

'His Majesty instructs me to remain a while. It is so pleasant here. And he fears you might be starved for company.'

'His Majesty is most kind. And you are welcome, Brother. I shall be glad to hear your news of Angouleme, and to thank you for your good stewardship there.'

At least my ladies would make him welcome, I thought grimly. It seemed that Pierre had chosen his knights for their looks for this visit. After I had received their greetings, I said that I would retire, and leave them to refresh themselves and continue the dance. Another ripple of sighs followed me as I left the pavilion, which meant Pierre was behind me. The girls would have to make do with the bishop, I supposed.

My chambers at Woodstock occupied a tower at one end of the palace. I quickened my pace as I crossed the walk. I had no wish to speak with Pierre, but in the doorway I wearily told my guards they might wait below. I could not avoid listening to him, he would not leave until I did, and I did not believe for a moment that he was come with John's good wishes. Agnes was already sleeping, so I waited for him in my closet, seating myself in the deep recess of the window, drawing up my knees beneath my light summer gown.

'Well?' I would make no more show of courtesies, at least.

'It is Lammastide, Sister.'

'And what of it?'

'I need you to come with me, tonight.'

'Where?'

'Why, to the sabbat, Sister. We will fly to the sabbat and dance beneath the moon.'

The scar on my shoulder twitched at his words. 'I will not.'

'You must.'

'Is *must* a word you would use to your queen? You forget yourself, Brother.'

'Do you recollect, *Sister*,' he drew out the word, the sound recalling the time he had come to me in Paris and begun the slow poison-drip of the Lusignans' schemes. 'Do you recollect a certain Gilbert, who served your husband in Rouen when he still called himself Duke of Normandy?'

The crouching figure in the passage the night of Arthur's death. One of the old religion, a man of the south. What had I promised him? That he should dance with me skyclad, and twine his fingers in his queen's unbound hair? 'No,' I lied. 'I pay no mind to servants.'

'Perhaps your nurse will. He is with her now.'

'Agnes!'

'Of course. Agnes. Would you have that her last sight on earth, Sister? To open her poor old eyes to my man's knife, before he closes them forever?'

I rushed to the door of my chamber. Sure enough, there he was, in a coat of my brother's Joigny colours, squatting like a gargoyle at the head of my bed, leering at me. He waved the dagger in his hand in insolent greeting, its blade gleaming in the starlight from the casement. I stifled a cry, stepped backwards. *Think, Isabelle, think.*

'Have him kill her. As you say, she is old. I have no need of her. She will be gone soon, one way or another. You may bid him proceed.'

It was dim in the closet, but my brother's eyes found mine and held them, so long that I no longer knew whose gaze was whose, so like it was to looking at my own face. I lowered my eyelids, eventually, and tried a small, careless shrug. 'As I said, Brother, have your man murder the nurse. She is not heavy, the two of you should be able to carry her body. You may float her down the river to Oxford as a gift for the bishop. But I shall not go with you, this night or any night.'

'Anyone might think you really were a Taillefer. You have courage, Sister. Or indeed a talent for sacrifice – I recall another body, in another river.'

'I am tired of this discussion. Do as you wish. But it would be more polite, I think, to murder my nurse in the gardens. More discreet, too. I should not wish to have to explain the blood in the queen's chamber. You may leave me.'

He laughed, low in his throat, and reached out a hand towards my face. His knuckle traced the line of my jaw. 'Such a pity that you consider me your enemy, Sister. I like you so very much. But I cannot leave you just yet. You can save your nurse, though I am impressed to find you so prepared to lose her. Very well. You shall not fly to the sabbat with me tonight, at least. But there is something else we must do.'

'What?' I hissed. 'I told you, you tire me. Make up your mind and leave me.'

'You know what. You know very well.'

I did know. I had known since Rouen, when I had decided to pay my brother to fight for me in the south, knowing that he would encounter Lord Hugh there. I had thought on it when I summoned the witch Susan to me, when she had sent me the draught of which I had taken a few drops in a cup of wine each day since. It was bitter, and the fumes from the vial made my head swim, but I had swallowed it dutifully in anticipation of this moment. Still, it suited me that Pierre should think me reluctant.

The Lusignans made children with their own. That was what I had missed when my mother had told me the story of Melusina. Count Raymond had killed his uncle with his spear, he had lain with Melusina and the result was two children, one good, one evil. The monster had destroyed the good brother, and that was the warning in the tale. Perhaps Pressine had had another child, with her king in Poitou, a son. Perhaps that son was Raymond of Lusignan, so that the fairy bride was also the Count's sister. My mother had been telling me something quite different than a thrilling legend of magic and fairy fountains, something about what I was, and of what I must beware. That was why she had sent Pierre to me in Paris, since if the Lusignan plan for Arthur failed, there would be another way, the darker way of the old faith. The Lusignans wanted a royal child, well then, they should have one. John could not get a child on me, and since I was queen, since I was never alone, my own brother was the only man I could trust to do it.

Pierre spoke to the man in my chamber. 'Leave the old woman. Wait at the door. I would be alone awhile with my sister.' He was already loosening his belt as he turned back to me, unhurried, like a long-married man coming to bed to his wife.

'My sword is there, as you see. And I will put my knife here, on this chest. I trust you will do nothing foolish, Sister. I doubt your lord the king would be so understanding of a man in your chamber a second time.' He put his arms about me and drew me close. 'Shall I kiss you, Sister? It can be sweet between us, you'll see.'

His lips were warm, so soft on mine. As his tongue wandered into my mouth I felt a treacherous thud of pleasure deep inside me, even as his grip tightened on my arms and he pushed me to the floor. I pulled back my head. 'No.'

But the length of him was already on me. He laid a forearm across my throat, almost tenderly, slowly crushing the air from my lungs. 'You know they call you whore, Sister? John's Whore. For your bed, they say, he lost a kingdom. I would wish to know,' he parted my legs, pushing harder against me, and I could feel that my body betrayed me, even as I struggled against his touch as helpless as an un-nested lark, 'I would wish to know how my sister bewitched her king. Come. Show me.'

And for a few shameless, helpless moments, I abandoned myself to the throb of my Lusignan blood. He no longer needed to hold me beneath him. When he raised his head at the moment of ecstasy, I saw the horned man behind my eyes, and felt my own pleasure rise to meet my brother's.

And that is how, as the year turned and I wore my crown next to the king at the Christmas court at Windsor, that I was able at last to tell my husband I was with child.

CHAPTER FIFTEEN

D EAR AGNES HELPED MY SON INTO THE WORLD, AND
it was the last duty she performed for me. I named him
Henry, for his grandfather. When I had been churched and
was able to walk out, I carried his tiny body against me in the
meadows of Winchester, where I had taken my chamber, and
whispered in his ear that he would be a great king, greater
even than his namesake, and that he should take all the lands
which were stolen for his mother's cause, and more, and that
when he was grown, he should give me back my father's city
of Angouleme, and that I would rule it for him. I was glad
to have chosen Winchester for the birthing, the long meadows
there, plump and green with autumn rain, recalled a little
the Angouleme plain where Agnes and I had watched the
Lionheart's messenger come, and if she could not be buried
in her own place, at least in the abbey of England's old capital
she might hear the streams as they played down to the river,
and feel the roots of the poppies in summertime as they swayed
before an English breeze.

'Don't be afraid, little one,' she had whispered to me when the first pains came. 'You see, it has come right, all along. Don't be afraid now, you are so strong. Always such a stubborn child. You can bear this.'

I twisted and writhed on the low birthing pallet in my chamber, struggling to breathe in the thick air of the closed room, heavy with incense from the oratory and the rancid stink of the sheepskins nailed to the casements to keep out the light. Agnes washed my face with rosewater, pulled the bloodied nightgown from my swollen, pulsing body, gripped my hand with her old fingers as hard as ever a crusading knight held his broadsword, and breathed my son into life with the last force of her waning strength. When the baby was washed and swaddled, it was Agnes who brought him to me, her eyes shining in the dim candlelight. 'It's a boy, little one. You have given England a king.'

And as my baby squirmed blindly to my wet nipple, she took her delight to rest with her, and slipped away that night. Perhaps it should have broken my heart, but I had I not known for some time that I had no heart left to break? As Henry fed, I cried out as my womb sank and sucked inside me, but even amidst that new pain, I felt the mark of my shoulder throbbing, to remind me of what I had done. And I was glad, so glad, that Agnes had died believing that at last, she had kept her promise and cared for me to the end, that we had stayed safe, that her little warrior had lived, and borne a son.

Later, much later, there came news from Ireland of a man who called himself Peter the Fair. He died of quatrain fever in a monastery there, a handsome lad, they said, with hair as pale and gleaming as white gold. He was known as the son of the English queen, wrote the monk who recorded his passing. The story skimmed its way across the sea, and it was said that the Angouleme queen had taken many lovers to her bed, and given birth to a secret son. They said that John had discovered me in my adultery and hanged my lovers from my own bedstead, but like much that was spoken of me then, it was not true. Whoever poor Peter was, he was no child of mine, for all that he might have been named after my brother. Cuckoos all, my children, true, but my brood of Lusignan bastards knew no ignominy on their birth. Henry, Richard, Joan, Isabelle, Eleanor. God was generous to John Lackland with his children, if nothing else, for all five were beautiful and serenely healthy, with no sign of having been born between the bed and the wall.

Of all my children, Henry was the only one I was permitted to rejoice in. Everyone I had ever loved had been taken from me, even Othon, but on Henry I could pour out all the love that had been thwarted and twisted in me, little dammed streams of hope and joy that I thought had run dry, but had merely been returning to their true course. I will always love him for that, my son. I would have no wet nurse to him, no matter how much my women clucked and said that giving milk was for peasants, and that ladies were not strong enough to feed their children. My breasts were fat and full of sweet milk, I would give it to my baby on my fingertip to encourage him to suckle, and stroke his little downy head, bald as a baby bird's, as he snuffled and grew stronger against me. I would laugh to see him falling off my breast like a little drunkard, dazed with milk, as happy as a summer bee dizzy with pollen. Henry had two cradles with gilt arms above them, and hangings of blue silk, and four women appointed with no other task than to rock him, but when he was not resting in my arms I liked to have him on my bed, wriggling plumply on a thick square cushion that I could wrap my arms about and doze with him safe within their circle, his milky breath on my face. When he cried I would whisper to him the stories I had invented for Agnes as a child, of Saracens and deserts and monkeys and palaces of pink marble, and I invented new tales, of the wild men of Scotland and Ireland, of giants and dragons, until the sound of my voice soothed him and he let his tiny fingers play happily in the curtain of my hair.

John was delirious with joy. He even took my hand as we watched our son sleep on the day he was christened. A son was a sign that God was pleased with him, however the Pope fumed at Rome against his realm of England. For a time, at least, the discontent among my husband's barons was quashed, now that the kingdom had an heir. He talked of returning to France, of pushing Philip from his borders in Gascony and Poitou and reclaiming the birthright of the Angevins for his boy. So prideful was he that it never occurred to him that his poor squirming over my body could have got no child at all on me. He granted lands to my brother Pierre in recognition of his loyal service. But before Henry was a month old, he left us at Winchester, to resume the wanderings over England, which his ever-restless spirit could not live without.

I was glad to have him gone. With Henry, I remained in the south, circling the royal manors and parks that surrounded London, happy to be alone again with my ladies and my child. My boy travelled in my litter with me as we moved from palace to palace; when we passed through a town I was sure to have the curtains drawn wide, even in the winter weather, so that the citizens should see their prince and remember it. I wanted Henry to hear the voices of his people calling out, 'God save Him', for a great king must have the love of the people, I told him, and then his men will always ride out for him, and die if they must for his lands. It surprised me to learn that John was not so unpopular among townsfolk as he had been for so many years at his own court. He was known as a firm king, who interested himself in justice and the rights of the small people and saw that his laws were fairly obeyed. Perhaps Henry might learn that from him, it comforted me to think. John was no true warrior, but then Henry had none of his blood. He was Courtenay, and, though I did not care to think it, he was Lusignan. But mostly he was mine, and in my love for him I felt as mighty as the elephant I had once seen at the French king's palace.

My mother knew, of course, that Henry was Lusignan. Lord Hugh had his wish at last, though I was gleeful to think that I had tricked the pair of them. They might rejoice that England would have a Lusignan king, but what use could they make of a power that depended on his being John's son, rather than Pierre's? And when Henry was grown, he would take back not only the Angevin lands, but the Lusignans', too, and they would have to kneel to him and declare themselves his men if they wanted to hold their castles at all.

I was so happy, so happy just to have my baby's delicate little body close to me that I began to forgive my mother a little more. She had loved me when I was tiny as I loved Henry, and now that I knew the overwhelming depth of that love, I began to think on what she had done, and the terrible pain it must have cost her. I questioned whether I should have the strength to hurt my child, if I believed it was the best thing for him. I had thought I could never survive the guilty agony of what I had done to Arthur, yet besides even that, the thought of hurting Henry was abominably unimaginable.

Perhaps my mother had had no chance to resist Lord Hugh. Perhaps her faith in the old religion was so strong that she believed herself to belong to him, as she could never to my Taillefer father. I began to forget the sabbat at Lusignan, my wedding night at Bordeaux, the torment of Paris. More and more, as I laughed over Henry as he splashed in his little bath, or played, fascinated, with his toes, whose existence always seemed to surprise him, I remembered instead my sweet maman, who sang to me and kissed me when I had tumbled down, who told me that she loved me more than anything in the world. Only now that I had a child of my own, I knew that love, and I softened towards her, for had she not suffered greatly to the best of other's desires, and in so doing to protect herself and her child? I had done terrible, sinful things myself, and I knew I should be capable of even worse if it was to pre-serve Henry.

So in time, I wrote to my mother, declaring that she might return to Angouleme if she wanted, to pass her widowhood peacefully. Perhaps, I dictated, when the present difficulties between my husband and the French king were over, I might even visit her there? I almost wept to imagine us sitting together in the gardens where I had played, with my maman watching proudly as Henry took his first staggering steps, and I wished that Agnes could be there, to dream it with me.

My mother accepted my offer, and returned to Angouleme. The next summer we were at Berkhamsted, deep in the bluebell woods, where John's ancestor the Duke of the Normans had first accepted the English crown, when three mules arrived, loaded with gifts from my city. Tiny clothes stitched by the nuns of Langoiran in linen so fine it caught the light like glass, a pearl-lined cedar chest to store them in, and for me, her daughter the queen, a heavy cloak of yellow velvet lined with white fox fur. My mother sent olive oil soap, of the kind I liked to bathe with, scented with rose and jasmine, and a length of the lightest sky blue silk to be made up as a summer gown. The silk man must still visit in the springtime then, with secrets and wonders in his cart. There was a further gift, a nursemaid named Aliene, a stolid, sensible-looking girl who would be to my boy, my mother wrote, as Agnes had been to me. 'He will hear our tongue, Daughter,' she wrote. 'For will he not one day be a king in the south, also?'

I was delighted, foolishly delighted. I prattled to Henry all the time in French, and I was delighted that he should also hear the langue d'oc. The last gift came a year after Henry's birth.

By then my little court was at Ludgershall, far from the capital. Henry was walking properly now, swaying importantly along on his stout legs, bumping down on the lawns every few paces with an outraged expression, then marching on, busily, for he always had a great deal of business to attend to. The package was sealed with my mother's mark, and the bearer came from Angouleme, yet when I broke the wax and opened the grubby oilcloth, soiled with its long journey, I started to see a silk ribbon in the green and white Lusignan colours. I thought foolishly of poppets and dried toads, peasants' mummeries, but then came a memory of Lady Maude, kneeling stolidly beneath a nailed up sheet, and I thought of poison. I had not seen those colours since Lord Hugh and Hal had been bundled so disgracefully at the cart's tail after Mirebeau. I called for a ewer and washed and dried my hands, then told a page to fetch a pair of gloves and put them on before opening the parcel.

First he removed the letter, also sealed with my mother's sign. Then a small wooden box, a crude, cheap-looking thing, but when he opened it, he gasped, then controlled himself and handed it to my usher, who passed it, unfastened, to me. Inside lay Lord Hugh's brooch, the serpent I had seen on his cloak at Lusignan, the serpent whose twin writhed beneath my skin. I sent my attendants away, and taking a corner of my gown to cover my hands, opened the letter.

Lord Hugh was dead. He had died at Lusignan, some months ago, it must have been, for the time it took for the letter to reach me. John would have known earlier perhaps, but I had been here, remote in Wiltshire, and seldom apprised of the precise whereabouts of my husband's restless court. How had my mother come by the brooch? What did she mean in sending it to me? I held up the parchment to the candlelight, but there was no more script beyond the formal salutation from the Dowager Countess of Angouleme to Her Grace the Queen of England. Gingerly, I took up the jewel. It felt heavy and very cold, even through the cloth that bound my palm. I turned it, examining the fine work, the delicate tracing of the serpent. It was an ancient thing, an emblem that might indeed have dated from the time when Melusina walked by the fountain at Lusignan, when fairy goldsmiths worked their tiny burins to form the shimmer of her scaly tail. I turned to the reverse plate, and there were the Lusignan arms, and beneath them, a scratch in the metal's tarnish, much cruder, as though it had been done with a pin or the tip of a sharp knife: the word '*necieros*'. The Occitan word for need. Whose need? Mine? Was this some sort of trap so that the horned man might watch over me even as Lord Hugh descended to the Hell he surely deserved? Or was it a message from my mother, an attempt at an explanation that she had acted out of need? I passed the rest of the day thinking on it, but I could not make it out. I wrapped the brooch back in its gaudy silk and had it locked in one of my jewel caskets. After all that had happened, surely the only thing that mattered was that Lord Hugh was dead, and I was free.

I was sure that my maman had understood, that she had broken now with the old faith and that we should rejoice one day together in seeing Henry a great and a Christian king. Perhaps he would even take the cross, as his uncle Richard had done, and maybe there might be another Courtenay emperor in the Holy Land after all. I had judged right in what I had done then, had I not? I had protected John and given England an heir, I had wriggled free of Lord Hugh's wickedness and found a means by which even his ambition could be made right and good. One day I would tell everything to Maman, and we would forgive each other, back home, in Angouleme.

CHAPTER SIXTEEN

A T LAST, MY HEART WAS EASY. MY CHILD WAS STRONG; my city was safe. John's troubles with his magnates had not ceased, but I thought that whatever became of him, I should be untouchable, for was I not the mother of the king? I saw John seldom, but with Henry's birth he had ceased to treat me scornfully, and when he came to my bed I no longer felt like a whore. He drank as much as ever, but at least in my company he was jovial, and I could pretend, in the darkness of his chamber, that he came to me as a man. Henry was followed quickly by Richard, then by Joan, and John rejoiced in them.

That they were not my husband's children no longer felt like a sin. I no longer feared that my soul was as damned as Lord Hugh's. I could never forgive him, but once he was gone, I began to see things differently, just as I had with my maman. I even began to think that there had not been such madness in his scheming after all. I was Lusignan, Pierre was Lusignan, Henry was Lusignan. We were descended from Melusina, and perhaps it was the destiny of our line to breed together and finally bring peace to those lands that had been sown in blood for so long. I had long since finished the draught I had from Susan, but my body, it seemed, was apt for children. And since my husband trusted Pierre, and had given him a place in the household, my brother followed the king, and would come to me, always a night or two after he knew I had been summoned to John's bed. Perhaps I lay with him as many as twenty times. It was never sweet, as he had promised me at Woodstock, as sweet as it had been that night in the valley with Arthur. It was something different.

I could not say that I ever wished it, with Pierre. I never ached for him. But as soon as he touched me, it was as though I became someone else, as though my body opened for him like the tendrils of a sea anemone unfurling beneath a wave, or perhaps like the slow uncoiling of a serpent's tail beneath a heavy weight of water. We moved together like that, slowly, swimming through a red dew, his teeth in my neck, savage, so that I answered him bite for long bite, taking his blood into me. He would strike me, cuffing my face, squeezing my neck, lifting me from my waist and hurling my body onto him, so that I writhed in his arms to escape him even as I crammed my fist into my mouth to stop the screams of the craving he summoned in me. It was cruel, what we did together. And when we were done, he would kiss the tears from my eyes and I would lick the marks on his body, and he would smile that long vicious smile and leave me, soused and sobbing in shame and pleasure. And thus the king's children were made.

*

Since I liked to have my babies about me, I did not establish a household for them, as was customary in England, but had them move with me as the court made its slow perambulations, circling London like a sundial. We seldom stayed more than a month in one place – the houses quickly needed to be cleaned and refreshed, while the demands of the royal purveyors might soon exhaust the provisions of the local country if we remained too long. I felt a child's excitement at the preparations for each departure, as the wagons were loaded and the furnishings and hangings were packed up. My children's necessities were packed in a cart of their own, while we travelled last, in a train of litters, in order that the servants might get a start upon us on the road, and the new place be made ready by nightfall. Henry was toddling about everywhere now, still tumbling over with a surprised expression, and he too loved the bustle of moving, climbing earnestly onto a cart to inspect the canvas covering, or being lifted onto the high shoulders of one of the huge dray horses, so that though I praised him for his bravery, my heart was always in my throat lest he should fall. Holding Aliene's hand, he would often climb down from the litter where his smaller brother and sister were drowsing and stump along the hedgerows, gathering flowers into a battered posy, which he would present to me in his hot little fist, with an expression of love in his eyes that always melted my heart.

Though she was young, I quickly appointed Aliene as the chief mistress of the royal nursery. I wished my children to speak with the clear accent of my own country, and to hear from her of the lands of the south that Henry would one day reclaim. As we travelled, I often spoke with Aliene, first of my mother and the changes in her household, then of my memories of Angouleme. Was the gingerbread seller still keeping her stall in the market place? Had the niches on the cathedral façade been filled with finished statues of the saints? I had been so long from my home, but as we journeyed laboriously through the thick mud of the English roads, or moved along one of the high ancient roads of the hillsides near the coast, Angouleme lived for me again in Aliene's tales. I grew fond of her, though her manner was always respectful and never over-familiar, so fond that I did not see what she truly was until it was too late.

Though my husband saw little of the children, he was always pleased to visit the nursery when he returned to court. Aliene would solemnly report on their progress, how Henry had learned to count, or Joan to hold a spoon. Sometimes we would even play games with them, John pretending to be a dragon and chasing us round the chamber, or, a great treat, putting out the candles and hiding in the dark. Once, as we were watching the children eat their supper of bread and milk, Aliene began to sing, a Provençal song *Lanquan il jorison long e may*. She had a sweet voice, pure and clear, and I noticed John looking at her in the soft light that fell on her warm brown hair through the casement. Aliene was not beautiful, her features were wide and plain, but her mouth was large, with full red lips, and her skin was the colour of new cream. I watched them as though from a long distance away, as she caught his eye and modestly lowered her own. The silence as her singing died away screamed between them.

'That was very pretty,' John said softly.

'Thank you, sire.'

'I would hear something else in that tongue.'

Aliene threw a questioning glance towards me. 'Perhaps my lord might be amused by some of the sayings of my country? I'm sure my lady the queen will recognize some of them.'

'Go on,' John smiled.

'Well, something the people say is "Ten le gendre lens e le tiu femourie proche".'

I laughed, and so did John as I translated, 'Keep your son-in-law at a distance and your manure close at hand.'

'Or this one?' Aliene continued. 'Femo morto, capel nou.'

'Dead wife, new hat,' I capped.

There was a sudden, awkward silence. John rose to his feet and formally bid me good evening, he inclined his head courteously towards Aliene. 'Thank you for your singing.'

It had been so long since he had used such a gentle tone to me; strangely, I felt an echo of the sadness I had known when I had lied to him at Rouen. But the next day John was gone again, and I thought no more on it, until we returned to London for the Christmas crown-wearing at Westminster. That winter was bitter, there was ice on the river and I worried that the children would catch an ague in that huge draughty place, so I asked John if I might order them some new furs. I rarely consulted him about the ordering of the household, but for something so costly as furs it seemed wifely to do so. He gave permission and I ordered three little ermine capes, with hoods and mittens, of Flanders pelts. When I went to the nursery on Christmas Eve, I found Aliene prinking herself in a long mantle of red squirrel with a thick black satin collar. At first I thought the cloak must be from my own things, it was much too fine for a nurse to wear, but I did not recognize it, so I asked her why she had it. She blushed.

'It was a gift from the king, Majesty. It came with the children's things. To warm me when we walk out, his Majesty said.'

I gave her a cold look. 'The king is very kind to permit you to wear such a thing. I hope you thanked him fittingly.' And then I could have bitten my tongue, for of course that was just what John would wish. After that, I watched them.

John visited the nursery frequently, but I could hardly chide him for that. At dinner and supper, though, I saw his eyes searching her out across the hall, where she sat among the upper household servants, far from the fire, snuggled cozily into her new cloak. He did not call for me to his bed during the twelve days of the feast, and on the last, Twelfth Night, when we broke the bean cake and crowned the Lord of Misrule, he danced with her. Again, this was not so very odd – John's manner towards ladies was always gracious, in public at least, and he had even danced with Agnes at Twelfth Night before, but as they turned to the music, their palms touching, I recognized the expression on his face. How could I not? It had been mine for so long. I danced myself, with William Marshal and my brother Pierre and several of the other barons. I clapped and smiled at the antics of the fools and tumblers, I poured wine for my husband, and as I did so I remembered another proverb, 'Qui beu amarguent pot pos escupi dous' – who drinks bitter cannot spit sweet. And then

John spun Aliene, lifting her in a high turn so that her gown rose up and in the red glow of the torches I saw another band of red, a flash of scarlet thread bound about her leg. And then it was as though I had swallowed a bitter poison, the room began to turn and the flames of the fires rose higher, casting shadows like cavorting demons on the walls. I spoke to one of my ladies and said I felt unwell; she summoned a maid who accompanied me discreetly to my chamber.

'Do you wish for the apothecary, Majesty? Or something to help you sleep?'

'No, I am merely tired. You may leave me.'

I sat hunched up before the fire, wanting Agnes, that she might brush out my hair with a comb dipped in scented oil, to soothe me. My mother. Always my mother. My mother had sent Aliene to me, knowing that I would take to a girl who reminded me so pleasantly of my home in Angouleme, that I would let her near my children, that she would cuckoo her way into my household and my trust – but why? I did not doubt that John had become Aliene's lover, or thought that he had, and for that I cared not a farthing. Kings had mistresses, and better even a servant than the wife of one of his barons. It was no loss to me to be spared his grunting and probing. And I could not blame the girl, might even have been sorry for her, for what young woman could refuse her king, even if she wished to? But I had seen the garter, and knew her for what she was.

Might Pierre help me? Between us there was understanding, but no affection. I was not such a fool as to think that my brother cared for my interests, except where they suited his. But then I groaned aloud. Pierre was of the old faith, just like my mother. He had known all along, had deceived me yet again.

I must send the girl away, I thought. Declare myself dissatisfied with her and simply send her away. I rested my head in my hands, massaging my temples to ease away the ache, but then I started and called out, frightening myself with the high, thin panic of my own voice. 'Who's there?'

A shadow, a shifting log. Nothing, I told myself, nothing. There was no horned man lurking in my bed hangings. But the shadows were circling me once more, plucking at me with their goblin talons seeking to drive me mad.

CHAPTER SEVENTEEN

U NUSUALLY, THE KING REMAINED AT WESTMINSTER AS winter froze and dripped towards spring. He received visits from his bishops, and from the Pope's legate at Rome, some business to do with an ecclesiastical appointment, and from his seneschals, bringing in the New Year's taxes from across the country. And when he was not hearing charters or quarrelling with the churchmen, he spent his time in his chamber, with Aliene. I had not succeeded in having the girl removed. When I sent to John to inform him that I wished to appoint a new mistress of the nursery, he returned that he wished the children to remain for the present at court, with their maids around them. When I sought him out to complain of it, he gave me a bored look, as though I was a tiresome petitioner, and said that I had heard his wish. I tried again, going to him after Mass, most civilly, requesting that I should order my children's household to my liking.

'I have told you, my lady, what I intend.' He was stalking along the inner court of the palace, muffled as always against the cold, which he seemed to feel so much more than other men. I had to trot to keep up with him, which made me feel small and angered me, but I attempted to keep my words sweet.

'I wish the Angouleme girl to leave. The children need an English maid, now. And soon Henry will require a tutor, and a squire of his own.'

'Indeed. Perhaps the children should keep their own house, at Eltham perhaps, or Berkhamsted. Do you wish that?'

'You would send them away?'

'It is not healthy for them, here at court. I was brought up far from London.'

I knew that. John had not seen his own mother, Queen Eleanor, for years at a stretch. I had often wondered if that was what had made him so angry, so vicious. I could not have my boy sent away.

'I wish the Angouleme girl gone.'

'And I do not. Would you defy me?'

'Of course not, my lord. It shall be as you wish.'

The halls of Westminster were full of the delicious news that the king had taken a mistress. I saw my maids pitying me, a gloating pity that triumphed in the loss of my power over the king. Aliene was not stupid enough to flaunt her success, but I could hardly avoid the sight of her in the fine clothes which John permitted her to order, or the jewels which she now wore each day at supper, a string of grey pearls, an opal ring, which I and every woman at court knew to be gifts from the king. I wondered what other women might do in my place. It was not such a strange position, after all. Many wives tolerated their husbands' whores as part of their households. I could find ways to make Aliene's life unpleasant, I thought. I was still queen. I could taunt her, humiliate her, but I was too proud for that. Besides, I wished to remain with my children, and she knew it. I wondered what poison she dripped into his ear, night after night as she lay in his arms. I wondered what tricks she contrived to make him feel like a man. She was the nightbird now, the cosseted darling. I had served my purpose, bred his heir and now I should be left to grow old and ugly and bitter like so many a royal wife before me, while she grew sleek on the king's pleasure. At least I did not have to endure any sardonic expressions of sympathy from Pierre; the Lord de Joigny was gone to the west country to see after the wardens of the ports.

John had not loved me since Arthur's death at Rouen, but with Henry's birth he had softened once more, still treating me, as best he could, as a wife. Now, each day, I watched him grow colder towards me, as though he had to force himself to speak even the few words that courtesy demanded from us. The palace was so vast, and the king's business so pressing, that I might have gone for weeks without ever seeing him at all, except for his formal message each morning, to ask how the queen did, yet I sought him out. Sought, as I thought many wives had been obliged to do, to win him round with gentleness and patience. I arranged a supper party in my room, with musicians newly arrived from Germany, but he sat there glowering, picking at his food, and remained no more than an hour before bidding me a brusque goodnight and going to Aliene's bed. I ordered a bear baiting and a wolf hunt along the banks of the livid winter river, the beasts brought in cages from the wild northlands of the country, to be released, starved and slavering, for the huntsman's sport. But John did not attend. I heard that he had ordered white bearskins for Aliene's bed, and merchants arrived each day from the city with bales of velvet and furs for her to pick over like a housewife cheapening goods in the market. I had a consignment of strong red Spanish wine served at supper, thinking to tempt him that way, but he swilled at it from the alabaster cups I had thought might please him as though it were coarse common ale and dragged himself bleared and belching from the table, so that I was ashamed of myself for stooping to allure him.

And then the comet came. It was February, the feast of St Bridget, and though the day marked the change of the season, the world remained grey and sodden with melting ice, the dung heaps in the yards frozen and reeking, the stabled horses fat and restless. That night the sky was clear, pierced with stars above the smoke of the humming city, the hall at Westminster was thick with wood smoke and the scent of roast meat. A monk had come from the abbey at Wendover some days earlier, with a set of curious metal instruments and a heavy manuscript of charts, which showed the movements of the moon across the heavens. God was sending a sign, he said, in the sky, and the king would do well to mind it. It seemed like sport as we trooped dutifully out onto the palace walls, huddled in our furs, peering eagerly at the dark heavens. I could not see Aliene among the crowd, and for a few blessed moments I forgot her, and looked eagerly for the comet.

I had seen it like a huge shooting star, a red blaze across the heavens but it was not like that at all. The little monk in his dingy habit was hopping with excitement, his sandals slipping on the frozen stones, gesturing at the moon, which hung low and heavy in the sky. Slowly, the surface of the moon dimmed, from silver to pearl and then to the colour of blood. There was silence on the walls as we watched. God was not making fireworks for our pleasure. This was something else. The bloodied moon gleamed malevolently through its shroud, then dimmed to a greasy grey. For a few seconds, the whole of London was still. The cries from the alehouses, the watermen's calls, the creaking of carts, the bustle from the kitchens, all ceased. We were entranced, watching the sky that seemed as though a huge vial of ink had been upset across it. Some of the maids made the sign of the cross, the little monk was praying into his cowl. Then the murmurings began. It was a sign, people whispered, a sign of God's wrath. And then the eyes of the crowd slid towards their king. John was standing apart, his eyes fixed upon the skies, one hand resting tautly on the hilt of his sword. I made my way towards him, my women trailing carefully behind, holding up their gowns away from the treacherous stone. From the city beneath us now came the sounds of prayer, and the church bells began to ring. I came up beside John and removed my glove, trying to work my fingers between his own. 'What does it mean, my lord?'

He started as though roused from sleep, and stared wildly at me for a moment. 'Nothing. It means nothing.' At the motion of his hand the heralds sounded and the servants began to light torches and braziers, burning the night back into its familiar state. The king would return to the hall, he began to make his way along the walls. Then there was a sharp whistling sound, and a whip crack of impact, and the page that walked before my husband fell to his knees. There was a shout from the street beneath us, 'There he is! Henry's bastard!' Then a wave of thin, humming noise that I recognized from Mirebeau. Arrows. There were arrows being fired on the palace. John's face was barely visible in the torchlight under the dimmed moon; for a breath his eyes gleamed black as the sky, still transfixed by what they had seen, then he shook himself to life as the barons rushed up around him and the screams from the street told us that the guards had found whoever was firing. The little monk, Roger, his name was, was flapping and babbling frantically about God's anger. John pushed him aside so violently that he almost toppled from the wall, and he strode towards the court, calling over his shoulder that the queen and her ladies should be escorted to their chambers. As I was hustled along amidst my maids, I saw the orange glow of fire begin to crack and shimmer across the rooftops, and where a few moments before the town had been so still, now a great yell of sound bellied up towards us, like the explosion of a fool's bladder. The curtain of blood across the moon had been drawn back, exposing the roiling anger of a people whose discontents I had simply not known. Why were they so furious? What did they mean to do?

'What's happening?' I called, stumbling on the hem of my cloak.

'A riot in the city, my lady. Nothing to fear. His Majesty's guards will quell it in no time,' a soldier responded.

The walls were writhing in a confusion of bodies, John and his men trying to descend, the guards roaring as they barred the palace gates, the servants in the kitchens below running about like startled fowl. The children. Were the children safe?

'Take me to the nursery,' I hissed at the soldier who had answered me. The good man squared his shoulders against the shoving cluster of courtiers and pulled me in front of him.

'Make way! Make way for the queen!' he bellowed, and then we were moving, his arms keeping off the crowd, down through the wall gate and along the passage, until we came to the great staircase, where I stooped and threw my slippers aside, feeling the hard stone beneath the wool of my stockings, and then I ran, leaving him behind me, passing a kitchen hand with his arms full of plates, who screamed in terror and dropped it with a great clatter – was he stealing in the commotion? I ran across the hall and up to the gallery, turning left, shocked with the cold again as I came out on the open balcony, then plunging back into the palace, my mind ablaze like the burning town with what I might find. There was no guard at my children's door. I pushed it ajar quietly and walked softly into the room. The nursery was a large square chamber, where the children ate and played, with four rooms off it on either side. On the right, the river side, the casements were fastened tight, but the nightlight was burning in its dish of oil and I glimpsed Joan, sleeping soundly, her brother Richard likewise, both children sprawled half-out of their bedclothes, their faces flushed with dreams. I released the huge breath gathered in my lungs. They were safe. But where was Henry?

236

I passed out of the sleeping chamber and crossed the main room to the left side. The first alcove was empty except for the small altar where a candle burned. My son's room lay beyond.

'Henry?' I called softly, so as not to frighten him.

Aliene was stooped over my child's bed, the low hanging cloth of estate touching her hair. Henry lay before her, sleeping soundly on his front. But his nightshirt was off, the pale glow of his skin illuminated in the candle the girl had set in its bracket by the bed. She was muttering something, a high drone in a tongue I might have recognized if I had listened, but I did not listen, for in her right hand she held an awl, bright as an icicle, and she was reaching her left hand to my boy's mouth, to stay the scream that would come when she marked him. I had not felt such rage since I had fought with Hal, so long ago in the garden at Lusignan. No. I had never felt such rage. I sprang at her, knocking her off the bed, grabbing for a handful of her hair to twist her face towards me. She stabbed at me with the awl, though I did not feel it pierce through my heavy winter cloak, and tried to scrabble to her feet, even as I battered at her with my fists, the pair of us fighting in silence while Henry, improbably, slept on between us. I managed to force her down on the carpet and straddled her body, pulling her throat back and banging my knee against her heart. Her eyes were wild, unseeing, I think that she did not know me, so entranced had she been with her task. I pulled up her gown, feeling for the red thread I knew would be bound about her leg. I grasped it and pulled against her flesh, snapping it in one movement. Perhaps I thought to strangle her with the evil thing, but just then I felt

237

myself pulled off her, kicking out at her prone form as I did so, and I turned, limp but unsurprised, to face Pierre.

'Sister, you shock me,' he drawled. 'Brawling with the servants while your husband's city burns? Hardly queenly conduct.'

I was limp against him, panting. In full view of Aliene, who remained prone on the floor, he insolently dipped his head to my throat and traced my collarbone with his tongue.

'Or were you missing something else, Sister?'

I had no strength left to strike him for the outrage. I glanced towards Henry, who still slept on. 'Get her out of my sight. Now!'

Pierre released me and stooped towards Aliene. Her neck showed red weals where I had grasped it. Good. He helped her tenderly to her feet and smoothed her gown, holding out his hand for the garter, and then he whispered something into her ear. She made me a dazed curtsey and staggered from the room, feeling for the doorframe as though intoxicated. I seated myself next to Henry and fussed with his nightshirt, covering him with his linen sheet and woollen blanket, stroking his tumbled hair from his face. He stirred, but did not wake. I rested my lips a moment against his warm brow, breathing him until I had recovered my countenance. 'When did you return?' I asked Pierre.

'Today. It is an important night, Sister. Imbolc The time between the winter solstice and the summer. You ought to have paid better attention to your old nurse.'

'And this? That girl?'

'Your son is one of our own. As are you, however much you deny it. It was time.'

'I will not have it.'

'What will you do, Sister? Have you heard the people outside?'

'There is unrest. The comet has disturbed the people. They are angry with the king.'

'And why?'

Always this slow drawing out with him that I hated so much, the agonizing drip of his knowledge, filtered like amber through pine bark. I always felt like a child with Pierre, stumbling to catch up. I did not know why the people were angry. I had paid so little attention to John's business of late.

'The taxes? The bishops? The war in France? For God's sake, tell me clearly!'

'Come. They shall tell you themselves.'

He guided me, unresisting, towards the casement, reached up to unbolt the shutters. Henry's room lay on the city side of the palace, and with the sharp air that rushed in came the sound of shouts and the smell of smoke. I glanced anxiously towards the bed where my son lay.

'Listen,' instructed Pierre.

At first, I could make nothing out amidst the babble of voices and the thud of rushing feet. Somewhere a horse was shrieking wildly, perhaps a stable was burning. I had a sudden vision of Othon, rearing in panic. And then I caught my name: 'Isabelle', 'the queen, the queen!'

'They are calling for me.'

'They want you.'

'Why?' I breathed, pushing my hair back from my face. 'Please, Pierre. Tell me what is happening.'

'They blame you. It was unwise, Sister, that merciful business of yours with the witch. Susan, wasn't it? They blame you for all the evils the king has visited on them. They called you whore, and now they call you witch.'

'But why? The people love me. I have heard them, when we pass through the streets? I give them charity. They bless me. I am their queen, the mother of their prince! I have done nothing.'

'Yet they seek a source for their discontent. Much easier to blame their queen, the foreign slut, than their true-born English king.'

'Does John know of this?'

'He has ears.'

'This is your doing. You are conspiring with that-that Angouleme bitch!'

'Very good, Sister, very good. It does not suit me to have you at court at present, or to see you recover your husband's favour. So touching, those little entertainments. And so now the citizens of London are calling on the king to put you aside. The comet is a sign of God's displeasure towards England. They are afraid.'

'I will not leave my son.'

'Oh you will, Sister. You will.'

CHAPTER EIGHTEEN

THE DAY AFTER THE MOON TURNED TO BLOOD, IT seemed that the sun had lost the heart to rise over London. Like clouds of slut's wool billowing from a beaten blanket, great clouds of wet mist rolled up the Thames to Westminster, where they met the hanging wood smoke of the rioters' burnings. The mist and the smoke crept stealthily into our lungs like death's own fingertips. Even in the palace, where torches had burned all night and the fireplaces were stoked high, there was a tangible humour in the air, as though the fear and suspicion borne on the comet's tail were made solid. We were a house of spectres, and in the streets the market carts rolled against the corpses of dead men, their vitals blistering in the cold.

I was to become a spectre, too. I had lain awake all night in my chamber, frantically passing over in my mind the names of anyone I might call upon to help me. Not my mother. The king of France? Even if I were to succeed in sending a messenger, claiming our kinship and seeking his royal protection, it should be days before he received my appeal. William Marshal was a good man, but he had not attended the Christmas court and I had no notion of where he might be. Among my women there were good Christian ladies, whose husbands had castles and manors where I might seek shelter, but which of them could I oblige to take the risk of harbouring me? I was queen, and therefore I was powerless if the king's displeasure was fallen upon me. I was property. I could enter a convent, I thought wildly, as I had once feigned I wished to do. I could ride for Winchester, where I had birthed my boy, but John's disputes with the Pope, so far as I understood them, would not encourage any abbot to further anger his king. And if I entered a convent, I should be shut away from the world, and never see my boy come into his own. I wondered on Hal of Lusignan. He would be lord of the castle, now. Could I trust Hal? I, who had witnessed his shame? Perhaps he had forgotten our childish misliking of one another? But I was being foolish: he would never forgive, even if I could fly to him over the sea and the Poitou hills like Melusina herself.

I expected John to summon me the next morning. Would Aliene tell him that her lover's wife had attacked her? Or would the aldermen of London already have made suit, calling on the king to give up his wife to keep the peace? But no page came with any message, and there was no sign of John, or of Pierre, or of Aliene. I spent the day sewing with my women in my great chamber, my presence suppressing the gossip that shivered through that cloying air. My maids were respectful as ever, but I knew that as soon as I left them their tongues would be flying swift and sharp as their needles. We ate dinner and supper in the hall, once more a court of women as the barons had followed

John downriver to the Tower to meet with the justices over the riot. Before I retired, I visited the nursery and asked that the children should be bathed. The nursemaids looked askance at such a request, did I not know of the dangers of washing in the wintertime, but I had never had any patience with such filthy English customs, and less so, now. I wanted to see my babies' bodies, smooth and clean and flushed with warm water, to see that Aliene, wherever she was gone, had left them at least unmarked. I watched the children at their baths, and we ate a dish of raisins together, counting out rhymes with the stalks on the brim of the platter, and I helped each of them into their nightshirts, warmed before the fire. I heard their prayers, and blessed them, and returned to my chamber to sit out the night hollow eyed in the darkness. I should not have done so if I had known then that I would never see Henry again.

*

I was wakened from a restless doze by the sound of hooves in the palace yard. All through the first hours of the day I heard them, a gathering, urgent rhythm that sounded a counterpoint beneath the slow rituals of my rising, my dressing, my prayers. As my maids sponged my face and hands with rosewater, as they handed my shift and laced me, as they combed my hair and fitted my mantle, as I knelt and turned the leaves of my breviary, I listened for them, and heard grooms calling and the sound of spurs on stone. When I had sent my chaplain away and taken some milk with honey, I sent to the chamberlain's rooms to discover the news. While I waited, I sent to the buttery to ensure that the guests, whoever they were, were served. Even while my heart scratched in my throat as brittle as a bird's nest, I tried to move as slowly and graciously as if the king of France himself were leading me out to dance. Perhaps those men had ridden through streets where my name was being proclaimed as a witch at street corner crosses, perhaps even now my husband was having faggots piled for me in the Tower yard, but I should be a queen still. The mist and the smoke of the riots had dissipated, but we were old acquaintances, death and I, and I was not afraid.

The visitors were the sheriffs of the counties close to London, ridden in on the king's command. Many of them must have been on the road all night. When John finally summoned me to the council chamber, some time after noon, they knelt to me as I passed, some with their hands to their breasts, and if I had not known better it should have lifted my heart to see them so loyal, so good, so willing. John handed me courteously to my chair and I remained next to him as he received each of the sheriffs in turn, charging him to keep the peace after the disturbances in London, and directing him to the treasury for funds. One by one, the men made their bows and departed, so as each left I felt the dryness in my throat ease a little, the stiffness in my smile relax. Until the last of them rose from his knees. A huge man, a good two heads taller even than I remembered Lord Hugh, his massive shoulders straining his muddied surcoat. His face looked oddly small, smooth and pink, with close set periwinkle eyes. He looked like a cunning pig, I thought, a forest boar with a coarse tuft of fair hair and dimples where his tusks should be.

'Terric!'

It was not John who spoke, but Pierre, entering the council room with familiar ease, behind him, between two liveried servants, Aliene. She was no longer the haunted, frenzied creature I had caught on the night of the comet. Her hear was braided and modestly covered in beautiful ivory lace. My lace, a New Year's gift from the wife of a Marcher baron. She wore a soft gown of blue wool and a cherry-coloured velvet cloak with a gold fur trim. Quite the lady. At least she had the sense not to look in my face.

'Majesty,' the gross man was lowering his bulk before John's throne, then turning and inclining his head towards Pierre, 'My Lord de Joigny.'

'My lady.' It was the first time John had addressed me since the evening of the riot. 'May I present Terric, Sheriff of Berkshire.'

'Known as Terric the Teuton,' put in my brother conversationally, as lightly as though we were gathered for a hunting picnic. I inclined my own head half an icy inch.

'My lady is in danger,' John announced, in a similar tone. Had they repeated this, practised this scene like players before a fair? Was Terric to be my perfect knight, carrying me away to an enchanted tower?

'I hope you will keep my dear sister closely, Terric,' put in Pierre. 'The king's Majesty entrusts you to keep her from harm.'

'You have my word, Majesty, my lord.' His voice, like his face, sat curiously with his bulk, thin and reedy, his tongue thick on the English words. Did they not speak English in Berkshire?

'Then I bid you farewell, my lady.' John rose, and bent to kiss my cheek. His face had a crazed look of malice as he came close. I smelt wine on him, and something else. Something black and strong, like a sleeping draught, like poppy gum. His breath was foul with it. 'I hope you will prove obedient, Isabelle,' he whispered.

'As ever to your command, my lord,' I managed.

And then Terric took my arm and the strength of his grip belied his attempt at a pleasant smile. I was his prisoner, as clear as if he had bound shackles about my wrists. As I walked with him down the length of the hall, I turned back to send one last, imploring look to John. If any of my old power over him remained, I begged God, let him feel it now. But he did not even catch my eye, his head was thrown back and Aliene's hand rested on his brow as she seated herself calmly in the queen's chair beside him, as though she were born the daughter of a great lord, not some brat out of a Poitou cowshed.

'Godspeed, Sister,' whispered Pierre. And then the guards banged the door of the council chamber behind me as sure as a prison cell.

Terric escorted me first to my chamber, whence my maids, all but one, were gone. I barely recognized her face, she was an underservant, a trimmer of candles and a holder of fire baskets. She trembled as she held up a dark gown and a heavy furred travelling cloak, and her fingers were clumsy with my gloves and slippers.

'What is your name?' I asked.

'Hilda, Majesty.'

'Hilda, please,' I had little of value on me, my jewel caskets would be gone, I knew there was no sense in sending her to the garderobe. But my girdle had a silver clasp, 'take this and—'

And what? What should she do with it? The girl shook her head miserably. She could not pity one such as I, nor could she understand. I sighed and refastened the girdle around my waist. Perhaps the silver clasp might be of use to me, wherever I was going.

*

I saw Corfe in the February dusk, as the closed plain litter in which I had travelled from London was hauled, the horses straining up the last of a line of steep chalk hills. Terric insisted I travel with the curtains drawn, which I had been glad of for four icy days on the road, but now I twitched the leather aside and stared greedily at the massive stone wall, surrounded by a banking of timber. Terric's own horse, as huge as his master, plodded in front of me, only four grooms and a page completed our party. On the road, Terric had given out that I was a widow, travelling privately, and I had not sought to contradict him, though the wretched, verminous inns where we had broken our journey were like nothing I had ever seen before, even when I had ridden on campaign with John. I could not eat the greasy bowls of pottage, beans and barley swimming in rancid bacon fat, which were offered to me, nor could I sleep on the straw-filled ticking where I was expected to rest without even a maid to lie next to me. I thought wistfully of the hot honest sweat of Othon's flank, which had made my pillow before Mirebeau.

That had been no bed for a queen or a countess either, but it had been nothing like the squalor which John now imposed upon me. Terric was respectful, though he did not kneel to me, procuring heated water for me to wash and thin white wine to accompany the hateful pottage, and I did not fear him, yet. But I saw that I could not hope to beguile him into friendship with me, even had I bent to try. He was immutable as a moss covered rock, a lump of humanity, not a man.

We rode into the inner bailey, where a few servants came out to meet us. They were a poor lot, no livery and a grubby, unkempt look that contrasted with the new buildings of what was clearly an important stronghold. I tried to recall what I had heard at Westminster about my husband's building here, I knew he had spent a vast amount of money on Corfe, which had been built by his great-grandfather, but beyond that I knew nothing. Still, what did it matter? One prison would be very much like another.

Terric handed me down, my limbs stiff and sore from the joltings of the litter. 'This way, my lady.' None of the servants knelt, though a few of the slatternly girls attempted a curtsey. I followed Terric to the largest building, to the west of the inner courtyard, up two flights of stairs and along a passage. 'Your chamber, my lady.'

A wooden bed with a cloth of estate above it. A chest, a stool and a small table. One casement giving onto the castle walls. I thought that somewhere I could hear the sound of the sea.

'Where are my maids? Where are my things?'

'Why, here, lady,' Terric gestured to the empty room.

'But—' I knew that I should be a prisoner. I knew that Pierre and Aliene had contrived that. But royal prisoners were kept in some sort of state, surely? Not like common thieves? I had a horrible recollection of the poor girl Susan, of her mangled wrists, stinking from the shackles.

'A woman will be provided to wait on your needs. You will be quite comfortable.'

Tears were pricking behind my eyes, but I should not let him see them. 'A priest, a clerk, a carver?'

'There is a priest in the town and we can fetch a clerk if you find yourself in need of one. But the king says you must rest, lady. And I must protect you.'

Desperately, I asked, 'And how long must I remain here?' I could not help the imploring tone in my voice.

'As long as it pleases the king's Majesty.' He took his own pleasure in that, I saw. And since the king's Majesty's pleasure endured for another three years, I had abundant time to become cognizant of Terric.

I had known different kinds of cruelty, the cold ruthlessness of Lord Hugh, the frenzied rage of John, the dark sensuality of Pierre. I had been cruel myself, to Arthur. And beneath all that, there was the other darkness, the Lusignan taint I carried in and on me, which was not cruelty, quite, but the blood call of Nature itself, the paying of sacrifice embodied in the horned man who for so many years had stalked my dreams. Yet Terric was different. His cruelty had no motive, no end beyond itself. It was blanketed in quietness, in that dull manner of his, by his slow movements and the heft of his vast body. But Terric's cruelty had no gain at its end. He was cruel in the manner of an idle musician, who would toy with his lute while awaiting his master's summons, cruel because he simply could be.

When first I understood that I was to remain at Corfe, I thought to make a friend of him. I thought he might respond, if not to my state, to myself, to a gentle tone in my voice, a pretty flutter of the eyes, the small tricks that women use to bind men and which I had after all studied for so long. Yet not only did he remain dull as a brick to my overtures, he took pleasure in tormenting me. In the first few weeks of my captivity, what few accoutrements I had brought with me from London disappeared. A scent flagon, my combs, my wine goblet, all vanished. And then began a long game of begging, where I, his queen, was to ask him for something so simple as a napkin, and it would take days to appear, only to be withdrawn again before I had the use of it. Sometimes the pot beneath my bed was left stinking for days, sometimes I was served no food, or my washing water was mislaid. When I asked for news of my children, or my accounts, when I requested a clerk that I might write for information, I was put off, day after endless day. I was permitted to walk as much as I wished on the walls of the keep, Terric plodding behind me like a malignant dog, yet as the weather turned and the days grew long and warm, I was told that the king had forbidden me to walk to the river or the meadows, and only those bare dusty stones might make my exercise. Perhaps the moment which captured the man most clearly was the day I picked the poppies. They were growing in a chink in the wall, just three of them, brave red against the greyness, which by that first summer seemed eternal to me. I picked them and set them on the casement sill in my dreary chamber and gloated over that small patch of colour as though it were the most beautiful tapestry hanging from Flanders, so pinched and confined had my eye become. And the next day, they were not gone, but crushed and mangled, crunched in a huge fist and left a dry mess, to remind me that I could expect no joy there at Corfe. I wept over them, those poppies, as I had never wept for the loss of my jewels or my fine clothes, for they had seemed a talisman to me, a delicate beacon that drew my mind to the meadows of my childhood and promised that one day, I should once more be in Angouleme.

*

It was not until autumn that we heard from the king. A courier arrived in the royal colours and a great splattering of mud. From the walls where I stalked away my days like the ghost I feared I should become, I watched him hand a parchment roll to Terric. Since I knew he could not read, I thought he might bring it to me, but three days passed and I saw nothing of it. I knew better than to ask a question, for if he sensed it might bring me pleasure to learn my husband's news I should be sure not to learn it at all, and it was only when I saw a scruffy mule trudging up the causeway from the town, carrying the equally scruffy priest who served Mass in the castle, that I thought I should learn its contents. As it was, John came himself the next day, in a great company of knights, my brother riding beside him. I peered humiliatingly from the walls like a nosy serving wench, desperate to see a lady's litter, so that I might know if Aliene had

251

accompanied him, but his company was of men. From the carts of sacks and tally sticks which rolled in that evening I imagined that his purpose in coming was merely to extract the royal taxes from the country, or perhaps to see about the defences of the castle, where the masons were still working. That John no longer cared even for the appearance of civility was made plain when he did not summon me to supper or to sit with him in the hall, from where I could hear the men carousing, and smell the now-unfamiliar aromas of roasting meat and spiced wine. I dined myself now like a peasant, on coarse bread and onions, herbs and tough smoked fish or hard cheese. John remained two days, and the only moments I spent with him were when he lumbered to my chamber at dawn, stinking like a wineskin and senseless to the small questions I made him as he laboured fruitlessly as ever over my scantily washed body. When Pierre followed him, before I had had time even to scrape the stench of my husband from my skin, he cuffed me into silence, and I was even grateful for the short time of the things we did together, for the brief jolting cruelty of his embrace. And a month after they rode out, I knew I was again with child, and that I should have to endure Terric's leering as my belly swelled, and I wished then that I might die of it, so spiritless had I become.

CHAPTER NINETEEN

I WAS TWENTY YEARS OLD WHEN I LAY IN AT CORFE
for the birth of Eleanor. When the familiar pains began I
recalled how I had first taken my chamber, for Henry. The
whole court had assembled as I ceremoniously progressed to the
suite of rooms that had been selected for my enclosure, leaning
heavily on John's arm, my belly proud before me. The ladies
who would attend me entered the rooms while I shared sweet
spiced wine with my husband's lords, then bade them a formal
farewell. They wished me God's blessing in the bringing forth
of a prince, and then I heard Mass before the doors were closed
behind me. The walls were hung with carpets and fabrics, the
floors thick with rushes, the shutters tightly sealed. I would see
no man until the child was born. Now there was no one but me
and a maid, and a filthy old wise woman from the town, and
England's princess came into the world on a dingy straw pallet
unfit for a farmer's daughter. The labour was short, and much
less painful, and I was able to hold the scrawny bluish body
against my breast for an hour or two before Terric opened the

door, and there was the wet nurse come to take my baby away. I pressed my lips to her soft brow and blessed her. I did not think to see her again. She would join her sister in the royal nursery while I stayed here to rot.

I had the maid bind my breasts tightly with strips of linen torn from my bedsheets, to stop the milk, sent the old bawd away, and slept away a day or so, waking only to take a little gruel, glad of the exhaustion of my body. When I woke, I knew, it would be as if I had dreamed the birth, and a little of the pain would be gone. I floated on clouds of memory, stunned by the opiates a woman's body will make after childbed, as potent as any of dear Agnes's draughts. I thought I smelled a sweet posset, spiced with cinnamon and rich with egg, such as I had drunk when Henry came. I sighed and pushed it away and turned on my pillow to sleep some more, but the scent did not evaporate. I opened one sleep-gummed eye. There was a cup in front of me, steaming milk and honey, cinnamon and nutmeg and cloves. I was still dreaming then. I closed my eyes and prepared to sink away into another dream.

'Majesty!'

'Terric?' I sat up and peered drowsily over the edge of the tester. A woman knelt awkwardly on the bare stone, proffering the cup formally. Her hair was covered with a coarse veil. A new maid, it seemed. And a small kindness. I took the cup and drank the thick sweet liquid greedily. 'You may leave me.'

'Majesty!'

What was the woman doing? Had she no idea how to behave? 'I said, you may leave me.'

254

'It is Lady Maude!'

I sat bolt upright in the bed as the woman raised her head. 'Lady Maude! What are you doing here?'

'Please, Majesty, please help me. I haven't much time.'

I had not seen Lady Maude for more than five years, since she and her husband had left Rouen so hurriedly, in that lost time when I loved Arthur. The burly, commanding figure I remembered was quite gone. Her face was thin and lined like a field woman's, the wisps of hair which escaped beneath her cap were a dirty grey. Her face was besmeared with dust, as though she had come straight from the road. I was puzzled, but I tried to be gracious.

'You are most welcome, Lady Maude. Forgive me if I am presently unable to receive you properly, but please to stand. I will call for some refreshment.' She might see that I had remembered the lessons she had tried to teach me, even in this dreadful place.

'Majesty, you are kind. But there are no refreshments. I mixed your drink myself, from my own travelling necessaries. I should think they will be gone already.'

'Thank you, then, Lady Maude. You are kind.'

'It is you who are kind, Majesty. But I must speak with you.'

There was no seat to offer her, so I gestured that she should make herself comfortable on the bed. I hated to think how the room must smell; the maid had changed the linen but the pallet would still be soaked with my blood and worse. But I was queen. I would not acknowledge how low I had been pushed.

'Pray speak then, Lady Maude.'

I was even more surprised when she grabbed at my hand and held it tightly.

'They brought me here just now. The king's men came to our home. They are gone for my son, and when they return, they will lock us up.'

'But why? What has happened? I see no one here, I have no news. Has there been another rebellion?'

'No, Majesty. I am a loyal subject, and my husband too. But the king ... the king is angry with us. He knows that we know what happened, back then in Rouen.'

'Do you mean – to the Duke?' Even now I could not bear to say poor Arthur's name aloud.

'Yes, I do.'

'It is an old story, put about by my husband's enemies. It is forgotten now, surely?'

'Perhaps. But not by the king. You see, my husband was there. He saw it. He saw ... you, Majesty.'

'But you were gone when the-the calamity occurred!'

'My husband wished us to leave. He felt in honour that he could no longer remain. But as we were on the road that night, he felt remorse. He thought that it was his duty to return, to try to persuade the king not to do anything ... hasty.'

Neither of us dared to speak the truth aloud. I was tired of this.

'Lady Maude, you mean that your husband believed that if he returned he might prevent my husband from murdering his nephew?'

'Yes.'

'And then.'

'My husband road back, as fast as he could, alone. He entered the castle and went to the cell where the Duke was held. The door was barred, but he heard sounds inside. Dreadful sounds. There was a grille in the door, he tried to look through it, but as he did so it was opened from the inside and he saw that he was too late.'

'What did he do?'

'He was confused. He thought that he ought to detain the king, but dared not draw his sword on his sworn liege. He told me that the king was wild with rage, wild like an animal. The king asked if he would help them. There was another man in the room, and my husband said that in conscience he could not. Then he fled, fearing that the king would have him killed, too, for what he had witnessed. So we returned to England and have been living quietly on our lands ever since, keeping the king's peace on the border as is our duty.'

'But if my husband has not troubled you since then, why now? Why have you been brought here?'

'How long have you been here, my lady?'

I thought, then said, 'It is almost three years.' How quickly they seemed to have passed when I spoke it, and yet how long it had felt! 'I live very quietly, as you see,' I added scornfully. 'I keep no court here. The king has visited from time to time.'

'I understand. I congratulate you on your family, Majesty.'

'I have no family,' I muttered. 'They took my children from me.'

'But it is as a mother that I beseech your help, Majesty. They will bring my son and I am afraid for him.'

257

I bit down the tears that were rising in me. I was a queen listening to a petition, it did not behove me to weep. 'But why?'

'The country will come to war, before very long now. There is talk of a plot against the king. The men of the north are grieved. They feel that the king neglects them to continue to fight in France, where they have no lands. He taxes them too hard. They owe him huge sums. They feel angry, pushed aside. And they look to my husband to help their cause.'

'So the king will keep you here as a hostage? You and your son? For your husband's good behaviour?'

'Yes. The king has never forgiven him for his knowledge of what passed at Rouen. He suspects him.'

'The fault was not your husband's,' I said sadly.

'My son is William. William, like his father. He is a fine man, a father too. I have a grandson.'

'What do you want of me, Lady Maude?'

'I hoped that you could intercede for me, with the king. I do not care what he does to me, but my son must be free. Please, Majesty. Will you be so kind as to speak to the king for us?'

I gestured around the room. Lady Maude's eyes followed my hand over the piss pot in the corner, the clumsy wooden shutters, the sagging, stinking bed. The shabby cloth of estate above the tester looked like a spiteful jest. 'You see in what good standing I am with the king, Lady Maude. How can I help you when I am little more than a prisoner myself?'

'Majesty, I know I gave you no reason to love me, when we first met. But now, after all this time ...'

258

'I thought you were my enemy, once,' I replied dreamily. 'Before I knew what an enemy was. I am sorry for you, Lady Maude, deeply sorry, and for your son, too. I will send a letter to the king, but I cannot promise that he will read it. I have written many letters, these three years.'

'Thank you, Majesty. Bless you.'

*

I did write to John. That day, I summoned Terric and asked him once again to send the clerk from the church at Corfe. I explained that I had spoken with Lady Maude and that I was certain she and her son, William de Braose, were loyal servants, and that I hoped, for the sake of our own son, Henry, that he would deal with them leniently and allow them to return to their lands. I expected no reply, and I received none.

When I was strong enough to rise, some days later, I resumed my walks on the walls of the castle. Idly, I scanned the road from the town to see if I could make out any activity there. Would the northern barons depose my husband? Then Henry would be king and I should be free. But there was nothing, no riders, no trumpets, no proclamations. I walked and walked, spending hours each day on the walls until I had tired myself enough to sleep, for dreams were the only amusement I had. Terric accompanied me, pacing stolidly a few steps behind, watching to see if I dropped a token or a letter over the walls. One day, two Sundays after Lady Maude's visit, I did hear a noise, a woman, calling. 'Terric, what's that?'

'Nothing to concern you, lady. Will you continue your walk?'

'But I heard something.'

'The kitchens, perhaps,' he smiled grimly. 'Not that they're busy, down there.'

Next day, I heard it again, louder this time. A woman's voice, repeating the same word, over and over: 'Please … Please'.

'Terric, I feel unwell. I fear I may faint. I must sit. Fetch my maid.' Terric's huge head cast about him, anxiously, peering about him as though he feared a trap. Cruelty comes in two kinds, the cruelty of stupidity and of great intelligence. Terric's was of the first kind. I stumbled a little, put a hand to my head. 'Terric. I am faint. I need my maid. Fetch her.'

'I will help you to sit then, lady.' He took my arm and helped me down to the courtyard, where I rested on a bench. A few servers were passing, carrying firewood and greasy platters, but they barely looked at us. The sight of their bedraggled queen in her shabby gown was no longer an object of wonder. My room was in the north-west tower of the court, level with the walls. The noise had come from the south-west, opposite. When Terric had lumbered off towards the staircase, I jumped up and walked swiftly across the court, circling the base of the tower until it met the wall.

'Lady Maude,' I hissed, 'Lady Maude. Is that you?'

The base stones of the tower were covered in bright green slime and wet moss, with clumps of weeds bristling out in the corner. I heard the call again, 'Here, Majesty! Here!'

I looked up, but the casement on the first floor was shuttered. Where could the voice be coming from?

'Down here!'

Almost buried by the weeds was a rusty iron grille, just a few inches high. I squatted down and pulled away a clump of bindweed.

'Lady Maude?'

'They are starving us. We have had no food. Please, please help us.'

I glanced over my shoulder. Terric would return at any moment. 'I will try.'

I had just time to run back to the bench and compose myself before Terric returned with the maid. My hands were streaked green, I hid them in my dress. I spent the evening gently tearing another square of linen from my bedsheet, which I used to wrap the food I had saved from my own dinner and supper. All the bread, a piece of cheese, some raisins and a slice of salt pork. The gruel I ate, as I could see no way to carry it. I was still served wine, the only acknowledgement of my estate, but I thought it would be too difficult to conceal the cup, so I drank that, to keep off my own hunger. Lady Maude said they had no food, she and her son. Had they water? I imagined them licking the slimy walls of that dungeon pit to sustain themselves.

I was not permitted to attend Mass in the town. On Sundays and holy days of obligation, a priest from the abbey came with a communion table to serve as an altar, a plain iron crucifix and a leather bag containing a vial of wine, candles and wafers. I ought to have been churched after Eleanor's birth, the customary ceremony where a new mother is cleansed of childbed, but this had been forgotten, just as I was being forgotten. When Terric came to bolt my door for the night, I spoke to him of this and said that I was sure the king would not be pleased to hear it had been neglected.

'You might walk with me to the church. It is not far, I see it from the buttresses. I should like to offer to Our Lady, to give thanks for my safe delivery.' I knew he could not refuse, and accordingly, next morning, I was permitted my first outing from the castle in over a year.

I was accompanied by four guards and Terric, and we made our way down through the streets, to the church porch, where the priest who was accustomed to serving Mass to me mumbled hastily through the ceremony. For a moment, I was reminded of my wedding, so long ago at Bordeaux. I had hoped to be permitted to enter the church and pray, but Terric took my poor purse of pennies and handed it to the priest, saying that he would offer for me. He was clearly nervous to be beyond the castle walls, I wondered if the rebellion of which Lady Maude had spoken had already begun. Perhaps even now, Henry's riders were on the road from London, come to deliver me. I would take Lady Maude and her son to Westminster, I thought, find William a place in the new king's household to compensate them for the cruelty John had inflicted on them. As we re-entered the castle, I paused by the grille in the tower. I had the folded napkin hidden in the pocket of my gown. I stooped to adjust my slipper, its soles worn from my hours of pacing the walls, and as I did so I pushed the napkin I had made towards the overgrown bars, coughing as I did so to alert Lady Maude to my presence.

Then I saw a horrible thing. Three fingers shot out from the grille, scuttling spider-like towards the food, scrabbling desperately. They were filthy, the nails torn and bloodied. Then, as I knelt, Terric's great boot came down and stamped upon them. There was a cry, but the fingers continued clutching. He stamped again, and the thing, which seemed barely to be part of a whole being, withdrew. I was left looking up into Terric's face.

'So you thought to feed the prisoners, lady? Please to stand up.'

I stepped back. He knelt down towards the grille, scooped a broken lump of cheese from the mess in the napkin and held it towards the grille.

'Here, kitty kitty kitty. Here. Look what the kind lady has brought for you.' He waved the cheese before the bars. I could smell its thin reek. 'Here kitty,' he crooned. There was no movement from the darkness inside. Tentatively, the fingers reappeared, grasping blindly. Terric placed the lump of cheese under the forefinger, then as it scrabbled to gain purchase on the food, he whipped out his knife and slashed at it like a butcher. A howl of pain. The tip of the finger lay on the ground, oozing blood over the pale cheese. Terric bent to the hole.

'You can drink your own juice, woman. That's all you'll get for disobeying the king's orders.'

I was still staring at the livid finger, taking gasps of air, trying to stave off a vomit. Then the blood rushed from my head and I swooned. When I awoke, I was in my chamber, and the door was bolted. I never saw Lady Maude again. When they pulled the bodies from the dungeon, William de Braose's arms and legs were gnawed and tooth-marked. In her frenzy of hunger, Lady Maude had tried to keep herself alive by chewing on the starved corpse of her own son.

CHAPTER TWENTY

THE PLOT AGAINST JOHN NEVER CAME TO PASS. NO riders appeared from London to release me in King Henry's name. I could not close my eyes without seeing that terrible, desperate hand. Sometimes it ran like a crab over the pale body of Arthur in the waters of the Seine, sometimes it crawled across my face like a rat in the darkness. I begged Terric to fetch me a sleeping draught, or even some strong drink, until I perceived the pleasure he had in refusing me. Seeing the lines of exhaustion in my face and the black hollows beneath my eyes, so pronounced that I saw them in my washing basin, the only looking glass I had. The dull witted maid asked me if I was ailing, and shyly produced a lump of poppy seed paste from her apron. I gobbled it down, and slept again, and for a few days we might have been friends, for I grew as stupid as she. Since I had tried to help Lady Maude, Terric had not permitted me to walk outside, and I sank into a state of half-living, like a bear hibernating in a cave. The poppy gum stayed my appetite, and when I was lively enough to do anything other than watch the shadows of the clouds as they played across the daub ceiling of my chamber, I thought that I too might waste away entirely, and then I wept for Lady Maude and wished that I had had some poppy to share with her, before I recalled that she was dead now, with her son's congealed blood dry on her teeth, and then I would shift and scream in my flower-hazed stupor. So time stretched and narrowed, and my heart beat stubbornly on, until one day I did hear the sound of horses and voices beneath my window. I dragged myself to the casement, wondering if I was still dreaming, and saw that the yard was full of men in brightly coloured surcoats over their mail: my brother's colours. Was it to be that time again? My first thought was to call the girl and request a clean shift, have her brush my hair, but then, despite that I was ashamed of myself, I threw myself back defiantly upon the bed – let him see what he had brought me to.

When Pierre entered he did so bareheaded, kneeling to me as reverently as if we were in the great hall at Westminster. I looked down at him.

'Forgive me, Brother. I have had little time to prepare for your visit. It is very ... informal here, as you see.'

'Majesty—'

'Do not toy with me. Come. Close the door and do what you are here to do. I am very busy.' I raised my dingy shift and closed my eyes. Nothing. I waited a little longer. His weight did not join me on the bed. 'Brother?'

He was still there on the dust-clogged rushes. A quick spasm of disgust passed his face, but he composed himself and spoke to me courteously.

266

'I am sorry to find you have been so unwell, Majesty. I am come to escort you to court. The king commands it.'

I sat bolt upright. So it had happened! 'The king?'

'Why, your husband, Sister. Is there another king in England? The king commands you to court, and then you are to sail with him to Poitou.'

The last I saw of Corfe was Terric's startled face as my litter was carried through the gateway, surrounded by a hundred knights, their lances raised, three heralds riding in front, calling on the people to make way for the queen. His astonishment was perhaps provoked because he was being manacled by three of my brother's guards and bundled towards the south-west tower. I had no idea how long my new status would endure, but this was one thing I could do for Lady Maude, at least. The fresh air startled me after the long captivity of that hateful chamber, and when I looked between the curtains of the litter, I saw that the trees were full, their shadows deep on the flower-strewn meadows. It was summer. I had drowsed away a whole season since Eleanor's birth.

We rested that night at Wareham, at a long, low manor house by a ford. The jouncing of the litter had shaken the poppy from me. I was ravenously hungry and horrified by my matted hair and the grey skin of my hands. Surreptitiously I slid my hands beneath my gown, my ribs poked out like a pair of house eaves and the skin of my belly felt loose and slack. What had I allowed myself to become? Pierre had women waiting in the house to attend me. It was given out that I had fallen ill at Corfe and been the victim of neglectful servants. I saw nothing to be gained by objecting, at least until I knew what John's purpose with me was.

When I was bathed and dressed in new clothes, supper was served in the solar, with plate and silver ewers of rosewater to cleanse my fingers, my food was tasted and the pages knelt. All these things seemed strange to me, but then, I had never thought to see them before they were taken from me. I ate slice after slice of capon boiled in sweet wine, bottled figs, white manchet bread, a pudding of carp, quince jelly, almond custard and saffron cakes with honey. The meal was a battle between my quivering hunger and the dainty manners I knew I should use, I wanted to mop my plate and stuff the food into my mouth; it was difficult to hold back. I felt the strength flow back to my limbs with each bite. I did not take wine, since I feared it would affect me, and after I had eaten I knew I should have to speak with Pierre. After I had dined, I received the lady of the manor, thanked her graciously for her hospitality and made a few moments' pleasant conversation. I said that I should be sure to recommend her to the king and remarked on the beauty of the setting of her home. She was a widow with four sons, all squires in the service of the local lord. She asked me anxiously if her boys should be sent to fight in France, and I pretended I knew what she meant. Was John finally moving against Philip? I complimented her, saying that I was sure her boys would be knighted if they served their master well, and that perhaps they would be given lands of their own, in Poitou, when my dear husband had retaken his own, as surely God willed.

All the time my mind was tumbling over itself – why did John wish me at his side in Poitou? Why was I once more being treated as befitted his queen? Not from remorse, or affection, I was sure. He had a use for me. When the lady left me, I pressed her hand kindly and wished for her sons' safe return. I had once thought myself different from other women, from women like her. I had thought myself so different as a child, in my dreams of crusading and then as a queen who could ride into battle, who could destroy a royal duke, who could escape by her wits from the most powerful lords in France, who could birth a king. We were not different, though, she and I. We were women, and at best our part was to wait, and to suffer and endure as the wills that men forced us. What would she have thought, that good lady, if she had seen me just hours ago, filthy and ragged and dazed with misery? I was glad that I had never been permitted to love my daughters, for they should have a part of that misery in time, as I had, as all women had.

Pierre sent a page to ask if I was sufficiently rested after my journey to do him the honour of a few moments' talk. I wondered again at this courtesy from him. Or was it just another wile, to torment me? He knelt when he entered the solar, and the sight of his bright hair pained me. Henry's hair.

'I should leave you to kneel, Brother. For shame.'

'As you wish, Majesty.'

'I should have you crawl on the floor and beg your queen's forgiveness.'

Slowly, Pierre stretched himself forwards until he lay at my feet. He kissed the hem of my dress. 'Forgive me, Sister.'

'Rise. You bore me with your play-acting. Tell me why the king has seen fit to release me, and then let me rest.'

'I bring you a gift, Majesty.' He handed me a small velvet pouch with something heavy inside. 'From the king.' On one side was an engraving of a woman, robed and crowned, her hair falling in ringlets, holding a flower in her right hand, in her left, a bird. I made out the words etched into the iron: 'Isabelle: By the Grace of God Queen of England, Lady of Ireland'. The other surface showed the same woman, this time holding a cross with the bird perched atop it. 'Isabelle: Duchess of the Normans, of the Men of Aquitaine and of Anjou'. 'It is your new seal,' Pierre said. 'To go with you into France.'

'Why? Why should my husband proclaim me when he has imprisoned me and deprived me of my estate?'

'Because you are Countess of Angouleme in your own right. When Queen Eleanor raised the south in rebellion against her husband, he imprisoned her for nine years. Then, when his lands were threatened, he released her to return to Aquitaine. She was … useful. Her presence encouraged the men to rally to the king's standard. You will do the same.'

'My husband plans to fight again in France, then? It is true?'

'You are very ignorant, Sister.'

'I lay in that rat hole for three years. I had no visitors except you and the king. You know that well.'

And then Pierre told me of what had taken place in the time I had lain at Corfe. My husband had made himself the richest king that England had ever known. He had extorted vast sums from the Jews, from the merchants and moneylenders of

London and Bristol. When a man would not pay, he would be imprisoned, and one of his teeth smashed out each day until he agreed the fine. Lady Maude had spoken to me of the discontent of the barons of the north, and John's avarice had spared his barons no more than the Jews. He had called in their debts and taken their lands when they could not pay, so much so that many of the great landowners had fled to Ireland, to make a kingdom in exile. John had raised a fleet out of Pembroke on his thieved money and swept through that country, not sparing even the wives and children of those who had dared to abandon him to his wickedness. And when Ireland was stilled, John took two campaigns into Wales against Prince Llewellyn, and slashed and pillaged that province into submission also.

'There is no man in England now who does not obey the nod of the king,' Pierre told me.

'I wonder why God does not strike him down.'

Pierre raised one beautiful eyebrow. 'God, Sister? But did you know that God has left England to John's mercy?'

'What?'

I had wondered, idly, that I could never hear the carillon from the church tower at Corfe, for all that the church lay so close to the castle. John's feuding with the Pope over the appointment of an archbishop to Canterbury had caused the realm to be placed under interdict. The churches were locked up, the only rites that might be served were the unction of the dying and the baptism of children.

'You thought yourself cruelly served, Sister, but you had the privilege of hearing Mass, did you not?' The hurried, mumbling manner of the priest, the shabby altar table, my churching in the doorway – all this now had a reason.

'And the country has changed, Sister,' Pierre continued. 'With the bell towers silent and the priests and their tales of sin silenced with them, the people are returning to the old faith. There are scarce marriages made, now. Men and women lie together in the fields with no false blessing to unite them.'

I wondered. Could it be that the feeling I had had when I returned to Rouen, that the Lusignan way was the right way, was coming to pass? That what the Church decreed was truly no more than a ledger book, a set of accounts of indulgences and penance for the gain of a crowd of fat priests. God had not heard my prayers from that squalid room, nor yet Lady Maude's. He had not heard the laments of the poor Jews, or the cries of the barons' babies as they were cut from their nurses' arms. Could it be that God was not there, had never been there at all? The thought was so shocking that I gasped aloud.

'Do not take fright, Sister. Your husband is a great king, now. The greatest of his line, the chronicles will say of him. And now he turns his attention to France.'

'I want no part of it,' I said at last.

'I am to take you to Portsmouth, where the king is mustering his fleet. You will sail with him. Does it not please you, Sister? You are going home. John will give your people back their Countess.'

'I may refuse.'

'And return to Corfe? You would prefer to share a chamber with good Terric? Or to receive the king's hospitality the way the Braose woman did? I think not. You will go home, Sister. And if your husband should not return …'

'Then?'

He reached for the collar of my gown and slowly drew it back. His fingers snaked along my skin, seeking the mark on my shoulder.

'And then Henry will be king. A Lusignan king. Our king. Who would be more fit to govern while he is still a boy than his mother and his dear uncle?'

I could not dislike the thought, however much I might have wished to. He watched my face, that was his, and I watched his, that was mine. 'You see, Sister? I have always told you. We are not so very different, you and I.'

CHAPTER TWENTY-ONE

T HE COMING MONTHS REMINDED ME OF THE TIME
when I had first come to England as John's bride, as
though time were a fairing ribbon unspooling backwards. My
journey with Pierre became a progress as we travelled towards
the coast with the purveyors ahead and my baggage train behind.
I saw, as if for the first time, now, the great contrast between
my royal state and the squalid lives of the country people:
Corfe had taught me compassion, at least. Pierre had given me
a purse of gold as he helped me into my litter when we departed
Wareham, by nightfall it was empty, and the next day as we rode
out there were people lining the pathways, clamouring for alms
and calling blessings on their good queen, as though she had
not been locked up for three years and word given out that she
was a witch. I marvelled again at the power of money to smooth
over memory, not only among the poor men of the fields, whose
bodies were misshapen by labour and hardship into squatting
gargoyles, their filthy palms emerging crookedly from flapping
rags, but between my husband's barons, who had mustered

loyally at Portsmouth to campaign on my husband's taxes as though they had never loathed and planned to usurp him.

My thoughts, though, were all with Henry. Each tread of the horses' hooves on the road brought me closer to him, I hoped. Each long swaying hour in the litter was given up to dreams of seeing my boy again. He would be quite grown now. His hair would have been shorn. Would he remember me? Or had my place been taken by that Angouleme whore? I longed for him so fiercely that when John came out of his tent to greet me, as smiling and civil as though I had been absent for a day, it was easy to make my face light and happy, despite the contempt I felt for him in my heart. We greeted one another as the company looked on, but when I asked after Henry, John's face, which was paler and more hollow than I remembered the last time I had seen it at Corfe, twisted into a familiar snarl, which he suppressed with an equally familiar smile.

'The prince is at Eltham, my lady, with his brother and sisters. They wish you joy of your ... recovery, and send for your blessing.'

'They are not to join us, before we sail?' I managed to ask, squashing the tears that crammed my throat.

'I thought it unwise. I should not wish to distress them.'

'Of course, my lord. You are always so considerate.'

'You must wish to rest after your journey.'

'Indeed. I will withdraw, with your permission.'

It was so long since I had walked between bareheaded men on their knees that it might have lifted my heart, to see the barons humbling themselves to me, but I had no mind to con-

275

sider even their hypocrisy. Henry was not there. But I should see him again, when the campaign was over, some little time further could not hurt him, after so long. And perhaps John was right: it would be unkind to reunite us only to have me take ship for France. And then, as I tried to comfort myself with these thoughts as I lay on the Turkey cushions of the tent that had been prepared for me, I knew that I was wrong.

If I wanted to see Henry, if I wanted to teach him, to assist him, I would never be allowed to do so in England. I had to prepare myself once more to fight, and even to kill. I saw, as I had seen once at Rouen, what it was that I might do. I had to escape, I had to be free of John, to steal myself away from him, and the only way to do that would be to get rid of Pierre for good. So for now, I had to play again, to be as smooth and emollient as an olive oil salve, to dissemble to buy time, so I might lay my plans for flight. At last, I acknowledged to myself what my mother had been trying to do. It was the old faith that would save me. She had known that I would never make Henry part of it, as I had never accepted it myself. But in sending Aliene, with her awl and her dreams of queenship, she had made Henry my brother's ally, one with him in the shadow of the horned man's antlers. Need. Once again, I would do what was necessary. As the tented fabric above me shifted in the breeze from the sea, I knew that it was time.

*

We sailed two days later, in a great flotilla of ships and barges, paid for with the blood of the English soil. I stood with my ladies in the stern of the ship and watched the coast of that country recede. I thought that I should hate the sight of those chalk cliffs, so familiar were they from my captivity at Corfe, yet as they fell away in a mist of salt spray, I was surprised to find that I regretted them. England had been my home, after a fashion, the only home I had known since I was taken to Lusignan. I waited until the green brow of the hills blurred into the deep blue of the horizon, and then I crossed to the prow of the ship, where the wind whipped my hair back from my face, and stood there a long while, watching for France.

*

That winter, we kept court at Poitiers, the high-towered city where it was said that old Queen Eleanor had challenged her troubadours to make courts of love that she presided over with her ladies in their old-fashioned wide-sleeved gowns. The brutal strength John had shown in England in the last years had drawn his French liegemen back to him; each day more contingents of lords, knights and squires arrived to pay their respects and promise their swords, and John bade me to entertain them magnificently. There was no mention of Aliene, of her we did not speak; in fact, we barely spoke at all, and John made not even the pretence of coming to my chamber, for which I was thankful. Beyond the courtesies of dinner, supper and Mass we behaved as well-born strangers might, who found themselves obliged to share a tavern room for a night on the road. And since John did not come to my bed, neither could Pierre, and I was thankful for that, also.

I imagined that Pierre, who had never served any interest but his own, was in correspondence with King Philip, but of his plan for a Lusignan kingdom in England he said nothing. He would wait, I supposed, to see which way the first encounters between England and France came out, which way the pieces on the chessboard tumbled, and then, when it suited him, he would move against John or hold his peace. My own unspoken assent to his plan was all that he required of me, and like John, he maintained a civil distance, handing me down at supper when John was too drenched in his cups to do so, sending small gifts and delicacies to my chamber, and dancing with my ladies, who preened and gossiped and wondered which of them the queen's much favoured brother would take as a wife.

I passed my time making the appearance of a dutiful and proud wife who rejoiced in displaying her husband's anticipated glory. I had stonemasons from Germany, to flatter John's alliance with the princes there, at work on a new façade for the cathedral, I had musicians from every part of France to play in the hall each night, I gave the seneschal the liberty of the kitchens, and roast swan and peacock jostled on the trestles, their chargrilled feathers rustling between the great sides of blackened beef that the Englishmen preferred. I sent to Paris for cloth and lace and leather, to Castile for jasmine soaps and bottled peaches, and to Venice for Arab gum and fine woods to be brought across those treacherous winter mountains whose peaks, they said, soared vanishing into Heaven itself, and had John's campaign tent fitted new with stools and chests that smelled sweetly of cedar and sandal. I had the clerks write letters to my children, asking how they did at their lessons and telling of the great warrior their father should soon prove himself to be. I drank apple cider with the monks of the abbey and spiced wine with the nuns of the convent and granted lands under my new seal to both, in the name of Queen Isabelle and King John, that God might favour his cause when he rode out in the spring. And like a woman, I waited. I waited for one particular thing to emerge among the heaps of goods that the packmen unloaded each day in the courtyards, which made a tumbled market of all the goods of Christendom and proved to the world how rich and mighty my husband was become.

Among the newly loyal vassals who arrived to pay their respects to John were several of whom I had slight recollections. Grizzled now, they had fought beside my Taillefer father years ago, and though it was their sons now who would ride out against Philip, they still held their lands and presided in their halls in appanage. They thanked me for sending Pierre and the mercenary troops from Rouen. They had been hard pressed by the French, and I made great use of my seal, granting the revenues of mills and manors, so they should be bound to their countess when the time came to fight once more. They spoke courteously to me of my mother, and of the beauty of the countryside around my city, complimenting me on the news of my children and the fineness of my entertainments, the sort of light, pleasant remarks that were suitable for ladies. Some of them had brought their wives, stolid women in unfashionable dresses, whose wide hips and square, stub-fingered hands spoke of an attachment to the soil which a couple of generations of rank had not yet bred out. As we sewed and walked and prayed together, I wondered about them, these country ladies who seemed so placid. Where did they fly in their dreams? Were their husbands among the naked creatures who disported with my mother in the moonlight? Or were they themselves members of the old faith, brewing witch's grease in their kitchens alongside soap and candles? As another year turned and I looked out on the loveliness of the reawakening countryside, I thought that all which seemed so certain in the business of the great, the elaborate courtesies, the scented wine, the delicate gowns of my ladies and the sweetness of the minstrels' songs was only so much coloured ink on a flimsy scrap of parchment, an overlaying of brightness and order beneath which the land itself moved immutably in a very different rhythm, one of blood and death, the feral screams of wild things in the night, the frenzied writhing of storm-whipped trees and the slow tug of river tides, so that all the trappings of my restored state seemed to me as empty and foolish as a child's playthings, a collection of spangled baubles heaped like fool's treasure beneath the mocking gaze of the horned man, who was the only true king of this quiet country.

It came as it had come once before, on another spring day, so long ago. I was walking with my ladies in the garden above the river, which gushed and frothed with meltwater between the banks, a clear day in March with a huge empty sky bright above the Poitevin plains. The road beneath the town was busy with market carts and couriers, I could hear their harness jangling above the duller tread of the horses on the still-soft winter mud, when among them I saw a mule, fat as a cardinal with baggage slings, plodding with bowed head among the smart rapping trot of the liveried messengers. I was no longer a child. I did not shriek and point and dance with anticipation, but inside my blood was leaping, for he had come – the silk man had finally come.

I had a page summoned to my side and spoke to him quietly. I turned the fur trim of my cloak along the walk, and continued conversing with my ladies, though all the while my eyes sought that fly-patch of beast and man, humming and buzzing at the edge of my vision. And later, when he had refreshed himself and washed, and spread out his marvels in my chamber for my ladies to finger and goggle over, I took up a length of silk in my hands, a green so dark it was almost black, as a fir tree against a snowy sky, and drew him into my closet.

To me, he looked just the same. Those same pale eyes, dancing with the light of my once-imagined city. The same coppery, weatherworn skin. I wondered how he saw the changes in me, and how he liked them. I bade him sit and he did so with a calm and modest familiarity that spoke achingly to me of our long acquaintance, and of how different it might have been.

'I have not seen you since the French king's feast at Paris,' I began. 'I hope you continue well.'

'God has been kind to me, Majesty.'

'Which one? Yours, or mine?'

He smiled, 'I am afraid I do not follow your words, Majesty. I am only a merchant. Will it please you to choose among my poor things today? I have a piece meant for the queen of Sicily, but does Majesty choose to see it first? It is stitched—'

'With the hands of elves in the caverns beneath the glaciers of Persia,' I broke in. 'I know. And your wares are as beautiful as ever. I shall be glad to take something. But there is one thing, you may recall, that you gave me last time we met. I am afraid it was … mislaid. I would have another.'

'Majesty?'

'Red, I remember. A very particular piece.'

He continued to regard me quietly, only a tautening beneath his sharp cheekbones indicated his curiosity. 'And this piece? Another gift from your lady mother, perhaps?'

'Perhaps. I find myself in urgent need of it. I have received a request from my mother, of the gravest kind. It concerns her business, that is, my family's business, with the Holy Land. I take it that you understand me now?'

'I had known of some such thing,' he answered carefully, 'when Majesty's brother was with you that time at Paris. When you received the first gift.'

'To which I have been true ever since,' I replied. I stepped to the door of my closet and asked the maid to close it. 'I am choosing surprises!' I laughed gaily, news that as the wood swung shut against my back I heard being relayed to the ladies in the chamber, who clapped and giggled approvingly. 'Give them whatever they ask,' I said carelessly. 'Tell them each I chose their silk specially. You will not have to journey so far as Angouleme this winter.'

'Your lady mother will be disappointed.'

'I doubt it,' I whispered, allowing my gown to fall loose on my shoulder and fishing in my bosom for the strings of my chemise. 'She has more important matters than gowns in mind.'

I turned so that he could see my bare flesh, smooth and sleek again after a winter of hot baths and rich food. I reached over my shoulder and traced the thin line of the scar with my fingertips, slowly, that he might mark it with his eyes. When I was sure he had seen, I adjusted my gown and turned to him. His eyes remained fixed to what he had seen, like a cat enthralled and dizzied with a sunbeam.

'And now,' I said, 'let me explain to you what it is that I need.'

He smiled, not his wheedling pedlar's grin, but a true smile. His hand was already scrabbling beneath his cloak, but I stayed him.

'I have no need to see it. I know that it is there, and why.'

'Then please, Majesty. Let me know your command.'

And so, some few nights later, I found myself doing what I had sworn I should never do, fastening on the red garter which glowed like a brand against the pale skin of my thigh. My hair was simply braided under my hood. I wore a loose gown and a chemise that laced at the front. I picked up the looking glass that had been my gift to myself from the silk man's cargo. How I had longed for such a thing when I was a girl! I smoothed my skin in its silvery sheen, pinched my lips and cheeks to bring the blood beneath.

'You look beautiful this evening, Sister.' Pierre was waiting for me in the passage. He was too clever to let his triumph show in his face.

'Thank you. I am grateful to you, Pierre.'

'For a simple compliment? We are in Poitiers. Ought I not to make a trouvère verse on your complexion?'

'For your patience, Brother. I have tried it sorely. It has taken me such an unforgivable time to know what I am.'

'And what you shall be, Sister.'

'Indeed. And what Henry will become, in his turn.'

Pierre gave an ugly smirk, the only moment in all that we had been through together when that perfect mask slipped. 'With God's help.'

I curled my own lips in a smile of contempt. 'Quite. With God's help.'

'Come. We are on the king's business, after all.'

*

Pierre had two horses saddled in the courtyard. He helped me to mount, then swung himself into the saddle and walked to the gatehouse. The guards bowed respectfully as the queen and the Lord de Joigny passed through. The night was cold and clear, the moon a Saracen scimitar above the city.

'Is it far?' he called as we turned onto the Paris road and pushed the horses to a trot, then a canter.

'Our mother's message said just a few miles. Along the river, until we come to the tower. They wait for us there.' There had been no such message, but Pierre was so eager to believe it, it seemed a shame to disappoint him.

'Then let us fly.'

I had not galloped a horse for so long, I wondered if my limbs had lost the memory of it, but my hands and legs were as sure as ever. The euphoria was the same too, the same reckless joy in speed and sinew, of sharp air in my lungs and the sweet warmth of horseflesh. Pierre rode well, of course, but I found I could match him and for a short time as we raced along abreast under the stars, I did feel once again that we flew, as one body, surging through the night. I even closed my eyes for a while, squeezing gently but allowing the horse to find his pace, and remembered Othon, and Tomas, and riding out with Arthur, and allowed the tears to fall from my tightened eyelids, a burning cold in the wind on my face, until the sadness left me and I bared my teeth in the darkness with a savage pleasure.

'Here?'

I pulled myself awake from the daze of the gallop and drew hard on the rein. 'I believe so.' I had passed Pierre, who waited behind me on the road, the silhouette of a guard tower defined by the gleam of moonlight on his hair. 'Forgive me!' I laughed.

'Come now.'

We walked the horses along a narrow path towards the tower, then dismounted and led them past the empty structure towards the riverbank. Ahead I could make out the glow of a fire. 'This way.'

The place might have been the same hollow where I had first dreamed, or thought I dreamed, of the horned man. Fire, rock, water, moonlight. It might have been my mother who stepped from her cloak, her gown, her chemise, who unbound her hair so that its colour mingled with the flames that caught the red noose on her leg. And she who might have turned to her son, to my brother, and held up her arms so that the silver light caught the delicate veins in her wrists, as though to twine her lover through her blood and trawl him into her heart.

Somewhere behind the rock began the slow thud of a drum, and I began to move to its rhythm, curving my hips and raising my hands, inviting Pierre to dance.

'But where?' he whispered, his moon-paled face confused.

'Come, Brother,' I smiled. 'Come, dance. They will be here. And He will be here too. Come.'

Pierre fumbled at his clothes, first unfastening his sword belt and letting it drop, then his surcoat, shirt, hose, until he was naked as I. As he stepped towards me, I watched the lean lines of muscle on his torso stir beneath the skin and caught the smell beneath his arms, musky and high. I embraced him, filling myself with the scent of him, then turned away, twisting my back and thighs against his body as we began to circle the fire. The drum beat faster, and we kept time, describing an orbit like the celestial bodies that circle the earth, around and around. I felt my own limbs prick with sweat, and glancing down, saw that Pierre was ready for me.

'Now,' I whispered. 'We must summon Him now.' I lay on the bare ground with my head towards the fire, and slowly parted my legs. When he was with me, I gripped my thighs tightly around his hips and rolled us over, so that I sat astride him, his face now illuminated by the flames. I began to move, pushing my weight down hard upon him and allowing my lips to part. It was the first time I had feigned pleasure with Pierre. The drumming had stilled, to a steady double beat, the twinned sound of our bodies moving together as I carried Pierre with me, and as his pleasure came upon him I saw a shadow over my shoulder and saw that Pierre had seen it too, his eyes rolling back in stupid ecstasy. I scrambled his body from mine and we turned once more together, prostrating ourselves before the horned man, who stood above us, the leather mask of his face descending into the hides that covered him, the antlered head gleaming like birch bark in the glow of the flames. The drum had ceased now. As we waited in silence, I threw a swift glance to the tumbled heap of Pierre's clothes. How far? Ten yards, twelve? Pierre saw the movement of my head, and I wondered whether he knew what was to come, or whether he would die enraptured, in the presence of his god.

But he did not see Gilbert step out from behind the rock, or the long blade of the dagger behind his heart, nor, when he had fallen forward with a gasp no louder than the whistle of a candle, did he see the horned man pull off his hide face and stand staring over my nakedness.

'Hand me my cloak,' I asked the silk man. When I was covered, I stooped over my brother's body, already cooling where it lay away from the flame. Gingerly, I closed his startled eyes.

'It is as my mother wished,' I intoned solemnly, for the benefit of my listeners. 'A great sacrifice.'

The silk man began to sing, and Gilbert joined him, a high, quavering melody that hung in the air not unlike a psalm. I heard them out. I no longer scorned them. We served the same ends, they and I, and after all, our methods had not proved so very different, in the end. I did not even despise Gilbert, whose loyalty had been bought for a palmful of gold. As he hymned his dead master, I searched in my heart for remorse at all I had brought about, remorse, or pity, or fondness even, an echo of the shameful passion I had always felt in Pierre's arms. But I was done with thought, with reflection. Thinking had almost destroyed me in body and in mind, and I wanted no more of it. The old way, the way of other creatures, did not know thought any more than it knew regret. It sought only its own existence, and if it failed, it gave up life, as Pierre had done. I could not hate him for what he had done to me any more than a squealing rabbit, tearing off its own limbs in the snare, could hate the hands that set the wire. Perhaps I even understood him. I had not had him killed for revenge any more than my mother had tormented me out of cruelty. It was simply the way the old ways worked, taking what they needed without thought or remorse. My boy would rule, and do so freely, the last and only difference between Pierre's desires and my own. And then I saw that I had been thinking, after all, dreaming in the crackle of the fire and the night breeze, and that both men were staring expectantly at me. I stood straighter and stepped over my brother's body to retrieve the rest of my garments.

'Gilbert. You will bury him, as we agreed.'

'Indeed, Majesty.'

I struggled to find a phrase that would sound suitably solemn and portentous. 'You have done as my mother commanded, and I thank you. It is not for us to question a sacrifice.' They nodded like a pair of monks at a Latin oration. I turned to the silk man. 'And you. All is ready?'

'As you wished, Majesty.'

'Then we leave. You may leave those … things,' I gestured towards his costume. 'Come.'

As we turned away from the river, I looked back one last time at the father of my son. His hair still glowed, as Arthur's had done, once. And now they would be bone and worm together. I fingered my own loosened braid, and thought how quickly Pierre should have done the same, had he no longer needed me. Then the silk man untethered his horse and attempted awkwardly to mount. In the part of my mind that was not still there, but in the firelight, I recalled that one such as he would never have ridden a horse. Horses were for lords and knights. 'Where is your cart?' I asked him, as he eased himself gingerly into the saddle.

'A little way down the road, Majesty. Not far.'

I unbuckled his rein and took it in my hand so that I could lead him, and began to walk us quietly along the road. The animals were skittish, I wondered if they had scented the blood. Gilbert would take both mounts. They would not be seen in Poitiers again.

In a while, a good long while, John would receive word that Pierre de Joigny had ridden for the Holy Land and gave over his lands to the English crown. Thus Henry would possess his father's inheritance. And there were many knights who had died there, far away in the desert, fevered with wounds or plague, that lay in unmarked graves beside dusty mountain roads. Pierre would disappear, and only my mother might mourn him, should she choose. This was not a punishment for her, no. It was my acceptance of the ruthlessness of her own beliefs. Do hinds mourn when the wolf takes their fauns from them? Perhaps. But it was my own disappearance that concerned me now.

When we came to the clearing where the silk man had left his cart, I unlaced the red garter and tied it to a tree as a sign to Gilbert. Any country person passing would see it, and leave the horses alone. The silk man had bundled a feather bed among what remained of his wares, and as soon as I lay upon it, I fell into a dead sleep, even before he had untied the mule and set off, at last, for Lusignan.

CHAPTER TWENTY-TWO

WHEN I OPENED MY EYES, I SAW ONLY THE MISTY blue of the spring sky above me. For a moment or two, I thought myself still on the ship that had brought us to the coast of Normandy, until I realized that the swaying around me was not the pull of the waves, but the slow, lurching tread of the silk man's mule. A queen in a cart, I thought. What would Lady Maude think? And that made me smile, and I pushed the hair from my eyes and sat up to look around. We were moving slowly across a plain, dotted with clusters of trees, no house or village visible. 'Where are we?' I called to the silk man's back.

'We have come ten miles, I think, my lady. Still a great way to go.'

In the freshness of the morning air, it was as though the scene last night had never occurred. I swung my legs over the back of the cart and jogged along, eating an apple and a hunk of bread with honey, dangling my feet as merry as a peasant girl on a hay wagon. We had plenty of time, I thought. John himself would not miss me, and even if my women raised alarm, they would see that Pierre was gone and assume I was with my brother. It would be days before my absence would be questioned, and by then, I hoped, I should be safe at last. The strange, calm simplicity of my thoughts astonished me. Aside from the clothes I wore, I had brought two things with me from Poitiers: Lord Hugh's serpent brooch, and my royal seal. I fumbled in the pocket of my gown for them, stroking them over and over like a rosary. The brooch would prove me, when we got to Lusignan, and the seal? With that, I could give commands.

We saw no living soul that day nor the next. As it grew dark, and the mule weary, we pulled the cart into the scrub at the roadside and made our beds, I above and the silk man on the ground below. I watched him prepare soup over a small charcoal burner, and then we lay down between heavy sacks of fabric, covered with canvas to protect them from the dew. I loved that wandering time, and though it was cold, and we were dirty, though our food was scarce and simple, and there was nothing to break up the monotony of the days save the passing of the landscape and the progress of the weak spring sun across the sky, all these things which had at Corfe seemed abominable privations had become joyful, as though this were a game. I gave no thought to what I had left behind, or indeed to what was before me, and when the silk man shyly poured a little of his watered wine on the roadside, or muttered one of his strange prayers, I did not turn away, but watched him pay his obeisance to the land through which we passed as a thing which was right, and which could be contained by no church, or no palace.

It was on the third day that the French king's riders came. We had passed several villages by then, where the peasants came out to stare at the silk man's cart, where I would conceal myself under the canvas until we had continued beyond their curious eyes. I had thought the silk man travelled only with cloths for fine ladies, and it surprised me to discover that he had also a sack of ribbons and kerchiefs, gaudy worthless things that the poor women handled and exclaimed over in the same manner as my maids in the castle. Sometimes I would have to lie for hours, scarcely breathing, as they made their choices and handed over the small coins they had saved against his coming. I thought it wise to conceal myself, in case John sent after me, but I had no real fear of these people; after my time at Corfe I was glad to hear them plucking a moment of brightness out of their dull, weary lives of fieldwork. But I noticed that in the towns we passed many of the cottages were shuttered, and several were burned, and when the women came forward to cheapen the silk man's goods, the men waited in the doorways, with a scythe or an axe in their hands, watching. So as soon as I saw the French riders, I dived beneath the coverings and lay there trembling.

There were a dozen of them, mercenary troops from the north, un-liveried, leading a single loaded destrier with a ragged fleur-de-lys banner atop. Their harried French captain was as far gone in drink as the rest of them, reeling along the road with his sword catching ridiculously between his legs. We heard them before we saw them, and smelled them after that, roaring drunk-enly, though it was barely noon. I could see nothing except the road between a chink in the slats of the cart, yet I knew that the silk man would be hunched down behind the mule, hoping to pass them quietly, and I knew that he would be stopped. I made myself as small and motionless as possible and began to mutter a silent prayer that they would not accost us. For a moment all was silent, except for the straining creak of the cart's wheels beneath me, but then I heard their heavy, unsteady steps approach, and the protesting snort of the destrier as its halter was dragged towards the ditch at the roadside.

'You! Hey, you! Where are you going, then?'

This close, I could smell the filth on them beneath the high stink of the wine. I could hear the relish in their thick voices, the eagerness for the release of violence. The silk man spoke up bravely, his voice low, but measured and clear.

'I am a pedlar. Please to search my wares, if you wish, Captain. You will find nothing but women's trinkets.'

'Got anything to eat?'

'I will be glad to share what I have with gentlemen in the service of the king of France.' I heard a rustling, the silk man must be rummaging for our packet of bread and hard cheese – then a gasp.

'Chew on that, you foreign swine!'

'You're no Frenchman!'

'A spy, that's what he is, a spy!'

Another gasp, and the sound of something falling, the mule began to jerk between the carts of the shaft, shaking the coverings over my head. More sounds, soft thuds, followed by grunts, which grew sharper, until they bloomed into screams, and then I knew that they would kill him, and me too if they found me.

Even as this realization came to me, as slow and somehow unthreatening as the approach of terror in a dream, I felt what remained of the fabrics in the cart lighten over my body. Then, for a second, I was dazzled by the light of the sky across my exposed face, and then there was no time for thought, I was up and over the shoulders of the first of them before he had time to exclaim, my feet hit the hard mud of the road and I was flying.

Agnes's voice came to me as I ran, speaking across the years. Light as a fox, fleet as a hare, strong as a horse. That was what the old faith believed. Later, when I considered my escape, which could in reality have taken no longer than a cloud's journey across the sun, it seemed not that Othon was with me, but that I became his spirit, the spirit I had rejoiced to feel in the rides at Lusignan and later, when I rode with Pierre to his end. How else could I have escaped those cruel men, whose blood was raised against any living thing in their path? I took my dear friend into me, and it was his strength, which had bled out beneath me at Mirebeau, which carried me back along the road, so fast that even the exclamations of the French mercenaries were lost to me, so fast that it was not until I veered off into the scrubland and collapsed beside a thicket of gorse that I felt the searing ache in my lungs and the fluttering of my heart, which beat so loud that I was certain they should hear it, and find me, but which my blood would not allow me to bend around myself and disguise. I would make tribute to the silk man, as was fitting, but my first prayer was not for his poor soul, but of gratitude to Othon, who had come to me in desperate need for the third and what I knew to be the final time.

I lay there among the thorns until twilight came, and lay on until the moon bloomed in the sky. I had not heard the mercenaries pass back along the road, they must have continued on their way as soon as they had finished with the silk man. When I rose, I winced and gasped with pain where the thorn spikes had pierced me, spitting on the hem of my robe and doing my best to clean the cuts, awkward with stiffness. I crept back to the road and set off the way I had run, keeping close to the ditch and the overhanging shadow of the trees. I had no doubt what I should find, and when eventually I came to the cart – I had flown indeed – it was only with a dull sigh of shock that I absorbed the huddled figure lying beneath the shafts. Even as I turned the body over I felt the heavy pull of death in it. I ran my hands over the silk man's face, remembering it as he had removed the mask by moonlight, the night of Pierre's death. Now his features were blotched with the shadows of bruises, a hideous creeping mould, and at the back of his skull I felt the wound that must have killed him, a deep slit from a dagger or a spur. My fingers came away wet and sticky, as though dipped in cooling jam, and though from the temperature of his skin and the blood I knew that he could not have lived long after I left him, his clothes, when I fumbled beneath them, still contained an eerie vestige of warmth. As I gingerly worked off his breeches, I could smell him in the clear air of the night – sweat and the thin ammoniac tang of urine, an ancient tinge of lavender from the gloves he donned to handle his fine silks, and that made him tender to me, so broken, so human.

I tried to clean him, as best I could, to give him dignity. As I did so, I remembered the joy his visits had brought, the marvels that had billowed from his pack, the whole mysterious world bundled in the flaring colours of his fabrics, and I gave thanks. I closed my wet eyes and prayed to God for his soul, making the sign of the cross above his heart. At least, in his last moments, the silk man would not have wished for a priest. He had no need of that. At least he knew the manner of his going, and I prayed, too, that he had had time to speak to his own god. If only I could have known that he had died quickly. I did not feel shame at leaving him, he had believed that he was serving his faith in carrying me from Poitiers, and I knew he would have encouraged me to escape, had he had time for words. But I sorrowed for him, nonetheless. I wept for his brightness and his courage, for the breaking of the link that bound us together to Angouleme, however warped and ruined it had grown.

When I had got his britches down, I kept my eyes from his privities and slid my hand along his cold leg until I found the red string, which I untied and placed in my pocket along with the seal. I could not bury him, I had not even a tool to make a hole. The soldiers had emptied the cart, except for a few reels of ribbon, they had driven off the mule and availed themselves of our provisions. I had no food, no water, no coins, nothing. I took some time scraping out a shallow hollow in the mulch of the roadside with my filthy hands, then rolled the silk man's body into the dent. I scattered a handful of earth and gathered grasses and leaves to cover him decently. That would have to do. I thought to take his coat, to cover myself as a disguise, but it was stained with his blood and I did not like it. The darkness had thinned now, diluted with the first glow of morning, and the birds were beginning to wake. I laid a hand on the silk man's face, beneath its last mask, and set off along the road.

*

Even at Corfe, where I had been so neglected and deprived, I had never been truly hungry. As I walked into that day, and on into the next, it twisted in my hollow belly like a tapeworm, writhing with need. Even had I known how to beg I did not dare to seek out a farm or a village, for fear that John's men would be following me. And who knew what tales the mercenaries might have told of the strange apparition that had flown from the silk man's cart? As my hunger swelled, I laughed to myself at the thought of being burned now, for a witch. I knew that we had been close, and I knew that I had to walk west, but at nightfall on the second day I felt a strange coldness creep over me, and I began to shiver. The scratches from the thorns must have poisoned my blood, I thought. There was a patch of blue flesh above my ankle, and another, tracing down my arm. I thought to lie and rest a little, so exhausted that even the damp sod appeared a delightful bed, but I knew I must go on, or die of thirst and fever. I would see the towers of Lusignan, I thought. I should see the château and then I should be safe.

And then for a while, I stumbled through a world of dreams, where my mother waited for me beside a clear cold fountain in a glade, and as I reached for the cup she offered me, already feeling the blessed rush of water in my throat, I spied John and

Pierre, leading Henry by the hand, walking away into the forest. I cried out and tried to follow them, but the trees turned to the bodies of the men I had seen fall at Mirebeau, and I pushed my way through a maze of gore, dangling limbs with hideous sores sprouting like mushrooms of their trunks. As I pushed them from my path, my face was splattered with blood, which became Arthur's hair, slimy with river water, twining about my neck. I screamed, and came to myself huddled at the roadside, my temples throbbing now with heat and my eyes filmed with sickness. I hauled myself upright and took a few steps. I had to go on. But in time the coldness came on again, though I clenched my teeth against it, and I sank once more to the ground.

I must have continued like that, fainting and falling, until dawn, for when I woke again it was light and the hunger was gone. I felt weightless, as though I could glide along the road like a feather puffed in the breeze. My ankle throbbed, and the blue had grown, throwing out tendrils of deep colour along my veins, answered by the hum in my arm. If the two strands met, I should not live. I had to go on, I knew, but first I should rest a little. Just a little more …

*

'Does she breathe?'

'I think so.'

Two wrinkled faces peered down at me, pitted with deep lines like earth cracked in the summer. Agnes? I tried to speak, but my parched throat emitted only a low, rasping growl.

'She is ill. Come away.'

'It's not Christian. See, she is young.' I felt a twig-like finger brush the matted hair from my face.

'But she's sick.'

'Like as the soldiers have had her.'

I tried to shake my head, but somehow my muscles would not obey.

'It's not right, wandering on the road alone. Leave her, now.'

'We should fetch the priest. He'll know what to do.'

'I don't know. A beggar woman. She'll be stiff before we get back.'

'Still …'

'Very well.'

The voices floated away from me, drifting back to dreams. I rolled over on my face and reached in my pocket for my trio of charms, the garter, the brooch and the seal, bunching them beneath my body, then slept once more. This time, my fancies conjured Lusignan, I dreamed that I woke and saw the cobbled rise to the keep, where horses could ride into the great yard, and that I heard the noises of the château about me, those same noises which had been so familiar to me as a child, the clanking of the guards' drills, the bustle from the kitchens. The seal burned beneath my frozen hand; it would be a weapon, I thought, when they brought me to Lord Hugh.

'Isabelle?'

I was not Isabelle. I was a poor silk pedlar, selling my fancies through the villages.

'She raves. She must be bled. Fetch the surgeon, ask for leeches.'

I would not be bled. I had seen enough blood, at Mirebeau, blood shining the river at Rouen, blood on Pierre's pale body. So much blood. My seal and my brooch were gone, the old gleaning women had taken them from me. I was a ghost, at last, and the thought made me laugh, though all I heard was a strange croak.

'The snake,' I tried to whisper, 'give it back!'

'Hurry! The surgeon!'

Then I dreamed a halcyon's tail of a knife, dipping and cutting my flesh like marzipan, and a sweet liquid in my mouth that made me retch at the flavour of rot it carried. I was poisoned, surely. I was in a dungeon with Hal of Lusignan, and we were starving together. I would eat him, nibble him like a rat and then we should see which of us was the stupid girl. I screamed again.

'Isabelle?'

Hal's face, disappearing in a scowl strapped to the back of a cart. Charcoal eyes and soot for hair, black like all the Lusignan men, bound next to Arthur, my husband's heir. Where was the silk man? Where was Lord Hugh, my father, my lover? Hal. My betrothed, my brother. I could not see him, he was drifting from me along a black river, where the horned man waited the coming of the tide.

CHAPTER TWENTY-THREE

I LAY A LONG TIME SICK AT LUSIGNAN. WHILE I TURNED
and tottered through endless dreams, a wild hermit man in
the north of England made a prophecy that the reign of the
English king would soon come to its end. When John heard of
his vision, he had the poor man brought to court and questioned
before all the barons, where the man stood firm and declared that
he should lose his crown by next Ascension Day. John sent him
in chains to Corfe to wait out his claim, and all who heard it put
faith in it, they said, as though his prediction had been declared
from Heaven. The comet was recalled, and John's power, which
had seemed so assured, began once more to slide away as his
magnates began to call for new laws and justice in his kingdom.

It was Hal who told me of the prophet, Hal who sent word
to the court at Westminster that Isabelle of England was gone
to inspect her lands in the Poitou, a charter with her own seal
affixed. It was Hal who ordered a doctor, and women to tend
me, who sent for hangings for my bed and sweet herbs to burn
in my rooms. It was Hal who told me of the strange woman

who had circled the walls of his citadel like a lost fairy, and lain down by the roadside for the peasants to find. Of the priest who had run to him at dinner and told of the delirious creature who muttered of ships and courts and soldiers and carried a royal symbol in her bedraggled gown. Hal was properly Lord Hugh now, since his father's death, but I told him I should never call him by that name.

'You called me by plenty of others, I remember.' We were seated in the garden where once I had fought him. My hair, which had been shorn during the fever, was beginning to curl out under the edges of a neat black velvet cap. It had darkened to a warm brown, no longer the gleaming burnish I had shared with Pierre. I was too relieved to be vain of its loss. Hal's finger played idly with it, tucking it back against my cheeks. In turn, I traced my fingers along the taut strength of his arm beneath the loose sleeve of his mantle, finding the serpent curve of his mark in his flesh, tracing the shape I knew so well from my own. On his shoulder, the serpent brooch clasped his cloak. They had prised it from my hand in my delirium, and thus Hal had known me.

'But how did my mother come by it?'

'I sent it to her.'

'You?'

'When my father died. I wanted to remind her. That you were mine, and so was Angouleme. I marked it first, and I asked her to send it to you.'

'A love token?'

He was serious a moment. 'No. I did not love you. But you belonged to Lusignan. I knew I could not rule well here without

303

your presence. And I felt that you would come. Somehow, you would come, Sister.'

I had never liked to hear that word, before.

Then a smile broke across his face once more. It was Melusina's power, my husband joked, that had drawn me back to Lusignan, and kept me safe until he had found me. He had heard her, he smiled, the night of our father's death, shrieking like a storm around the walls, and she had come to him in a dream, a beautiful woman with golden braids that reached her ankles, the night before they found me at the roadside. She had twined herself around him, and whispered that his bride had come. I said that was a pretty dream to tell me, of lying in a snake woman's arms, and he smiled and said that there were consolations to be had in being the lord of Lusignan, and that I should thank her for a fairy godmother.

That was how it was between us. What was impossible to change, we made light of, and all the severity of sin and the recollection of blood, all the pain and confusion and loss, we put behind us, for how else could we live with what hovered in our blood except to make a jest of it, and live as best we could?

For we were married, Hal and I. According to the laws of the Church, we always had been, for we had exchanged the words at my betrothal. When I was strong enough, Hal took me one evening at dusk to the river glade where I had first seen my mother dance with the old gods, and told me we should seal our compact among them, in the old way. The poor silk man's garter was my only wedding fancy, and for a church we had the arch of the turning trees and Hal's sword, the blade laid crossways in the embers of a fire. We took off our shoes and stepped barefoot across the whitening ashes, and it was done. Once my son was king, we would hold a wedding in a cathedral, with singing and incense and all the rites of the church, so that our lands could be held securely together in the eyes of the world, but for now, he was my true husband. Already, I rejoiced that I grew fat with his child. I had a letter put aside, against the time of Henry's crowning, though the parchment had been left empty at the top, for the ink of the date. If Hal de Lusignan should take a royal French wife, the writing explained, then all the English lands in Poitou and Gascony could be at risk from the greed of her allies. Therefore, 'Seeing the great peril that should accrue were such a marriage to take place ... ourselves married the said Hugh ... and God knows we did this for your benefit rather than our own.'

Long ago, when I was still a child, I had liked to play at cat's cradle with Agnes. Sometimes we used red wool, winding and pulling it between our fingers, twining and separating them until the patterns came out, taut between our hands. If I traced the strands of my life back, was it really Melusina who had drawn me to Lusignan, or was it the horned man, or my mother? Perhaps it had taken them all to lead me back where I had no choice but to belong. I was not certain that I believed in the old ways any more than I did in the new, yet here I was, alive. In marrying Hal, I had kept many promises, those of men and those that were of something far older than men. It was true enough, that stately letter. Women were to weave peace, to bind lands and blood in a cat's cradle of alliances and loyalties, and this was done. My boy's lands were secured, and perhaps there could be peace, for a time. Perhaps Henry would hate me for the choices I had made for him, choices which he should never comprehend, yet I hoped that he would forgive me too, as I had forgiven my mother, who had given me what I needed, in the end, to steal myself home.

Love makes a honeycomb of the heart. Too much and it grows friable. Better to seal off each chamber of sweetness so that the whole will stay rich and endure. I knew that Henry would never again love me as his mother, that my beautiful boy was lost to me, but as I closed that little part of my aching heart, I knew too that I had done everything to keep him safe, and I believed that no god would judge me for it. I knew that Hal did not love me as Arthur had, or even as John had done. He loved my titles and my dower lands and the salving of a wounding score. And nor did I love him. Yet there was room for him in my heart, not perhaps the sweetness spiked with spring flowers that had flowed so abundantly for Arthur, but something richer, as deep as the sugar of old wine, sweetness preserved for one who had known me as a child, when I believed in pink marble palaces and Saracen pirates. I could love his strength, and his certainty, and the safety they would give me, after so long wandering. And I would breed sons to him, a whole quiver of Lusignan boys, and they he should love, and perhaps I might be allowed, this time, to love them too.

I yawned, and stretched, feeling the rise of my belly beneath my gown. The air in the garden smelled of lavender and quinces.

'Are you tired, Isabelle?'

'A little.'

'Then we shall go in. You must rest before the journey.'

I was tired, bone weary and drained, but not with the life that was in me. It was the lives I had lived that exhausted me, too many of them. I wondered if my mother felt that, too. Tomorrow we should begin our journey home, that I might repossess my city. This time, I would make a story for her. I would tell her of my journey, and of how Melusina had brought me home to Lusignan, just like her own long-ago tale had promised. My story should have monsters, and sealed pacts, betrayals and love. It would have fairies and changelings and fountains and banquets, jewels and silks and charging horses and crowns. She would stroke my hair, and I should kiss her.

'Come, then, Sister. Come, Isabelle.' Hal's voice was warm. There was no shame between us. We were unlike others, that was all. This is what my mother knew, that was the true story of Melusina. Royal blood takes magic of one kind or another. So in a little while, I should give thanks for my return alongside my mother in the church her husband built, and then, together, we should go down at dark to the waterside, and make our thanks in a different kind. I knew I should find her there, my maman, in Angouleme.